Praise for Anne Louise Bannon
and Fascinating Rhythm

Fascinating Rhythm is reminiscent of Agatha Christie or Dorothy Sayers' novels of the time period. A very nice story to cozy up to a fire with and imbibe. Legally, of course.

Literary R&R

Those who love a great (who-done-it) mystery will enjoy Fascinating Rhythm.

Sheri Wilkinson

JuniperGrove.net

Praise for Bring Into Bondage

Like the first book, it's set in the 1920's, and it follows the continuing story of my favorite writer/editor pair, Freddie Little and Kathy Briscow. The new story takes them out of New York City to the small Midwestern town of Hays, Kansas. This is a welcome twist, and Bannon's depiction of rural small town life is every bit as convincing and entertaining as the views of big city life we saw in "Fascinating Rhythm".

Carol Louise Wilde

Author of Gift of Chance

The Last Witnesses

Anne Louise Bannon

Healcroft House, Publishers

Healcroft House, Publishers, a subsidiary of Robin Goodfellow Enterprises, Altadena, California, United States of America

Acknowledgements

How to say thank you, especially to all the nameless folks who inspired me without intending to. A chance conversation turns into an idea that blossoms as a way out of a tricky scene or highlights the perfect setting. Such a conversation is why Freddie and everyone end up at the Ambassador Hotel, which is sadly, no more. Which is why I offer a big thank you to the nice folks who attend the Archives Bazaar, put on by a coalition of archives in Southern California known as L.A. as Subject. The Archives Bazaar is an annual event that is history Disneyland, and if you ever get a chance to go, do it. You'll be amazed.

The late author Mary Higgins Clark is mostly responsible for the plot of this story. I had the good fortune to hear her speak multiple times and she always pointed out that it is the author's job to ask, "What if?" So, I did.

Then there is the crew of people whose work helped make this book so much better. Petrea Burchard suggested using a four-act story structure that helped me get the plot laid out. Beta reader extraordinaire Nancy Raven Smith helped make sure everything is clear. And editor Janet Aird reminded me to show, not tell and cleaned everything up.

Michael Holland, historian and archivist, was always up for answering questions, even when he was trying to watch TV. Sorry about that, dear.

Finally, credit for the photo that appears on the cover belongs to Maynard L. Parker, photographer. Courtesy of The Huntington Library, San Marino, California.

Dedication

To Cornelia Ann Klarner

Chapter One

As the taxi pulled away from the curb, Honoria Little Wentworth let out a huge sigh, as if she were letting go of her entire evening. And, in many ways, she was. The party had been less than interesting. Honoria had only gone to keep up appearances even as she wondered why said appearances were so important.

She was a tall, slender woman with brown hair and hazel eyes. To all appearances, she was happy, carefree and a bit naughty, with the added allure and worldliness of being a young widow. She wore rouge and lipstick and even mascara, and her wardrobe was always elegant and up to the minute.

She'd done her duty by getting married. It had lasted all of four days before he'd shipped off to France to fight in the Great War. That he'd been killed almost as soon as he'd gotten off the boat was, to her way of thinking, only fortunate. She looked out the window at the city at night as the car slipped past, lights dancing in the autumn air. She fidgeted with her purse clasp.

She'd only recently given up smoking, at the behest of Dr. Rothmayer. She'd seen him a couple weeks before for a particularly bad case of the croup. Going without the cigarettes had definitely helped, as had his tonic. She looked back out of the taxi's window.

Maybe this time, she'd do it, chuck it all and go where she really wanted to be. She could. She had her own money, thanks to her late and unlamented husband. But she also had ties here in her home in New York City. Her brother and his new wife, for starters. It was odd that she felt safer talking to her new sister-in-law than she did when talking to anyone else. Honoria was tired of hiding. Tired of being all the different things that others expected of her. Tired of saying what everyone else wanted to hear from her.

Yet even as she yearned to do all that she really wanted, she had to admit, she had little idea of what it was that she longed to do.

The taxi pulled up in front of her building. She paid the driver, then waited for him to open her door. She graced him with her usual flirtatious smile, which she only marginally felt, then smiled again (this time with genuine pleasure) as she approached the doorman.

"Good evening, Mrs. Wentworth," said the man. He was a spindly fellow, almost swallowed up by his uniform. Yet Honoria always got the feeling that he was a lot tougher than he looked.

"Good evening, Mr. Carruthers," Honoria replied. She paused as he coughed. "It's a cool night. Are your lungs okay?"

Carruthers had gotten a good dose of mustard gas in the War a few years ago.

"Good enough, Mrs. Wentworth." He smiled. "I'm able to work. That's better than a lot of the boys can say."

"True enough. I'll send Virginia down with some tonic in a bit."

"Not necessary, Ma'am."

As he put his hand on the building's bronzed door to open it for her, Honoria stopped him.

"Mr. Carruthers, I do know a very good lung doctor," Honoria said, thinking of Dr. Rothmayer. "I'm sure he wouldn't mind seeing you as a favor to me."

Carruthers coughed and shook his head. "It wouldn't do any good, Mrs. Wentworth. When you've been gassed, it's permanent. And I'm not in bad shape compared to a lot of the boys."

"No, I suppose not," Honoria said as he opened the door. "Thank you and have a good evening."

"You, too, Mrs. Wentworth."

Honoria barely noticed the ornate beauty of the colonnaded entry hall as she walked past the concierge desk, smiling and waving her fingers at the two men behind the desk who had quickly sprung to their feet.

Mr. Ellroy, an older Negro with that ageless look apart from his gray hair, already had the elevator door open.

"Good evening, Miz Wentworth," he said as she got in.

"Good evening, Mr. Ellroy. How are you tonight?"

"'Bout the same as usual, Miz Wentworth." He snapped the door to the elevator shut, then pushed the lever to get it going. "Going to your apartment or stopping at your brother's?"

"My place, thank you."

"You seem a might sad tonight, Miz Wentworth."

"I suppose it's nothing," Honoria said.

"Feelin' like you ain't fittin' in again?"

"You know, Mr. Ellroy, you're absolutely right." Honoria sighed. "But what do I do about it?"

"You learn how to make a way out of no way. You'll get it, Miz Wentworth."

"Thank you, Mr. Ellroy. How is Mrs. Ellroy?"

"Doing well. Doing well."

Few people who lived in her building knew the names of the staff members and rarely spoke to them beyond ordering what they wanted. Honoria didn't understand that and made a point of learning everyone's name. It made it easier to spy on her brother, who lived in the apartment below hers. Not that he was up to anything interesting these days. In fact, when Freddie wasn't working on his next book, he was busy with his new wife, Kathy. Fortunately, the two really were in love with each other, so Honoria didn't begrudge them the time spent with each other. She just wished she could talk to Kathy a bit more often.

The elevator ground to a slow stop and Mr. Ellroy opened the door.

"Thank you, Mr. Ellroy," Honoria said, stepping

off.

She waited in the tiny elevator lobby just long enough for Mr. Ellroy to close the doors to the elevator and head back downstairs. She turned and opened the door into her apartment. Virginia, her lady's maid, was not there to get her hat and coat, which wasn't unusual at all. She was probably downstairs with Freddie's cook again.

Honoria took the cloche off and shrugged off the coat with the white fox collar, laying them on one of the small tables flanking the door. She sniffed. Thanks to the croup, her sense of smell was still off. Yet something did not smell right. She turned toward her bedroom.

The young woman lay sprawled at the entrance to the back hall, her eyes open and staring. Honoria gasped and screamed. She ran in the other direction, toward the empty servants' quarters and down the stairs to her brother's apartment on the floor below. In seconds, she was pounding on the door to his bedroom.

"Just a second!" Freddie called to Honoria's hysterical sobs. "Calm down, for heaven's sakes."

He unlocked the door, and Honoria fell into his arms, gasping for air.

"What happened?" he asked. Tall and spare, like her, he had strawberry blond hair and green eyes. He was also bare-chested and wearing only a pair of pants. "Are you all right?"

Honoria gasped and slowly got control. "It's in my foyer. A body."

"A body?" asked Kathy, coming up behind him. She was shorter, with brown hair cut to her chin and alert brown eyes. She, too, was mostly undressed and wearing only a silk Chinese print robe that was obviously Freddie's. "Are you sure?"

Honoria nodded. Freddie glanced at Kathy.

"All right, darling," he said soothingly to his sister. "We'll go look. Do you want to stay here, or would you rather stay with us?"

"Don't leave me alone!" Honoria grabbed him,

then sniffed.

Freddie paused just long enough to get a handkerchief out of his bureau.

"Did you take the elevator?" he asked handing the handkerchief to her.

Honoria shook her head. "The stairs. It's faster."

They were also in the servants' quarters. Kathy went straight there. It was her usual route in and out of the building. Only Honoria, her servants, and Freddie's servants knew that Kathy's presence in Freddie's apartment was blameless. As far as the building staff was concerned, Kathy lived in Honoria's apartment, and Freddie was still a bachelor.

The wide, staring eyes greeted them in Honoria's foyer. The body belonged to a woman with dark hair that was straight and longer than fashion decreed. Bruises marked her face, and her clothes were torn. Honoria watched as Kathy touched her wrists.

"It's still pretty warm," Kathy said, shutting the eyes.

Freddie sighed. "Honoria, do you have any idea who she is?"

Honoria's eyes flitted away. "I can't say."

Freddie glanced at the body. "She doesn't look like she was too well off. Could one of your friends have done this as some sick sort of joke? One of those Bohemian maniacs you insist on going about with?"

"I'd expect something like this from one of our set sooner," snorted Honoria.

"We'd better call the police," said Kathy.

"I'll do it," grumbled Freddie suiting action to word.

"Who would do a thing like this?" said Honoria.

Kathy glanced at the body. "It wasn't just a prank. That body's too warm. If my guess is right, she was killed around eleven-thirty right here in this apartment."

"How do you know?" gasped Honoria.

"Long story." Kathy eased back into the inner

vestibule and disappeared into the bedrooms.

Honoria shivered and wondered why Freddie wasn't freezing. He didn't even have a union suit on. Honoria tried not to think about whatever activity had been going on right before she'd arrived. A second later, there was a knock on the door. Freddie opened it to a tall, portly man in a new black bowler hat and a dark gray tweed suit that had seen better days.

"I'm Detective Jim Corcoran," said the man, flashing a badge. "You have a body here?"

"This way," said Freddie, taking over. "This is my sister, Mrs. Honoria Wentworth. This is her apartment. She came home a few minutes ago and found the body over there, then came downstairs to get me."

"And you are?" Corcoran asked as he looked over the body.

"I'm Freddie Little," he said.

"It looks like there's been a struggle in the bedroom," Kathy announced, coming out of Honoria's bedroom.

Corcoran, notepad in hand, turned to look at her. Freddie glared at her, clearly annoyed at his wife's badly-timed entrance. Honoria bit her lip. She felt a giggle coming on and this was clearly not the time for it.

Kathy smiled weakly. "You got here quickly."

"Connections," said Freddie. "This is Detective Corcoran, Kathy. Officer, Kathleen Briscow."

"She lives with me," Honoria added.

"Well, Miss Briscow, how did you manage to sleep through the struggle in the bedroom, I'd like to know," asked Corcoran.

Kathy glanced over at Freddie and turned pink. Corcoran looked at Kathy, who was wearing only a very masculine dressing gown with the sleeves rolled up, and at Freddie, who was only wearing a pair of dark tweed pants, and came to a very accurate conclusion about which apartment Kathy had been in, and what she'd been doing there.

Corcoran shook his head. "Mr. Little, I appreciate the effort to save Miss Briscow's reputation, but it isn't going to help solve the crime."

Freddie sighed. "Detective, with all due respect, it is not Miss Briscow's reputation that concerns either of us, as we have been married for some months now. We are merely trying to keep it a secret for a number of reasons that are really quite irrelevant to the matter at hand."

"I see." What Corcoran saw was the nude left ring finger on Kathy's hand.

Honoria noticed it, too, and held in another giggle. As Kathy was not supposed to be married, she only wore her wedding and engagement rings at home, and frequently forgot to put them on there. Honoria seriously doubted that the wedding band Freddie wore would make any difference to Corcoran. Not that many men wore wedding bands, and Freddie's, which he never took off, had yet to be noticed, let alone questioned.

"Detective, if you insist, I can go downstairs and fetch the marriage license," said Freddie, clearly trying not to get irritated. "In any case, we will tell you everything we know about what has happened here if you will only see to it that Miss Briscow's name stays out of the report and that her presence here tonight is kept confidential."

"Well, it depends," said Corcoran.

"I can and will make it worth your while," said Freddie with an insinuating nod. "However, I would bear in mind, that the consequences of revealing our marriage are relatively small compared to a complaint that an officer of the law not only accepted a bribe, but asked for it, and I am not without connections on the police force."

Corcoran glared at Freddie, then turned to Honoria.

"All right, Mrs. Wentworth, you say you found the body this evening when you came home. What time was that?"

"Somewhere between eleven and twelve, I guess." Honoria sniffed. "I'm sorry, I don't know. I don't run my life by the clock."

"It would have been roughly quarter of twelve when we heard Mrs. Wentworth scream," said Kathy. "It was twenty of when I'd asked my husband what time it was, and that was between five and ten minutes before."

"I decided to come home early tonight," said Honoria. "One of the Vanderbilts had a small party. It was deathly dull, so I left, and came home to find this...." She gestured at the body.

"We think she may have been killed here," said Kathy. "I can't be sure, but I thought I'd heard some screaming, it must have been around eleven thirty, perhaps a little earlier."

Corcoran glared. "So how did you hear Mrs. Wentworth, but not a girl fighting for her life?"

Kathy colored up, as Freddie rolled his eyes.

"We... eh..." he began, then paused. "Well, my wife did hear her but we had other business we were tending to."

Honoria bit her lip even harder. She couldn't understand why she felt the need to giggle at such moments, but it was devilishly hard to stop, especially once she started.

Corcoran looked Freddie and Kathy both over again and nodded. It wasn't his job to say how other people should be living, as long as it wasn't breaking a law, but he obviously wanted to. He didn't for a minute believe the married tale.

"And what about the servants?" he asked. "Where are they, and why haven't they heard?"

"I only have the maid living here," said Honoria. "There's a daytime cleaning staff and Freddie's cook also cooks for me. Between the two of us, she barely has enough to do as it is. The maid is probably downstairs, sound asleep. She does that fairly often, visits downstairs and falls asleep, I mean."

"And who knew it?"

Honoria shrugged. "Anyone who knows our servants, I'd imagine. I have no idea. I don't discuss my domestic arrangements with people, but I don't doubt I've called for something and had to call downstairs to get it. Anybody could have overheard and gossiped over it."

"And who is the victim?" Corcoran watched her carefully.

"She was a friend of one of my friends," Honoria said, glancing over at Freddie and hoping he wouldn't question her further. "I was offering her shelter. We didn't get much of a chance to talk, but her name was Flossie Walsh. She said she was from Caledonia, Ohio."

"Caledonia, Ohio." Corcoran finished writing then snapped the notepad shut. "Well, the boys from the morgue should be here any minute. Miss Briscow, if you don't want to be in the report, I'd recommend taking your leave."

Kathy obediently headed for the servants' quarters. The morgue crew showed up a couple minutes later and as they got the body onto their stretcher, Honoria slipped into her bedroom. The bed linens were all askew. Several perfume bottles had been knocked over on her bureau and the top drawer hung open. Honoria looked closer at the bed and then drew back gagging. The blankets and coverlet had been pulled back and on the white top sheet, a red bloodstain was slowly getting darker. Next to the bed, a vase from the foyer had been shattered.

Honoria went back into the foyer, breathing heavily.

"Are you all right?" Freddie asked, his voice thick with worry.

"As right as one can be," Honoria said. "Detective Corcoran, you may want to look in my bedroom. My sister-in-law was absolutely correct. There was a struggle in there, and there's a nasty bloodstain on the bed."

Corcoran's eyebrows rose straight into the hat he had yet to take off. "Indeed."

He stalked off into the bedroom. The morgue crew had already left, and Honoria noticed that there wasn't any blood where the body had lain. She looked at Freddie, who had apparently noticed the same thing and looked at her. She shivered again but waited until Corcoran finally emerged from the back of the apartment.

"Well, it looks like yours was the only room that was disturbed," the police detective said, sounding vaguely annoyed. "It would be a safe bet that your friend caught a burglar in the act and paid for it with her life."

"Detective, must you be so callous?" Freddie said with a glare.

"It's all right, Freddie," Honoria said with a sigh. "I'm sure the detective means well."

Corcoran managed to look a little abashed. "My apologies, Ma'am. I'm afraid I do see this too d—, uh, too often. If you don't mind, I'd like to take that stained sheet to be tested."

"Yes, please do," said Honoria. She smiled courteously, the sort of thing she thought she was expected to do.

Corcoran returned to the bedroom, got the sheet and left promptly.

Freddie looked at Honoria. "Do you want me to rouse Virginia and have her get your room back in order?"

Honoria shook her head. "No. I— I think I'd rather not stay here tonight. Would it be terribly inconvenient...?"

"Not in the least," Freddie replied. "Go fetch what you need for the night. My rooms are always ready."

Freddie brought her downstairs and only paused at the door to the room that had been his bedroom alone until Kathy had moved in. He peeked in and smiled softly.

"She's sound asleep," he whispered proudly.

"She does have to work tomorrow," said Honoria.

"She does." Freddie sighed.

"Would you rather she didn't?" Honoria asked.

"Oh heavens, no," said Freddie, closing the door. The reason Kathy and Freddie were hiding the fact that they were married was so that Kathy could keep her job as a junior editor at Healcroft House, Publishers. Freddie was happy to support Kathy's working, but he also worried about her. "It's… One of the senior editors was fired today. Sanders, I believe. She's hoping to get his job. I just don't see how that will take place. Her boss is open to reason, but he's still terribly Victorian in his outlook. It's woefully unjust. She does more work than most of the senior editors there."

"I know," said Honoria, knowing that she understood Kathy's situation even better than Freddie did. "But women are making great strides all over the place. Maybe Kathy's boss will change his mind."

Freddie smiled to imply that he thought so, too, but both knew the odds were very much against Kathy getting the desired promotion. There being nothing more to say on the matter, Freddie saw to making sure Honoria was comfortable in one of the three guest rooms in his apartment.

The next morning, Kathy poked her sleeping husband awake.

"Mm?" Freddie grumbled.

"I've got to leave now," she whispered. "I'll be late for work."

"Oh." Freddie yawned and sat up. "Have you talked to Honoria?"

"She's still asleep. I've got to leave now, darling. I'll call you at lunch."

Freddie kissed her warmly. "You'll need to come straight home from work tonight, and no working late."

"Oh." Kathy grimaced. "That party at your mother's."

"It is my birthday."

"I know, dearest, but we're not supposed to be on the sort of terms where I'd care about that. If Honoria hadn't made such a fuss about inviting me, I doubt I'd be attending. I absolutely must leave this instant."

She kissed him again and hurried out of the room. Roberts, Freddie's valet, waited in the foyer. He was an average-sized man in his middle years with dark hair and an impassive face. Kathy was afraid he didn't like her much.

"Breakfast is waiting, ma'am," he said.

"Oh. I don't have time, Roberts." Kathy paused. "Maybe I'll just take some toast with me."

Roberts' face remained impassive, but Kathy could see the internal groan. Eating in taxis and on the subway just wasn't done by people of Freddie's privileged background. But almost three months of marriage hadn't made a socialite out of Kathy. She remained a working girl at heart and doubted that she'd ever be anything else. She grabbed her coat, hat, and the toast, and ran through the servants' quarters, and up the stairs to Honoria's apartment, so the daytime elevator operator could see her leaving from there instead of Freddie's place.

She walked into the junior editors' office at Healcroft House, Publishers, just on time. Two of her fellow junior editors, Fisk and Norbert, were in the various stages of removing their outer-wear. Burton hadn't arrived, but then, he rarely made it into the office on time.

"I thought today was going to be a red-letter day," Fisk teased as Kathy took off her hat and coat. "The day Briscow would be late."

"Sorry to disappoint you," replied Kathy with a good-natured smile.

Norbert sauntered over. "Still, we got here ahead of you. Something must be up. Did your rich boyfriend finally give you a ring?"

"Do you see me wearing one?" Kathy asked,

holding up her left hand.

"When is he going to propose?" groaned Fisk, pushing his glasses up on his nose and leaning back in his chair. He was a medium-sized man with an exceedingly normal profile.

"Why do you gentlemen insist on assuming that I want him to?" said Kathy, remaining genial in spite of the annoying nature of the questions.

Norbert ran his fingers through his dark hair with the flecks of gray. He was medium-sized, as well and rather gaunt.

"Briscow," he said with a sigh. "Must I remind you that the Frederick G. Littles of the world are very few and far between."

Kathy laughed. "I don't know why you say that. There are three of them, you know."

Norbert sat on the edge of her desk. "This is not a joking matter, Briscow. You are not a young woman."

"Oh, dear." Kathy pressed her hand to her chest in mock amazement. "I had no idea."

"Quit fooling, Briscow," said Fisk. With a worried frown, he got up from his desk and joined Norbert. "Norbert's right. At your age, you won't get too many more opportunities, let alone a fat one like that."

"That Mr. Little is married," replied Kathy. She folded her arms and smiled severely at her office mates. "Honestly, gentlemen, I don't wonder you'd like to see me married off. I know you genuinely care, but something tells me you'd like it better if you didn't have to worry about me getting Mr. Sanders' job."

Sanders had been fired the day before having returned from his luncheon drunk. Fisk and Norbert burst into laughter.

"You?" gasped Norbert. "Mr. Healcroft would sooner disband the company than make a woman senior editor."

"Even if he did, who would he get to work under you?" sniggered Fisk.

Kathy remained unfazed. "Why not you? You both

know what I can do."

Fisk giggled and shook his head. "It'll never happen. You're good, Briscow, but Healcroft would never do it. He'd never get the authors."

"You'd better see if you can get your boyfriend to propose," said Norbert. "A woman senior editor?"

Still laughing, the two went to their desks. Kathy turned to her work. It didn't matter what the other two thought; she alone knew how determined she was. Still, Fisk had made a point. As a senior editor, she'd have three to five junior editors under her, and they'd all be men. It had been four months after her promotion before Fisk or Norbert would even talk to her. Burton still wouldn't unless he had to.

The battle for acceptance had been hard fought. Kathy had found herself subjected to all sorts of harassment at first, not all of it from the other juniors. Mr. Dillbeck, her immediate boss, had been less than kind also. The only reason she had more authors to edit than anyone else was actually the result of still more harassment.

None of the editors had liked the fact that Freddie, who was one of the house's best-selling authors, wouldn't let anyone but Kathy touch his work. Worse yet, everyone knew Kathy had done a superlative piece of editing on Freddie's first book, and, as predicted, the book's sales had been fabulous. Part of this was due to Freddie's name and social standing. That the book was still selling after several months was due to the fact that it was a very good book, and Kathy's efforts to make sure it reached its potential.

Freddie would have remained her only author if it hadn't been for Pierce Jennings. Jennings had established himself as an angry young voice in literature some years before. In reality, Jennings was officious and whined, and generally made himself so unpopular that more than one publishing house had decided even his phenomenal popularity wasn't worth dealing with him. He had driven the other two senior editors into abandoning him when Mr. Dillbeck decided in a fit of pique to give him to Kathy.

Kathy chose to correspond with Jennings at first, signing with her first initial and last name. Jennings was so impressed after two letters that he came into the office demanding to see Mr. Briscow. With several smirks, Fisk, Norbert, and Burton directed Jennings to Kathy's desk. Jennings didn't believe Kathy was the editor he wanted, so she let him believe she was the secretary. Pretty soon, Jennings' search for Mr. Briscow became the office joke.

Then another best-selling author, Harold T. Mennerly, began to ask for Mr. Briscow, and some of the other authors, all of whom Kathy had worked with when she was still a secretary doing her boss's work for him. Frustrated by all the noise, Mr. Healcroft had given them to Kathy, to the irritation of Mr. Dillbeck and to the amusement of the rest of the staff.

It was getting on for noon when Freddie wandered into the office. Kathy was engrossed in a manuscript and didn't notice him until he sat down next to her desk.

"Why are you here?" she asked, brightening.

"I was hoping you'd be free for luncheon," he replied, then leaned over to look at what she was working on, and spoke softly. "I want to talk to you about the disturbing incident."

"I wanted to talk to you about that, too." Kathy smiled and got up. "Well, Mr. Little, I think I can oblige you."

"Shall we, then?" Freddie was already on his feet and held her coat for her.

Freddie hailed a taxi outside the building and gave an address near Fifth and 34th. They chatted about small matters until they were at the tea room and had ordered.

"Have you talked to Honoria?" Kathy asked.

"Yes," said Freddie. "She confirmed what you said about the struggle in the bedroom. Corcoran seems to believe that her friend surprised a burglar."

"That makes sense," said Kathy. "Was there anything missing?"

"Honoria says no."

Kathy's eyebrows rose. "As in you do not believe her."

Freddie sighed. "I do, about anything being missing, at any rate. But there is something about Miss Walsh being there that is bothering me. Honoria is not being entirely honest about her. But I cannot for the life of me say why."

"She's probably afraid you wouldn't approve of her friend." Kathy frowned. "Or maybe there's something else. I sometimes get the feeling that Honoria has secrets simply because she needs them for some reason."

Freddie shrugged. "I don't doubt."

Kathy pulled a cufflink from her purse. "I found this in Honoria's bedroom."

It was a gold square, rimmed with tiny diamonds. The face was a bas-relief design of vines intertwined around what appeared to be a letter of the alphabet.

Freddie looked at it. "It's a nice piece. Looks like a monogram of some sort."

"But which letter? Looks like it could an A or a P or maybe an R."

He shook his head. "Why didn't you give this to the police?"

"I was going to. But Detective Corcoran wasn't exactly receptive. And I didn't want him asking any questions about Honoria and any male friends that might have dropped this."

"Kind of you to spare her," Freddie said then frowned thoughtfully. "And as disturbing it is to think about Honoria behaving so badly, this was not left by a lover. The daytime cleaning staff was in yesterday and they would have found it and given it to Roberts or Virginia."

Kathy smiled at Freddie. "We've done it before,

Freddie. And there's something about that cufflink that makes me wonder if this hasn't come from your set."

Freddie mentally debated whether the attack on Miss Walsh had come from his "set" of fellow socialites while the waiter brought tea.

"It's possible," he sighed. "I did talk to the police this morning."

"And..?"

"She was beaten, and her neck broken." Casually, but without drawing attention to it, Freddie filled his teacup from a hip flask, and replaced the flask inside his jacket. "One of the servants in another apartment did see a man in the service stairwell that night, collar up and hat down, so it wasn't clearly enough to recognize."

Kathy took a sip of her tea. "What about the blood in Honoria's bedroom?"

Freddie shrugged. "Who knows? It wasn't the girl's. The police are very certain about that."

"How?"

"The blood type doesn't match hers, and she didn't have any wounds."

"Then it probably belongs to the man who killed her. Whose else's could it be?"

Freddie shrugged. "It would seem the logical conclusion."

"She must have marked the man." Kathy's face screwed up as she thought. "There was a vase shattered in the bedroom. She must have hit the killer with it, which would account for the blood. I can't imagine a wound like that would be easy to hide, especially if it was on the face somewhere. Head wounds bleed a lot"

They waited while the waiter delivered their lunches. Kathy tucked in gracefully. Freddie refilled his cup.

"Drinking so much this early?" Kathy asked.

"I'm anticipating the need for considerable reinforcements tonight," sighed Freddie.

"I would imagine you're anticipating worse than shall actually be."

"Hm. I've heard rumors they've made some more discoveries about that Teapot Dome mess, which means Father will be up in arms. And Mr. and Mrs. Wright are supposedly going to attend, which means Mr. Wright is going to rub it in, and there shall probably be a nasty confrontation over the billiards table. All in all, I'd rather withdraw with you ladies and discuss charity drives."

"I'd much prefer the confrontation over the billiards table."

"Not if you'd heard it as many times as I have." Freddie glared at his teacup. "That's only part of the unpleasantness, though. The papers have found out about the body, and there are reporters in every nook and cranny they can get into in that building. It was no small thing trying to leave this morning. Detective Corcoran has kept his word, however, and your name does not appear in any report, and the press seems unaware of your presence. I recommend consistent use of the service door. That's what I'm using until this whole mess blows over."

"Oh, drat. We probably shouldn't look into it, either, in that case. The papers will never leave you alone, if and when we solve it."

Freddie frowned. "We're going to solve it. We've done it before. Honoria's terribly upset, and I don't blame her. There's something else behind it, and I want to know what it is."

Chapter Two

Pierce Jennings, small, balding and whining, was waiting when Kathy and Freddie returned to her desk.

"Hallo, Mr. Little," he said, then turned on Kathy. "Well, where is that blasted Mr. Briscow? I was told he was out to lunch."

"Oh, for heaven's sakes, Jennings," groaned Freddie. "It's been six months. Haven't you figured it out yet?"

"Mr. Little..." warned Kathy through her teeth.

Norbert and Fisk watched with intent grins.

"Obviously, the man does not want to speak to me," Jennings complained. "I know I can be a little difficult at times, but it's dreadfully unfair. I suppose you're waiting for him, too, Little. Does he see you? I wouldn't be surprised. My work is never given the consideration it's due."

"Now, now, Mr. Jennings," said Kathy. "Your work is given proper regard by everyone in this firm."

"Then why won't Mr. Briscow see me?"

"Because Mr. Briscow doesn't exist," growled Freddie.

"Will you please?" Kathy turned on him angrily.

"Well, it's a fact," retorted Freddie in righteous indignation. "And I'm sick and tired of seeing you not get your due because of a foolish, ignorant prejudice."

Kathy, blushing furiously, glanced at Norbert and Fisk,

"Mr. Little, will you please contain yourself?"

"What's going on?" demanded Jennings. "What are

you saying, Little? That this Briscow character doesn't exist?"

"She exists. She's standing right here in front of you." Freddie folded his arms triumphantly.

"But she's a secretary," insisted Jennings.

"Only because you insist on believing it," said Freddie.

Jennings gaped. Kathy took Freddie's arm firmly.

"Mr. Little, may I see you out?" she said pushing him to the door. "Mr. Jennings, please wait here."

She waited until they'd gotten to the elevator lobby before turning on Freddie.

"What did you think you were doing?" she snapped in a low voice. "You could have ruined everything."

"Jennings is an ass. He deserves to be shown up."

"Never mind Jennings. What about Norbert and Fisk and Burton? They're all waiting around for you to propose. And after that little outburst, what do you think they're going to suppose is the reason you're not?"

"Oh." Freddie's face fell. "I'm sorry. I didn't think of that."

"You're drunk, that's what you are."

"I am not."

"Just because you're still standing? Good heavens, Freddie, you've got more sense than to act the way you did. Now, damn it, either you sober up before this evening, or I'm not going."

Freddie sighed sheepishly. "That's your final word?"

"Yes."

"I'll do my best, then. It is my birthday."

"That's no excuse for public drunkenness, especially in the middle of the day."

"All right. I'll see you this evening, then."

"All right." Kathy glanced around to make sure there was no one about, then pecked Freddie's cheek. "I'll see you later."

Back in the office, Jennings was pacing furiously.

"It's impossible!" he groaned. "It can't be."

"What can't be?" asked Kathy, going behind her desk.

"Are you really K. Briscow?" Jennings demanded. "A woman editing my books?"

"You've always said how pleased you are with the editing," Kathy pointed out calmly.

"I am, I am, I am. But a woman. This is preposterous."

"Well, you can have Mr. Healcroft try to find you another editor."

"No!" Jennings screeched. He planted both hands firmly on Kathy's desk and leaned over it. "That would be disastrous! No one else understands my work. No one else does it justice."

"No one else puts up with you."

"That's nonsense," snorted Jennings. "I make good money for this firm. I've even outsold that Little bastard, in less time. I merely insist on the best editor for my work. And that was Briscow."

"I resent the past tense reference, and your sales are only slightly ahead of where Mr. Little's were after a similar lapse of time after publication." Kathy blithely shuffled through the papers on her desk.

"You'll still handle me, won't you?" Jennings asked nervously. "If you think Mr. Healcroft will be angry because I found out you're a woman, I'll gladly tell him I won't have anyone else. I will. I won't even tell the others. Mennerly will stand by you."

"Mr. Mennerly already knows, as do Mrs. Petrie, and Mr. Davidson, and Mr. Kettner. Now, Mr. Jennings, was there anything specific you came in to discuss?"

"Oh." Jennings puffed himself up. "My next book. We need to set a publication date for it."

"I need a manuscript first."

"But Davidson..."

"Mr. Davidson does not have a reputation for missing his deadlines. Manuscript first, Mr. Jennings, then we'll talk about publication." Kathy sighed with relief as the phone on her desk rang. "If you'll excuse me."

The summons did little to relieve her beyond getting Jennings away from her desk. She hurried down the corridor to Mr. Healcroft's office, her heart pounding. Her immediate boss, Mr. Dillbeck, was there also, with a sour look on his face. Kathy tried not to smile.

"Miss Briscow," said Mr. Healcroft, an aging man with old-fashioned ideas and tastes. "We've got another job for you."

"Really." Kathy's heart took a jubilant leap.

"Odd as it may seem, another author has requested that you handle his manuscript." Mr. Healcroft sighed as Mr. Dillbeck frowned. "We are not in the habit of allowing our authors to choose their editors, but we have been wooing this gentleman for some time. Therefore, in spite of Mr. Dillbeck's protests, I have decided to hand the job over to you."

Kathy's heart fell. "Thank you, sir. I appreciate your confidence in me."

"Here it is," growled Dillbeck, handing her the box. "It's Lowell Winters' first novel."

"Lowell's?" Unable to contain her smile, Kathy opened the lid and looked at the first page. "That sneak. He must have finished it before he ran off to California." She noticed the bemused glares from the two men. "Mr. Winters and I have met before. Mr. Little introduced us. I believe they're quite good friends."

Dillbeck snorted. Mr. Little was quite a thorn in his side, for whatever Mr. Little wanted, Mr. Little got, and all too often he wanted his fellow authors to insist on Miss Briscow taking their books. The annoying thing was that the woman was so damned good at what she did. Why she couldn't go off and get married and raise babies, instead of taking work from men with families to support, Mr. Dillbeck had no idea. It was rumored she wanted the position left open by Sanders' departure. He would see to it that she got it over his dead body.

"Yes, well, I expect a report on this new project by the end of next week," said Mr. Healcroft.

"Yes, sir." Kathy closed the box. "Mr. Healcroft, have you made any decision about who is to replace Mr. Sanders?"

"Not yet. In fact, I doubt I shall. As you know, my son has been working with us for some months now. I've decided to leave the choice to him."

"I see." Kathy smiled in spite of the sinking feeling in her gut. "Well. I've got work to do. If you'll excuse me."

She left wondering what to do next. Thaddeus Healcroft was not only a notorious misogynist, he particularly hated Kathy. There seemed to be little hope of a senior editorship going to her with Thaddeus making the decision.

She was still brooding about the situation as she got ready for dinner. Freddie, fortunately, had sobered up and was very sympathetic.

"I could withdraw my new book," he offered as he buttoned up the back of her white silk gown embellished with vines of silver sequins running up and down the length of the dress. "And possibly get Mennerly to, and Davidson."

"That would help," Kathy replied sarcastically. "It would truly ingratiate me with Thaddeus. Besides, what makes you think you could get them to?"

"Darling, they don't want anyone else touching their work any more than I do. All you have to do is threaten to quit." Finished with buttoning, Freddie took a quick look at himself in the bureau mirror

"That's nonsense." Kathy moved away and picked up a pair of gloves. "And even if they did, it would only make my position there more awkward. No, Freddie, if hard work, excellence, and dedication aren't going to get me promoted, then nothing will. At least I still have a job that I enjoy."

Out in the foyer, the phone rang.

"I suppose." Freddie slid into his tail coat. "I still

don't like watching you take it on the chin because of a silly prejudice."

Roberts knocked then entered. "Excuse me, ma'am, sir, but Mrs. Wentworth just called. A Sergeant Callahan is coming up to her apartment to visit Miss Briscow."

"Criminy!" Kathy grabbed a purse and fled. "I'm on my way."

Sergeant Daniel Callahan, of the New York Police Department, was also Kathy's uncle, on her mother's side. He was a medium-sized man, sporting a small paunch and graying brown hair. He, along with everyone else in New York, was unaware that Kathy was married to Freddie, and thought, like everyone else, that Kathy merely shared Honoria's apartment to keep Honoria company.

He seemed gratified to see Kathy come from the back of Honoria's apartment, where the bedrooms were. Kathy suspected that he'd been hearing rumors about which apartment Kathy was living in.

"It's good to see you, Uncle Dan," she said, bussing his cheek. "What brings you over here?"

"I'm surprised you haven't guessed," said Dan. "What with all the excitement here last night."

"Oh, that. It was rather unpleasant, but I suppose you've heard I wasn't here. Honoria, do you mind if I show my uncle into the living room?"

"Of course," said Honoria. "How many times have I told you? This is your home, too."

She followed at a discreet distance as Kathy led Dan into the living room.

"That's quite a dress you have on, Katie-girl," Dan said, looking at the gown.

Kathy blushed. "I'm going out tonight."

"It's my brother's birthday," Honoria explained quickly. "My mother insisted that I bring Kathy. I loaned her the dress."

Dan took a long calculating look at Honoria's tall, slender figure adorned in a deep blue dress of lace and golden beads, then compared it to Kathy's smaller, better-padded form.

"It's all perfectly legitimate, Uncle Dan," said Kathy quickly. "Just complicated. But about last night."

"Yes, that." Dan turned on her. "Where were you if you weren't here?"

"Out. I went to a show, then met with some friends."

"On a work night?"

"Uncle Dan, this is hardly fair. You know I've done it before. I'm not under suspicion, am I?"

"Not of murdering that poor girl."

"Now really, Sergeant," cut in Honoria. "I must take issue with this. Last night was dreadfully traumatizing as it was. To make such insinuations, well, I won't have it."

The doorbell rang. There was a tense silence as Virginia, a small rounded woman with light brown fluffy bobbed hair, admitted Freddie wearing a dark overcoat over his white tie and tails and carrying a shining top hat.

"I hope you ladies are ready," he announced cheerfully. "Good evening, Sergeant. It's a pleasure to see you again. What brings you here this evening?"

"A certain disturbance that occurred here last night," replied Dan grimly.

"Yes, that was nasty, wasn't it?" Freddie smiled and put his hands behind his back. "Have you found anything out about the burglars?"

"Not as yet."

"That's too bad. I'm afraid you'll have to excuse us. There's a taxi waiting downstairs for us, and I don't doubt the meter is running." Freddie took Kathy's arm.

"Not so fast, Mr. Little. I've just as much cause to be talking to you."

"Uncle Dan..." protested Kathy.

"Enough, Katie-girl. Rumors is one thing, but when you tell me you're staying out all hours the night before you have to be at work the next morning, and a perfectly trustworthy officer tells me you were here, but in a state of undress, and you weren't here for the murder, then I have to wonder what has been going on."

"Well, you can just keep wondering, Uncle Dan," snapped Kathy. "I haven't broken any laws, and I've a right to my own private life. Mr. Little, are we ready to go?"

"Katie-girl, don't you smart off to me now. I'm only watching out for your best interests. And I find it mighty funny that your Mr. Little is standing there wearing what looks to me like a wedding band, and your ring finger is bare."

Kathy's face colored up as Freddie's hands found his pockets. Honoria gasped, then giggled.

Dan ignored her. "The funny thing is, Katie-girl, last summer your mother wrote a very strange letter to us telling us not to worry if any rumors about you and Mr. Little got around. But I do worry, young lady, and I don't see how you're going to come out of a situation like this on top."

Freddie smiled softly. "Sergeant, with all due respect, while I understand your concern, I must assure you it is not warranted. Nothing has passed between myself and Kathy that is not honorable and legitimate. I can promise you that."

"Then what was she doing in your apartment last night, without a stitch of clothing except your dressing gown, and with you not wearing much more? And you can't tell me she weren't down there. Not with the report I got."

"Uncle Dan, Freddie is telling you the truth," Kathy groaned. "Are you going to take someone else's word over mine?"

"No. But I notice you're not denying it, either. Now, what in the name of all the saints is going on here?"

Freddie looked at Kathy. "It's up to you."

"You're too kind," Kathy grumbled back. She took a deep breath. "Uncle Dan, I guess we're going to have to take you into our confidence. The reason Ma wrote you that letter is that we're trying to keep it all secret so I can continue working. But the fact is, last July when Freddie and I were in Kansas, we got married. And you know what kind of publicity Freddie gets. If anyone found out, I'd get fired, and I doubt I'd be able to get another job, at least not an editing post. You know how conservative some of those people can be."

"Married?" Uncle Dan stepped back and thought it over.

"As I said, perfectly honorable," said Freddie. "If you like, I'll go fetch the license."

"Married," repeated Dan. "And you want to keep it a secret? From your own family?"

"Well, it's not you so much, but one of the cousins might like a fast ten spot from a reporter." Kathy held her breath.

"One of Colleen's brats'd do it for sure." Dan sighed. "And probably wouldn't hold out for the ten spot. All right, Katie-girl, you made your point. You can count on me to keep mum. But if Michael and any of the others start asking questions, I won't be telling tales."

"Don't tell them anything," suggested Honoria.

Both Dan and Kathy laughed.

"Well, Sergeant, if you will excuse us," said Freddie. "I was quite truthful about that taxi. Ladies?"

Dan allowed himself to be shown out, with Kathy, Freddie, and Honoria close behind. Dan left the building shaking his head and muttering pleasantly to himself. There was tense silence in the taxi.

The front hall of the Little mansion was brightly lit and almost welcoming. It was too vast and too filled with art treasures and glowering portraits of ancestors to ever be completely homelike, even to Freddie and Honoria, who had grown up there. Briggeman, the slightly stooped butler, signaled a footman to take the coats, then escorted them to the salon, where he announced their arrival.

It was a relatively small group. Intimate, as the senior Mrs. Little put it. Only twelve people total. Freddie introduced Kathy around, first to his grandfather, Frederick G. Little, Senior, then to Aunt Theadora Corning, a sister of Freddie's mother, apparently there to keep Frederick, Senior, company, as he had already outlived three wives.

Then there were Edward and Dora Roundhouse, a brother and sister. Freddie decided they were there to tempt Honoria and him. Edward was Freddie's age, and the two were supposedly good friends with each other. Freddie had spent time with Edward in the same way he'd spent time with most of the people of his social set, more because it was expected than because Freddie any genuine liking for them. Edward looked as though he'd been in a fight recently, with fresh bruises all over his nose and a fat lip. He only said he'd taken a nasty fall. Edward's sister Dora was nineteen, blond and bored. Both she and her brother were of little substance and there was very little chance of attracting either of the Little siblings.

Arthur and Delia Wright were also contemporaries of Freddie's, and great friends, at least Freddie let them think so. They were supposedly the ideal married couple, but Freddie knew that both Arthur and Delia had lovers on the side, hated their children and barely liked each other.

Only one face was new to Freddie.

"This is Mr. James Ryland," said Mrs. Little, an imposing woman with graying blond hair piled neatly on top of her head. "No, no. Please don't get up, Mr. Ryland. He's had a little accident in his automobile. This is my son, Freddie, and my daughter's friend, Kathleen Briscow. In fact, Mr. Ryland, you and Miss Briscow should have a great deal in common. She's a working girl."

Freddie sighed silently. So, Mr. Ryland was there to keep Kathy company and probably keep her away from Freddie. Mrs. Little remained blissfully unaware of her son's marriage, and Freddie was all too happy to avoid enlightening her.

"A working girl, eh?" Mr. Ryland smiled cordially. He was square-shaped, with a square face, and body. His hair was graying slightly at the temples, but very black otherwise, and he kept a pince-nez in his breast pocket. If he'd been injured, it was hard to tell where.

"Yes, I'm a junior editor at Healcroft House, Publishers," said Kathy, somewhat coolly. "I presume you are also employed?"

"More or less. I work for the Republican National Committee, and also as Mr. Will Hays' aide."

"How nice." Kathy nodded and looked for an excuse to move on. Philosophically, she had little use for Republicans and wanted to be elsewhere before Mr. Ryland's sympathies provoked her into a full-scale argument.

She was keenly aware that Mrs. Little's acceptance of her was a tenuous thing at best. The fact that Kathy was not in the Social Register of New York's famed Four Hundred millionaires was the most serious fault, as far as Mrs. Little was concerned. But that Kathy also worked for a living made her a less desirable companion for Honoria and even Freddie. Kathy's good manners and the fact that her family were landowners in Kansas somewhat mitigated her less-than-desirable status. Being a Democrat certainly would not help.

Freddie was freely imbibing cocktails, as was everyone else in the room. Kathy wondered if they'd still be standing by the time the dinner gong rang. Mr. Ryland seemed to be focusing his attention on Honoria, who seemed largely indifferent to him as she nodded blandly at something Delia Wright was saying. Kathy excused herself and drifted about.

"Whoa, there, young lady," said Mr. Little, Sr., from a couch. "Come over here and brighten an old man's evening, will you?"

Kathy smiled. "I'll do my best, sir."

Freddie's grandfather was tall, gaunt, and white-haired, and very lively, with Freddie's congenial disposition. He looked as though he might be even younger than his son, Freddie's father, although Kathy had heard Freddie say that the old man was well into his eighties.

"Deathly group, aren't they?" Mr. Little, Sr., continued, sipping from a martini glass. "I was hoping Lowell Winters would show, but five will get you ten, he wasn't even invited."

"He's in California, anyway," said Kathy. "Apparently on movie business."

"Good for him. It's a growing industry, mark my words."

"What? You don't think movies are just a fad? Stiff dumb shows?"

The old man laughed. "That they are, but they're making a lot of people very rich. I won't say what they're producing is all that good. Well, there's some good stuff coming out of it. And there's plenty of trash to be had on Broadway this season. I've told my son more than once it's worth investing in. But he's so provincial. Fortunately, Freddie has a head on his shoulders, and knows how to listen."

"Indeed." Kathy couldn't help glaring at Freddie who was working on his third martini. It wasn't terribly obvious, but he was talking somewhat faster than normal and occasionally listing to the right a bit.

"Drinking too much again, is he?" Mr. Little, Sr.'s pale green eyes flicked back and forth between Kathy and his grandson. "Can't really blame him. It requires plenty of anesthesia to face this crowd. It's nice to see someone with a little less blue blood flowing in her veins. I'm sure Dora Roundhouse is after Freddie, but take my advice, and go after him yourself. We need some fresh breeding stock in this family."

"And what makes you so sure I'd be desirable breeding stock?" Kathy couldn't help feeling amused by the old man's suggestion.

"You're not in the Register. Come now. You're not

suggesting you're not interested, are you? Freddie's not as bad as all that, even when he drinks to excess. Being Honoria's friend gives you an enormous advantage, you know."

Kathy laughed. "Perhaps. But I've a few dirty secrets in my past, and my ancestry is hardly top drawer."

"Oh, really. Sounds interesting."

"Can you keep a secret?"

"Of course."

"My mother's family is Irish."

Mr. Little, Sr., sat back and laughed loudly. The others in the room smiled indulgently at the faux pas of their elder and went back to their conversations.

Mr. Little, Sr., gasped merrily. "I knew it. Good breeding stock, indeed. That settles it. I will ply your suit personally."

"I don't think you need to," said Kathy, holding in her giggles.

The old man's eyes flicked back and forth again.

"No, I don't think I do. Let me guess, you are relying on discretion, as Gloria is not likely to approve."

"Nor Mr. Little, Jr."

"Fred won't even notice. I don't know how I did wrong by him. As for Gloria, leave her in my hands. She's certainly the more sensible. And I promise I won't breathe a word about your unfortunate, hee-hee, ancestry. Now, my dear, tell me all about your work, and this marvelous book that Freddie has penned. I was very impressed by it, by the way. It's such a pleasure to see the boy making something of himself."

When they were summoned to dinner, Mr. Little, Sr., insisted on escorting Kathy in, leaving Mr. Ryland to take Delia Wright in. Edward Roundhouse got stuck with Aunt Theadora.

"The seating arrangement will be miserable, I guarantee it," Mr. Little, Sr., whispered in Kathy's ear. "I suppose I could raise a fuss. It's wonderful the license advanced age gives one. But I think we should rise above it, don't you?"

"Most certainly," said Kathy.

Freddie was seated next to his mother, and Kathy at the other end of the table, next to Mr. Little, Jr. Mr. Ryland was on her left, and Edward Roundhouse was across from her, with Honoria at his right. The tedious and terminally Republican nature of the conversation was bearable, but only just. Furthermore, Mr. Ryland, who was supposed to be plying Kathy with his charms, was much more taken with Honoria, who largely ignored him in favor of smiling blandly at Arthur Wright. Edward talked almost exclusively about football, a sport that interested Kathy. However, Edward was mostly interested in what the final scores were, and how much better the Ivy League schools were than the actual game. Mr. Little, Jr., who was tall with reddish white hair, all but ignored Kathy and discussed scores and the stock market with Edward. Kathy decided she was supposed to sit enraptured by the masculine brilliance around her, but found little to be enraptured about, and instead concentrated on eating.

After dessert, the ladies withdrew to have coffee in the drawing room, and the men to the billiards room, presumably to have the interesting conversations. Somewhere in all the shuffle, Honoria pulled Kathy aside.

"I have to leave," Honoria said quietly. "I just wanted to say goodbye to you, first."

"Are you all right?" Kathy asked, worried. There was something odd about Honoria's behavior, even if Kathy couldn't put a finger on what it was.

"I've got a headache, that's all." Honoria patted Kathy's hand. "You stay and help Freddie have a good time. And please don't worry about me."

Kathy nodded and allowed Honoria to make her escape. She stayed in the drawing room as long as she could, hoping that Freddie would soon escape from the billiards room. But the constant prattle and gossip about people Kathy neither knew nor wanted to know, along with her concern about Honoria, finally pushed Kathy to a decision.

She quietly excused herself and found Briggeman in the hallway.

"May I help you, miss?" the aging, but solid, butler asked.

"I'm just curious," said Kathy. "Mrs. Wentworth seems to have left."

"Yes, miss. Shortly after dinner."

"I know. Did she leave alone?"

"Yes, miss."

"And her brother is still here."

"Yes, miss."

Kathy pondered. It was possible that Honoria had made some assignation during dinner, or perhaps before, although Kathy had no reason to believe so.

"Have any of the other gentlemen left?" Kathy asked. "I was just wondering, in terms of planning my departure, you understand."

"Of course, ma'am. Mr. Ryland left a few minutes after Miss Honoria."

"Did Mrs. Wentworth take a taxi?"

"Yes, miss."

"We were supposed to go out later. You wouldn't happen to know the address she went to, would you?"

"No, miss. She gave it directly to the driver, and would not tell me."

"And that Ryland fellow. You don't know where he went, do you? I was hoping to meet up with him again."

"I'm afraid, miss, he left in his own limousine."

Kathy debated for a moment. It was possible that Honoria had decided to meet Mr. Ryland elsewhere. But she had been so cool to the man during dinner. A roar of male laughter drifted in from the billiards room. Freddie was not only still in there, he was probably very drunk. Kathy shuddered at the thought, then decided she might as well go home.

"Well, that settles that," she said. "I guess I'd

better say my good nights. Will you fetch my coat, and summon a taxi, please?"

"Certainly, miss."

Kathy felt a twinge of guilt at leaving Freddie behind, but not much. They'd argued about his drinking a couple times before and he'd agreed Kathy had a right to do as she saw fit when he over-indulged. Back at the apartment building, she was surprised to find that Honoria wasn't there. Kathy called down to the concierge desk and found out that Honoria hadn't come home at all, but that Mr. Ryland had come by. Kathy grilled Virginia briefly, but she didn't know anything. Perplexed and fully worried, Kathy went downstairs and changed clothes.

"Roberts, I have to step out for a short bit," she told the valet. "When Mr. Little returns, see to it that he's put in the guest bedroom. If, on the off chance, he is still conscious and protests, kindly remind him that there is no reason I should have to give up my bed when he is the transgressor, and he knows I will not tolerate his drunkenness."

"Yes, Mrs. Little. May I tell him where you are?"

"You could if I knew. Just tell him I'm looking for his sister."

Kathy hurried out into the night, leaving through the service door, and all but running to the subway stop. Considering the situation logically, there was no real reason to be concerned. After all, it was hardly the first time Honoria had lied about something, and she was certainly capable of looking after herself. But it didn't make sense that she'd fib about having a headache just to get out of the party. She'd have simply left without pulling Kathy aside. Also, Mr. Ryland and his convenient departure after Honoria's bothered Kathy. It wasn't for an assignation with Honoria. It didn't make sense. After all, Mr. Ryland had been injured recently.

Admittedly, Mr. Ryland seemed inordinately interested in Honoria. But Honoria had shown absolutely no interest in return. She hadn't even flirted with the man. And while Kathy had to admit there was a lot she didn't know about her sister-in-law, Kathy did know that Mr. Ryland's political leanings were such that Honoria would have had even less interest in the man than Kathy had. And it wasn't like Honoria to just disappear without at least saying something.

Chapter Three

Hidden underneath a long black wig and several red silk veils, Honoria moved about the Greenwich Village speakeasy, ostensibly just another spiritualist plying her trade. It, like so many things in Honoria's life, had started as simply a lark. Except that Honoria had discovered she was rather good at telling fortunes and going into trances and otherwise dispensing spiritual advice, albeit without the aid of spirits and the like. Whether she truly had "Second Sight" was another issue altogether and while Honoria was inclined to take a more stoic, rational view, she couldn't entirely dismiss the possibility, either.

The speak was draped with red fabric, and the lighting was so dim it was actually easier to see on the street outside. The air was thick with smoke, not all of it from tobacco. Honoria sneezed softly. Miles, the bartender, had signaled that there was a newcomer in the speak. Between the smoke and her veils, Honoria wasn't sure how she'd find the new young woman. Or wasn't until she saw an average-sized woman in a sensible suit stumbling into a hookah. What was Kathy doing there?

Honoria slipped up to her sister-in-law and tapped her on the shoulder. Kathy turned and Honoria beckoned her toward the back of the speak. Honoria went ahead, then turned. Kathy was behind her. Honoria slipped through a doorway covered by oriental rugs and held her breath. A minute later, Kathy had slid through, as well.

The room was roughly finished and the walls

were grimy, but there was light enough to see by. Sandalwood incense didn't quite mask the stench of sweat, bad whiskey, reefers and opium. In the middle of the room was a table with a crystal ball. Honoria motioned for silence, then removed the wig and veils.

"Honoria!" gasped Kathy.

"Sh!" Honoria threw the veils aside onto a battered overstuffed chair and checked the door. "We can talk, but not too loudly. How did you find me?"

"I've been going everywhere."

"Good Heavens, Kathy, why would you take such a risk?"

"It wasn't that much of one. Why did you leave dinner, and where did you change clothes?"

"I have my hiding spots."

"But why?"

"It's Flossie," said Honoria. "The girl who was murdered in my apartment last night. My friend asked me to keep her safe."

"I don't understand."

"I don't entirely understand, either." Honoria frowned. "My friend, she sent Flossie to me. This friend has been in hiding for a couple years now. She said she witnessed something truly horrible and that her life is in danger from the person who did it. I don't know if Flossie is connected to the same danger or not. I don't even know what the danger is."

"But who is your friend?"

"I can't tell you. She's in hiding. And shortly after she hid, I noticed that someone was watching my mail."

"Your mail?"

"Letters were steamed open," Honoria said. "It's not always easy to tell when one has. But I'd see drops of water on the envelope. The sheets inside would be shuffled out of order. Little things like that. My friend and I decided that someone is watching me to find her. Whoever is after my friend is someone with enormous resources if he can watch my mail that closely. But I have enormous resources, too, and that's why I thought it would be safe to keep Flossie at my apartment, especially if I snuck her in through the servants' door and made sure she stayed there. No one knew she was there, not even you and you passed through that apartment every day."

"But why don't you think Flossie was the victim of a burglar?" Kathy asked. "There's no real reason not to."

"Except that nothing was stolen," said Honoria. "This burglar opened several of my jewelry boxes and didn't take any of it. You'd think he'd have at least pocketed one or two items before Flossie surprised him. And even if Flossie had surprised him, how did her neck get broken? He could have knocked her out as easily as not, even if she was fighting him. No. This was someone who knew what he was doing and killed her on purpose. And it wasn't a burglary."

Kathy went over what she'd seen the night before in her mind. "You're right. I was wondering why it didn't look like anything was missing, myself, now that I think about it."

"I decided this afternoon that I'm not going to take any chances. I'm going to stay hidden down here for the time being. I only went to the party last night for Freddie's sake. I've sent a telegram to my friend, and I may be able to get some information here in the Village that you can't." Honoria swallowed. "Do you think you can avoid telling Freddie? He'll be furious if he finds out."

"He probably will." Kathy took a deep breath. "But it would be better if we worked together. If I keep Freddie from chasing you home, will you please at least tell me what you find? I can get my uncle, the cop, to help us. He can dig up things no one else can."

"I don't like it." Honoria looked away and fidgeted with the corner of a veil. "There is something terribly dangerous going on. I don't want either of you to get hurt."

"Of course, you don't," said Kathy. She laid her

hand on Honoria's shoulder. "And I don't want you to get hurt or Freddie, either. And he doesn't want either of us hurt. But it's not going to help to work at cross purposes. Honoria, Freddie and I work as a team because neither of us alone can get the job done. If you work with us, we'll be that much more effective."

Honoria thought it over. "All right."

"Good." Kathy smiled and Honoria watched as Kathy marshalled her thoughts. "What can you tell me about this Flossie Walsh?"

Honoria shook her head. "Not much, actually. As I said, I don't know if she's connected to the same danger my friend is. It could be, which even if I knew was the case, is no help at all since I don't know what my friend is running from." She took a deep breath and centered her thinking. "Flossie did tell me that she's from Caledonia, Ohio."

"Yes. You told the police that."

"Right. She said that she had worked for a lung doctor here in New York. Dr. Rothmayer. He's very well thought of in his field and I went to see him when I had the croup so badly last month. But Flossie said she had to change her name and go away again last winter. She didn't say where." Honoria suddenly felt overwhelmed by grief and guilt. "I should have asked her more about her trouble and I shouldn't have brought her to the apartment. I don't know why, but I thought she was simply hiding from a husband who beat her. Or that's what I chose to believe."

"I don't see why you'd have any reason to assume that Miss Walsh was in hiding from the same thing as your friend," Kathy said quietly. "At least not until last night and even then, it still could have been a burglar."

"But I don't know what my friend is running from and why that would include Flossie, and I'm not sure I'll be safe until I do."

"No. I don't think you are. And I agree. You should stay in hiding." Kathy frowned. "We should probably maintain as little contact as possible just in case someone starts watching Freddie and me in order to try and get to you. But we need to find some safe way to communicate just in case one or the other of us finds out something important, especially if it could save one of us."

"Oh, dear." Honoria shivered. That Kathy was absolutely right did nothing to curb her fears. She took another deep breath to calm herself and as she let it go, her eyes fell on her veils and wig. "Wait. I've got an idea. Why don't you come to me for spiritual consultations?"

"Me? Spiritual consultations?" Kathy let out a short laugh. "Who would believe that?"

Honoria frowned. "That is a problem. No. Here's what you can say. You came down with me on a lark. You can tell everyone that I talked you into it. They'll believe that. And you were shocked at how accurate the spiritualist is. That it was as if she knew you."

"That's awfully close to the truth."

"That's what makes it such a good lie," said Honoria, a glint of mischief finally coming to her eyes. "The best lies are as close to the truth as possible. You can ask for Madam Krichevsky, Mistress of Mysteries."

Kathy looked at her. "Are you serious?"

"Yes!" Honoria laughed full out. "Ridiculous, isn't it? But I'm building quite a clientele. I even had Clara Browne come down for a reading. She didn't recognize me at all and we went to school together."

Kathy still seemed dubious. "And I can always find you here?"

"Almost. You can leave a message with the barkeep, Miles, but put it in code. Let me think." She paced, but then saw the deck of cards next to the crystal ball on the table. "Wait. I've done this before. We'll use the deck of cards. Freddie can be the king, you be the queen, and I'll be the knave, and our suit is hearts. We'll let our killer be the knave of clubs, and the alphabet can be spades and diamonds, with the letter 'A' being the deuce of spades, 'B' the trey, and so on, starting from the deuce of diamonds when the spades play out. You can write in some extra mumbo-jumbo around it all, questions, and the like. It'll be perfectly logical if I'm your spiritual advisor."

"All right." Kathy repeated the code to herself. "We're hearts, Killer is knave of clubs, A is the deuce of spades. And your friend is the queen of clubs and Flossie is king of clubs. It will look funny if we don't use those cards, as well. Just in case this place gets shut down, you can leave a message at a speak on 11th and 39th. Ask for Thomas Callaghan, and tell them I sent you. It's behind the candy shop, and if it gets shut down, just ask around the neighborhood, and use my name."

"Callaghan... Is he trustworthy?"

"He's my uncle."

"That's why it sounded familiar. But I thought his name was Dan."

"That's a different uncle. I've got them all over this city." Kathy yawned. "I've got to go. I've got work in the morning."

"Then let's go. And Kathy, please, please be careful." Honoria's eyes almost started filling. "You're the sister I never had."

Kathy's did, too. "You be careful, too, Honoria. In many ways, you're the sister I wish I had."

The two embraced tightly, then Honoria put her wig and veils back on and led Kathy back through the speak to the street.

Freddie awoke near ten the next morning feeling absolutely awful and knowing damned well he deserved every bit of it, even waking up in the guest room. Roberts appeared with a breakfast tray containing a glass of tomato juice, some cabbage leaves, and some aspirin.

"What's that?" Freddie asked, and winced.

"Mrs. Little recommended it."

"My mother?"

"No, sir."

"Kathy. She's at work."

"Yes, sir, and she asked me to tell you that she will be home promptly at twelve-thirty to spend the afternoon with you."

"That is assuming I can stand by that point. Damn, why do I do that?"

Roberts did not comment but set the breakfast tray on the bedside table. Freddie took a sip of the tomato juice and gasped.

"What the hell is in this?"

"Tabasco sauce, and red peppers, sir. I understand it's quite an effective remedy."

"If it doesn't kill me first." Freddie winced and downed the drink, then ate the cabbage leaves to soothe the burning in his mouth. He downed the aspirin after he finally stumbled into the bathroom.

He had to admit that he felt much better by noon, and when Kathy walked into the apartment from the servants' quarters, he was almost chipper.

"I owe you an apology, darling," he said after a quick kiss.

"Have you done your penance?" she replied lightly in spite of the glare in her eyes.

"Both with a miserable hangover and with the remedy."

"Then let's say nothing more about it." She gave him a quick smile to reassure him that he was forgiven, and headed for the dining room. "I've got some very interesting news."

She told him about Honoria's adventure over their lunch of a creamy tomato soup accompanied by cheese and toast points. Freddie was not happy about what his sister was up to but recognized there was little he could do about it.

"So who is this friend of hers?" he complained instead.

Kathy shrugged. "Honoria wouldn't say. I'm afraid we'll have to leave that part in Honoria's hands. In the meantime, what do you know about James Ryland? He seemed awfully interested in Honoria last night."

"Ryland. Ryland..." Freddie leaned back in his chair, his chin in his hand. "He's the right-hand man for Will H. Hays, formerly of the Republican National Committee. Rumor has it, he does some of Hays's dirty work, and of course you know Hays is up to his neck in the Teapot Dome scandals."

"How was Mr. Hays involved, other than being part of President Harding's administration?" Kathy asked. "He was postmaster, wasn't he?"

"Yes." Freddie returned to his soup and took a sip. "Apparently, there was a suspicious campaign contribution from Mr. Sinclair."

"Sinclair? Oh, Mr. Sinclair from Mammoth Oil Company. But I thought he simply bribed Interior Secretary Fall to get the lease to the Navy's oil reserves."

"I believe it was supposedly a loan." Freddie's brow creased as he tried to remember. "No, wait. The loan came from Edward Doheny. He's the Los Angeles oilman. I don't think they've found out what all Albert Fall got from Harry Sinclair. But Hays testified in the Senate about a year ago that Sinclair did give Hays seventy-five thousand dollars as a campaign contribution during the nineteen-twenty election. And there's a rumor about that the money was not all Hays received from him. I seem to remember my father asking me to contribute to the nineteen-twenty Republican campaign debt, in return for which, we could get some Liberty Bonds, and Hays was behind it. I don't know if that's significant or not. I do remember wondering where Hays was getting the bonds."

"Could it have been from one of the other oil companies?"

"Possibly, and it could have been a perfectly legitimate donation from a private party. Or it might not have had anything to do with the oil companies." Freddie shook his head. "It's just a confusing mess, is what it is. Good heavens, it took them six months after

President Harding died to confirm that his people had been up to no good. That was almost two years ago, and they still haven't gotten it sorted out. We're due for a few more scandals, mark me well, my dear."

"But it doesn't tell us a thing about Ryland." Kathy nibbled a bit of the Vermont cheddar. "And Hays isn't looking any the worse for his involvement. So Sinclair made a campaign contribution. It doesn't mean Hays was crooked. He's not entirely influential, anyway, except in the movie industry."

"Very true. Nor does this have anything to do with why that young woman was killed in Honoria's apartment the other night, which is what we're after. Why are you so hot on Ryland?"

"I don't know. Honoria practically gave him the brush off last night, but he still seemed very interested in her."

"A lot of men are, my dear, including your brother."

Kathy glared at him. "Leave Abraham out of this. As for Mr. Ryland, he spent most of the party last night trying to chat Honoria up, then left your parents' home shortly after she did. And I found out from the concierge here last night when I got home that Mr. Ryland spent a good part of his evening after the party waiting for Honoria to get here. He apparently left shortly after midnight and didn't leave a note for her."

"It wouldn't be the first time some love-sick swain has hung about, hoping to see Honoria." Freddie thought it over. "Maybe I'll arrange to have a chat with him. At the very least, I can ask around about him."

"Uncle Dan already is. I called him from work this morning." Kathy giggled. "He says he's been doing quite a few favors for us of late."

"Oh no. He's not upset about last night, is he?"

"Not in the least. Not only has he got me happily, safely, and well married off, he knows something Uncle Mike doesn't, a rare occurrence, I assure you. He's tickled pink."

"I'm glad. Does this mean he will share his

information?"

"I think so." Kathy shrugged. "He has good reason to trust our work."

"Very well, then." Freddie mused.

Kathy placed a small gift-wrapped box on the table. "I know you told me not to, but I did find something special the other day that I wanted to give you for your birthday."

"Really." Freddie looked at the box, then with a shrug, opened it.

The mother of pearl handle almost rippled in the afternoon light. It was about four inches long and almost another inch in diameter. Freddie pulled it from the box, inspected it, then pulled the knife blade from the handle.

"A pocket knife?" he asked.

"Given your tendency to end up in trouble, I thought it might come in handy," Kathy said, her grin wicked and teasing.

"Let's hope it doesn't," said Freddie, laughing softly. "Thank you, my darling. I should have known you'd come up with something truly unusual." He couldn't resist leering at her.

Kathy smiled receptively. "Does that smile mean we shall be staying in this afternoon?"

"For a little while, I think."

The phone rang once while they were occupied. Roberts had been told not to disturb them, nor did he particularly care to. When they finally emerged, freshly bathed and dressed, he presented the message.

"So soon?" asked Kathy, and went to the phone.

Some minutes later, she found Freddie in the study.

"Well?" he asked, looking up from his book.

"Uncle Dan says that as far as he knows, Ryland is perfectly respectable. We might try talking to Uncle Mike about him, though, because Ryland is a lawyer." Kathy flopped onto the couch, then reached over the arm to retrieve her knitting. "Also, someone on the force managed to find Miss Walsh's family. The parents are gone, but she has an older sister and her family who live in Caledonia, so the police are shipping Miss Walsh's body there."

Freddie smiled as Kathy's fingers went to work on the white, black and tan piece of fabric that was hanging from the needles. Freddie could see an argyle pattern forming as she knit. It was another of Kathy's attempts at adapting to her new lifestyle. As she had tried to explain, being idle felt very wrong and knitting was the one domestic skill she found rather soothing.

"Did you get the sister's address?" Freddie asked.

"Of course."

"But do they have any idea how Miss Walsh wound up dead in Honoria's apartment?"

"None." Kathy snorted. "We're the ones who'll have to find out. The police commissioner has requested that the department investigate in as inconspicuous a manner as possible, so as not to cause more publicity. It would seem that someone has decided that as long as it doesn't happen again, this one should slide under the rug."

"I wonder if it was my mother, although, if it was, she might have a point," said Freddie. "Why advertise that it's easy to get in here and steal things? Of course, that means the police are not going to investigate further. That's rather convenient. We'll have free rein, and no one to answer to."

"And what if Honoria turns up dead in her hallway? You know, it's entirely possible that whoever killed that girl was actually aiming for Honoria."

Freddie put his book down "Except that the two are so very different in stature and style of dress. Even if it was dark, the killer should have had some hint that he had the wrong girl."

Kathy let her knitting rest in her lap. "But it wasn't dark, Freddie. The lights were on in the bedroom, and Honoria didn't go back there first. Why would the lights be on? It would make it too easy to be seen from the outside."

"But a lot easier if you're looking for something. And why kill her in the bedroom, and leave the body in the front hall?"

"You're assuming she was killed in the bedroom. It's entirely possible that the struggle started in the bedroom, then moved into the hall." Kathy swallowed. "And it's still possible that the killer was aiming for Honoria. She was awfully frightened last night."

Freddie got up and paced. "Damn it all to hell! Who is this nameless friend of hers? And why would she involve Honoria in something so dangerous?"

"Sheer desperation from the sound of it," said Kathy.

"I can't help but wonder if somehow Honoria's radical friends are involved." Freddie grabbed his cigarette case and holder, mechanically fitting a cigarette in the holder and lighting up as he paced and talked. "I have investigated them and they seem harmless. Politically skewed, perchance, but not violent, like some of those anarchists. Unless one of the anarchists slipped in somehow."

"I don't think so," said Kathy, waving at the billows of smoke Freddie was puffing out in his agitation. "Honoria chose to hide down in the Village among those very people. If she had any reason to be frightened of them, she wouldn't have gone there. And she even said that she thought it was more likely that someone from your set was involved. Wait. Could it be that some anti-radical or Ku Klux Klan member decided to make an example of her? Maybe someone violently opposed to radicals? Honoria would make a good target that way."

Freddie's pacing slowed as he thought. "Now that's a plausible theory."

"Your mother might even know something. After all, it's possible that she was the one who suggested that the police not investigate."

Freddie shook his head. "I can't imagine Mother being that ingenuous. Or perhaps I don't want to think of her as being that rotten. I suppose I could have her to tea tomorrow."

"Then it's a good thing I have dinner at Uncle Mike's. I don't think my presence will encourage confidences."

"My presence doesn't encourage confidences. But it's all we've got, and I wouldn't recommend trying to get Honoria to do it. All we'd get is a non-stop lecture on appropriate friends."

There was a knock on the door, and Roberts stuck his head in.

"Excuse me for interrupting, but there is a caller for you, Mrs. Little."

"Where?" asked Kathy, a little nervously.

"He's downstairs in the lobby, but he called upstairs to Mrs. Wentworth's apartment, and he did ask for Miss Briscow. It's Mr. Edward Roundhouse."

Kathy gave Freddie a puzzled glance. "Why would he want to see me?"

"I haven't the faintest," said Freddie shrugging. He, too, was exceptionally puzzled. Not that Kathy was unattractive. She had a beauty peculiarly her own. But her intellect and forthright manner tended to drive men off, even as it attracted Freddie, and he was not used to someone sharing his liking for his prickly bride.

"Damn," Kathy grumbled, setting aside her knitting and getting up. "I'd better go up and get it over with."

Freddie held her back. "If you don't want to see him, just have Virginia say you're not in."

"But I am in." Kathy shook him off. "I'm sorry, Freddie, I just can't tell those little fibs."

"It's a euphemism, Kathy, and Virginia will do the telling, not you." Freddie flopped back on the couch, disgusted.

"It's still not right. The man went to the trouble to come over. The least I can do is see him." Kathy headed out towards the servants' quarters.

Roberts stepped aside as Freddie followed.

"Good heavens, Kathy, he's interrupting your day and your schedule. That's not a courtesy, that's an inconvenience. There's nothing impolite about making yourself unavailable."

Kathy paused and groaned. "I just don't feel right doing it. I'll be down as soon as I can."

Freddie stopped. Sighing, he went back to the study and morosely thumbed through the latest New Yorker.

Upstairs, Kathy picked up Honoria's phone and told the downstairs staff herself to send Mr. Roundhouse up. She also opened the door herself when Roundhouse rang. He looked at her surprised, then smiled. He was a dandy, his clothes and manner jaunty and just so. He carried kid gloves, a fedora, and a walking stick, and wore a crease in his tweed trousers that was honed to perfection. A white carnation boutonniere sat snappily in his lapel. His smile, once he recovered himself, was equally snappy. His nose and lip, however, still looked very bruised and swollen.

"Well, Miss Briscow, I'm glad to find you at home."

"Will you please come in?" Kathy held the door open.

Roundhouse sauntered in. Virginia had his things in an instant. Kathy led him into the drawing-room.

"Is there anything I can help you with, Mr. Roundhouse?" Kathy asked, cautiously.

"Oh, Miss Briscow, this is purely a social call."

"Well... That's... interesting." Kathy remained standing, and so did Roundhouse.

He laughed deprecatingly. "That I wish to call on you socially? Perhaps it is. I don't know. You were rather quiet last night at dinner."

"There wasn't a lot to be said."

"I suppose that was rather unkind of us men to dominate the conversation. Football must seem pretty boring to you."

"Actually, I find the game itself rather interesting. I don't have the time to keep up on the scores. And speaking of that, I'm afraid I am rather busy this afternoon."

Roundhouse held up his hands. "A thousand apologies for intruding. Might I accompany you to tea tomorrow?"

"Tomorrow?" Kathy swallowed. "I'm sorry, I can't. I have another engagement."

"I hope it's not with those blasted radicals Honoria usually hangs out with."

"Not those." Kathy's interest suddenly flared. "Another realm altogether."

"Thank heavens. I can't abide radicals. Perhaps I could entreat you to be my guest at dinner some evening?"

His eyes looked so soulful and helpless, that Kathy was somewhat charmed against her will, and had to repress a chuckle.

"You can entreat all you like," she said with a smile. "But I'm afraid it will not be possible."

Roundhouse nodded. "Yes, it could be considered a little indiscreet. I know. You're a working girl. What about luncheon? Say, sometime this week?"

"I suppose that won't do any harm, as long as I meet you somewhere." Kathy held her breath, hoping that he'd gotten the hint that this was not to be a date.

"Corking. Sherry's, on Tuesday?"

"That's a bit far. Oh, never mind. I'll see you at noon on Tuesday."

"At noon on Tuesday."

With a pleasant nod, Roundhouse took his leave. Kathy followed him out to the foyer. While she waited for him to leave, she browsed through the mail on the hall table. Virginia usually brought Kathy's mail downstairs, but it sometimes took a while for her to do so. Kathy wondered how long the current stack of letters had been waiting. There were two letters for her, one from her brother Joshua, in California, and another from Henri Bendel and Co.

Downstairs, Freddie was on the telephone. Kathy

opened the envelope from Bendel while he finished his conversation.

"Well, you were saying the other night how little we see each other," Freddie told the party on the other end. He chuckled warmly, but as he did, he rolled his eyes. "No, Mother, I invited you, you should come here... Wonderful. Three o'clock?... I shall see you then."

He hung up sourly.

"Freddie," asked Kathy distractedly. "What time is it?"

Freddie checked his pocket watch. "Around a quarter of three. I tell you, I'm a glutton for punishment."

"Darling, do you mind if I run out for just a little bit? My new suit is ready at Bendel's, and I'd like to go get it."

"What?" Freddie gazed at her in mock amazement, although some of it was genuine. "You bought something?"

Kathy flushed as she went to the vestibule closet. "It was in a fit of madness, but, yes, I did. Honoria had me out shopping with her again. I saw it and fell in love. And I needed a new suit, anyway."

"Did I hear you say Bendel's, too?" Amused, Freddie took her coat from her.

"Yes," Kathy sighed as she waited for Freddie to help her on with her coat.

"Now, it seems to me that I remember hearing somewhere that Henri Bendel and Company is one of the most exclusive couturiers in New York."

"It was your sister who insisted on going inside, and, Freddie, please may I have my coat. I'd like to get there before the shop closes."

"No." Freddie hung the coat back up.

"But, Freddie..." Kathy gaped, then sighed. "I suppose I can pick it up Monday, then."

"Darling, they will send it around. We shall ring them up, they will deliver it upstairs, and Virginia will handle the money." Freddie escorted her back into the foyer. "You needn't lift a finger, just the handset to the phone. Here you are."

Taking a deep breath, Kathy got the shop and directed them to deliver the suit. The lady at the shop said she would be happy to do so, and that the suit would be in Kathy's apartment within the hour. Kathy hung up, feeling a little shaken.

"Freddie, did I do that right?"

"Of course, darling."

"It was so easy."

Freddie laughed. "Sweet, sweet Kathy, please don't let your fear of silverware gull you into thinking there is anything complicated about being rich. If anything, money seems to make life easier."

"Oh, it does?" Kathy turned on him, her eyes glowing with mischief. "Then why do you have five sets of table knives in your dining room, each to cut something different, not to mention all the forks. I don't want to even start talking about all the spoons."

"Then let's not." Freddie grabbed her and pulled her close. "How would you feel about seeing a play tonight?"

Chapter Four

Gloria Derby Little was in fine fettle as she sipped tea in her son's drawing room. She was a woman of no small achievement. Her charity work raised untold amounts for those less well off than she, which included practically everyone not on her social stratum. She was well-regarded by her peers. Perhaps not as famous as some of them, but then again, she considered publicity vulgar.

Her manner was always gracious, even when being vicious. There was a regality to her bearing the source of which could only be the sincere belief in her own worthiness as a woman of position. Aristocratic, most people called her, even though in her youth she had spurned the practice of her girlfriends of chasing down foreign, titled husbands. Unkinder tongues whispered that it was because she couldn't get one. She knew better and as such did not care about the whispers.

Her son's infancy was lost in those careless years. She'd loved holding him as a baby. But watching the tall, spidery figure, it seemed hard to believe he had grown from that tiny creature so long ago. He resembled his paternal grandfather, and to a degree, his father. A perfectly charming, quick-witted young gentleman, Freddie was, and the only thing that diminished his mother's pride was that he refused to marry.

"Dora Roundhouse seemed to like you a great deal," she remarked, casually.

"Dora Roundhouse is a foolish sweet young thing, eleven years my junior." Freddie smiled as he offered a plate. "Another sandwich, Mother?"

"No, thank you, dear. But, seriously, what am I to do? All the young women your age are already married."

"And many of them are divorced."

"Now, Freddie, you really don't want to spend your life with a bitter divorcée, now do you?"

"Of course not, Mother. However, there are other women in New York besides bitter divorcées and sweet young society girls."

Mrs. Little blanched. "Freddie! I hope to heavens you're not talking about taking after one of those ghastly radical women your sister seems to like."

"I'm not talking about taking after anybody, actually. I know it distresses you, Mother, but I'm very content as I am. And Honoria's friends are harmless. I've made very sure of that."

"Harmless! Why, they are chipping away at the very foundation of our civilization. Freddie, I'm worried. Honoria has been going about with all sorts of riff-raff. Labor people, like that Mr. Gompers."

Freddie laughed. "He's an old man, and no, she hasn't."

"Well, people like that. One of them is a Miles Yeager, and I know that for certain. It's a German name, isn't it? And he has connections with Mr. Pinchot, or Mr. Slattery, or perhaps both of them. I'm not sure which."

"Yeager." Freddie thought it over. "Do you know of anyone else?"

"Oh, heavens, no." Stifling back a sniff, Mrs. Little set down her cup. "Freddie, she tells such tales, it's impossible to tell the truth from her lies. And she won't tell me anything about her friends unless she's angry and wants to shock me. Even then, I don't know where the truth ends and the lies begin."

"That is a problem," said Freddie nodding. It was indeed a very big problem. Honoria lied so readily if it suited her, Freddie was not sure she didn't believe her own tales.

"Freddie, I simply don't know what to do about

her. I'm at a complete loss."

"There's not much you can do, Mother. She has her own money, and she is over twenty-one."

"I don't know what to make of the younger generation. I was hoping the other night that Edward Roundhouse would take a liking to Honoria. But that ghastly Mr. Ryland intervened and would not let Honoria go."

Freddie gazed idly at his teacup. "So how did you come to invite Mr. Ryland?"

"He's your father's friend," Gloria said with a dismissive little wave. "The two met at the Republican Club some time ago. They go to luncheon together every so often, I believe. Your father has asked me to include him at dinner, and when Honoria asked me to include Miss Briscow, I thought it would be a good opportunity to please your father."

"Well, at least you can't complain about Mr. Ryland's politics."

"Of course not, but it's only obvious his interest in your sister has very little to do with her charm and grace. I don't wish to be vulgar, but I believe he's one of those horrid types who are only interested in a woman with position."

Freddie smiled. His mother meant money, although as far as Mrs. Little was concerned, position and money were synonymous. It was merely vulgar to mention the latter.

"But speaking of Edward Roundhouse," said Freddie. He gazed at his teacup again, hoping his mother wouldn't notice his more than casual interest. "It seems to me he's been rather vicious when the subject of radicals has come up."

"There isn't a kind word that can be said for them."

"Still, one doesn't have to be nasty about it."

"I suppose not. But the sooner we're rid of the red scourge, the safer this country will be."

"Don't tell me." Freddie adopted a lazy smirk. "You've been rousting them out yourself."

"Oh, Freddie, stop teasing." Mrs. Little smiled warmly at her son. "That's not my position. There are plenty of good, brave men doing that already."

"Such as the despicable Mr. Ryland, perhaps?"

Mrs. Little laughed. "Freddie, you are absolutely impossible when you tease. Well, why not? He's not all that bad a sort, even if he isn't quality. He has my blessing on that venture."

"Have you made any donations to that cause?"

"Since when is that any of your business?" Mrs. Little pulled back imperiously.

Freddie smiled and disarmed her. "It isn't. Pray forgive me, Mother, but I couldn't help being curious. After all, you seem to consider it quite an important issue. I just wanted to know how important."

"It's of the utmost importance. But if you're thinking of donating to the cause, there isn't any that I know of, at least none that I would consider giving to. I heard there was a reverend somebody going about collecting, but he was Baptist, for Heaven's sakes."

"What about Edward? I've heard rumors that he's been getting his hands dirty going after radicals."

Mrs. Little put down her tea cup. "My darling, I don't care to be rude, and the only rumors I've heard about Edward Roundhouse are of the sort one doesn't care to repeat, but none of them had anything to do with radicals. Furthermore, you know better than to believe that nonsense. I have no reason to believe that Mr. Roundhouse is anything but a gentleman, and if he is going after radicals, then there are worse pursuits."

"Certainly, Mother."

"Now, let's talk about something more pleasant. Oh, I meant to tell you, I read your book, The Old Money Story."

"You did?" Freddie looked up, completely surprised.

"Of course, my darling. Well, I must confess, I did hesitate after hearing about how shocking it was." Gloria tittered. "In fact, I do believe some of my friends read it simply so they could be outraged. But it wasn't that terribly shocking, certainly not any worse than the Beautiful and Damned."

"You read Fitzgerald?" Freddie tried to keep his jaw from dropping.

"I read a lot of people. I love to read. Always have. You didn't come by your fondness for books all by yourself, young man." Gloria smiled triumphantly.

Freddie mused. "I don't think I've ever seen you read."

At that, Gloria sighed. "That, I suppose, has been my failing. Oh, Freddie. It's no wonder I know so little about you and Honoria and you two know so little about me. You had such a good nurse and my friends all spent so little time with their children. I think that was rather a mistake now. I kept thinking that as I was reading your novel. It was so beautifully written. If only I had known you were writing it." Gloria lifted an eyebrow. "I could have told you a few more stories."

"Mother, I— I— I had no idea."

"I know. But it's like that nonsense with Edward Roundhouse. I will not spread gossip, Freddie. And as your mother, I do feel as though I should lead by example. But as you pointed out regarding Honoria, you are no longer a child and there is no longer the need to protect you. I do forget that, don't I?"

"I suppose." Freddie took a long swallow of tea.

"So, are you writing another story?"

"Uh, yes."

"Oh. please, tell me all about it."

Freddie gathered his muddled wits together and began to speak.

Kathy was on the other side of town. She smiled at the spread in the Upper West Side apartment. Uncle Mike had done well for himself. The apartment wasn't as fine as Freddie's place on the other side of Central Park, but it was fine enough. Aunt Marian was hosting a crowd, as usual, including her six children, their spouses, and their children. Michael's brother

Thomas had brought his wife Jane and their youngest son Jimmy. Aunt Bridget and Uncle Morris were there, although their three adult children were not.

Michael Callaghan was the family patriarch, a role he'd taken over from his father, Michael Callaghan, Sr., who had immigrated to the States as a young boy fleeing the Irish potato famine of the eighteen-forties. Michael Sr. met his wife, who had also immigrated around the same time, in New York, and the two had produced thirteen children, eleven who survived into adulthood. Those eleven then went on and produced their own families, including Kathy's mother Katie Marie, who had gone so far as to marry Jacob Briscow, a farmer in Kansas.

Kathy had found the clan both intimidating and familiar when she'd finally met them upon moving to New York after she graduated from college. They were a boisterous group, quick to take umbrage and even quicker to forgive. Uncle Mike (the lawyer) and Uncle Patrick (the doctor) were the most well-off, but the rest of the siblings didn't seem to resent it. If anything, there was the general attitude that when one of the Callaghans prospered it was sure to benefit the others. Never mind that there was the occasional carping when Uncle Mike said no to a request for one hand-out or another.

Kathy moved among her cousins and aunts and uncles, answering questions about her job, asking even more about their lives. It wasn't until dinner was well over that Kathy managed to pin Uncle Mike down alone in his study.

"Well, Kathleen, you've been gunning for me all afternoon," he said, patting his expansive girth. "What's going on?"

"Oh, nothing much, Uncle Mike," Kathy said, sliding onto a couch.

The room's walls were covered by filled bookshelves. There was a small writing desk in the corner, but the room was mostly crowded with comfortable overstuffed chairs and the couch, all covered in buttery soft leather. Uncle Mike eased himself into a chair across from Kathy.

"My friend Honoria has run into someone rather…" Kathy bit her lip, wondering how to describe what she wanted. "Actually, this man seems to be overly interested in her and since he's a lawyer, we were wondering what, if anything, you knew about him. We're assuming he's all right, but I told Honoria that I'd ask you about his reputation just to be on the safe side."

"And who are we talking about?" said Uncle Mike, truly enjoying his avuncular role.

"A Mr. James Ryland? We understand he works for Mr. Will Hays, the new movie person."

"Him." Uncle Mike grimaced. "Ryland doesn't practice law, you know. And the few times he has, well, let's just say there are rumors he wasn't the most ethical fellow. It's no surprise to me he's working for Hays." Uncle Mike shuddered. "They are a pair, they are."

"But have you actually met either of them?"

"Mr. Hays? No. I've just heard the bad bit of business here and there. He likes to pretend he doesn't have much power, but he seems to have most of the Republican party eating out of his hand. I think that's how he got his job with the movie people, and I wouldn't say that job is without influence. But I have met Ryland and I did not care for him."

"Uncle Dan said that as far as he could tell, Mr. Ryland is perfectly respectable."

"That he is." Mike paused. "In a way. Kathy, if it weren't for your friend, I wouldn't be saying squat about the fellow. You definitely don't want to be on his bad side. And he is perfectly respectable in that he doesn't do anything illegal. But if anyone knows how to play the letter of the law against its spirit, it's James Ryland."

"Well, that's not altogether encouraging," Kathy

said. "I'll have to warn Honoria."

Mike looked at her closely. "And how are you doing, Kathleen?"

"Well enough, Uncle Mike." A clock began chiming and Kathy checked her wrist watch. "Oh, good lord, is that the time? I'd better get back home. I've got a manuscript to get read tonight."

"And what about your beau?" Uncle Mike asked as Kathy jumped up.

"Same as it's been, which is fine with me." Kathy tried to look reassuring. "Truly, Uncle Mike. You do not need to worry about Freddie. Whatever his reputation is regarding dissipation, he is a genuine gentleman."

"But he hasn't proposed yet."

"Who said I wanted to get married? I wouldn't be able to keep my job and I love my work. Which is why I am perfectly content as I am." Kathy reached over and kissed her uncle on the cheek. "And I really must go. Give my love to Aunt Marian if I don't see her on my way out."

Kathy hurried away before her uncle could question her further. She caught a cross-town bus that got her within a block of her apartment building, then took the service elevator up to Honoria's apartment.

There she paused. It was true that she had Lowell's manuscript to read, but someone had been looking for something in Honoria's apartment, so Kathy thought she might as well try to find whatever it was. She searched Honoria's bedroom first, but the only items of interest were her jewelry and there was little enough of that. Kathy found several letters in Honoria's writing table in the study. Two were from Henry Wentworth, her husband. One had been sent from London and the second from Cherbourg, France. Both were rather sweet, but not terribly interesting. The other letters were from relatives and friends, most of whom had names that sounded a lot like they came from the Social Register. Kathy pocketed the letters to look over later, if necessary.

Kathy moved on to the guest bedroom where Miss Walsh had been staying. There were few personal effects. A couple of extra dresses, fresh step-ins, and bras. No books, but two framed photographs. The first was of a family, including four adult women and one man. They looked enough alike and close enough to what Kathy remembered of Miss Walsh's corpse, that Kathy guessed this was the dead girl's family. They were gathered on the porch of a Victorian-style house, with gingerbread cut-outs hanging from the porch roof and several posts along the porch railing. Kathy pulled the photo from the frame. Sure enough, there was the stamp of a photographer in Caledonia, Ohio.

The second photograph showed Miss Walsh and an older woman standing next to President and Mrs. Harding and a third man carrying a doctor's bag. Both Miss Walsh and the other woman wore nurse's uniforms. That seemed surprising, but then Honoria had said that Miss Walsh had worked for that lung doctor, Dr. Rothmayer. It would make sense that Miss Walsh had some connections to get a job with an important and well-known doctor like that. Kathy slid the photographs into her dress pocket, then continued her search.

In the nightstand drawer, Kathy found several letters, most sent from Caledonia, Ohio and bearing the names of Miss Walsh's sisters and brother. One asked how she was bearing up, but mostly the letters dealt with the miscellany of life in a small town, raising children and the usual gossip.

But there was one envelope with the name Ellen May written on it, but no address. Inside was a short note: "E - This is my friend. Thank you for helping her. I." There was also a small piece of paper with Ellen May's name and an address on the lower East Side of New York. Kathy slipped the envelope and note into her pocket. She was about to leave when she decided to take the empty frames and the other letters, as well.

The rest of the apartment was empty, at least

of anything personal or interesting. Kathy went downstairs to find Freddie hard at work on his new book. Or supposedly hard at work. Mostly, he was pacing the study and smoking too fast.

"Is it not going well?" Kathy asked emptying her pockets onto the heavy oaken office desk Freddie had bought for her the previous summer.

"What?" Freddie asked, blinking at her through the cigarette smoke. "I suppose I should open a window."

"That would be nice." Kathy walked over and laid her hand on his arm. "You don't usually smoke so fast when one of your characters is getting troublesome."

"That would be an easy problem to solve," sighed Freddie. He pulled his cigarette from the holder and snubbed it out. "I'm trying not to worry about Honoria."

"And succeeding, I see." Kathy's eyes got that wicked glint in them. "I suppose the fact that there's not much we can do at the moment isn't helping."

"I searched her apartment this afternoon," Freddie said.

"Really? I just finished searching it as I came in."

Freddie went over to the credenza and poured brandy into two snifters. "I didn't find anything that shouldn't have been there. I did take Honoria's bank books and some of her more valuable jewelry to keep in my safe down here."

"You didn't read her letters, did you?" Kathy accepted the glass Freddie handed her, then sat on the couch.

Freddie made a face. "I probably should have. I was thinking I should go get them. I can't believe I'm saying this, but there's something dreadfully unsavory about prying into her affairs like this. Only I can't think how else to protect her." He went back to pacing.

"I brought the letters down. They don't look that interesting, but hopefully, you can identify some of the writers. I suspect most of them are relatives of some sort. And the rest I'm guessing are friends. Oh, and there are two from Henry Wentworth."

"Henry? That's odd. Honoria has never struck me as being that sentimental about him," Freddie looked around for his cigarettes. "She didn't even cry when she got the telegram that he'd died."

"That you know of," said Kathy. "And based on the letters, I suspect there wasn't that much about him to be sentimental over. However, he did signal a major change in her life and status. And she was only seventeen at the time. But why didn't you search Flossie's room?"

"I didn't have time before Mother arrived for tea," Freddie said. "I was just thinking about going back up there when you came in."

"So how did tea go?"

Freddie flopped into his favorite reading chair. "Quite nicely, actually. I should make a point of visiting with Mother more often. She told me she'd read my book and that she liked it. She even gave me an excellent idea for the next one."

"How lovely." Kathy had never understood entirely Freddie's ambivalence toward his mother. "So is it safe to assume she doesn't know who would be inciting violence against radicals down in the Village?"

"I think so." Freddie went back to glaring and fidgeting with his cigarettes. "Did you find anything out at your uncle's?"

"Not much, except that Uncle Mike does not like Mr. Ryland. Says he's very good at skirting the law."

"Hmph. Doesn't sound like someone who would get his hands dirty with a murder, does it?"

Kathy sipped her brandy. "No, it doesn't, I'm afraid."

"Mother seems to think he's interested in Honoria for her position."

"Really?" Kathy frowned. "But he's already working for Mr. Hays. How would Honoria's social class help him?"

Freddie chuckled grimly. "Mother meant he's after Honoria's money. Or at least, Mother thinks he is. I don't know how much of that is her general assumption that anyone not on our social level is after our money and how much of that is genuine instinct."

"That would be a good question," said Kathy with a soft sigh. She got up and went to the desk. "Here are Honoria's letters. Do you want to help me go through them? Maybe you'll see something I didn't."

But Freddie didn't see anything, pointing out that almost every letter was from an older aunt or family friend, several of whom had died already. He shook his head over the Ellen May note, as well.

"Honoria doesn't seem to have very many friends her own age," Kathy said after they'd looked at all the letters.

"She's friendly with several of the young women in our set," said Freddie. "But she's probably not friendly enough to be saving their letters. Honoria has never been terribly sentimental that I know of."

"And it's not unlikely her closest friends are not from your set," Kathy pointed out. "Though where she would have put those letters, I couldn't say." She looked over her desk. "Oh, and look at this. I found it in Flossie's room."

She handed Freddie the photo of Flossie with President and Mrs. Harding.

"This is interesting," said Freddie. "That's Dr. Charles Sawyer with the president and his wife. He was the president's physician if I recall correctly. I wonder who the other woman is."

"Another nurse?" asked Kathy, looking at the photograph more closely. "I wonder when and where this was taken."

"When would be some time before Harding died. As for where, my first guess would be outside the White House," said Freddie. "At least, the background looks like it could be."

"I do believe you're right," said Kathy, examining the photo. "How interesting. And here's the second photograph - Flossie and her family. This one has a photographer's stamp on it."

"Chas. Kling, photographer," Freddie read off the back. "Caledonia, Ohio."

Kathy took the picture back and put it back in its frame. "Did I tell you about Flossie working for Dr. Rothmayer?"

"Arnold Rothmayer, the lung specialist?" Freddie asked.

"I believe so," Kathy said. "It does seem unlikely there would be two of them in the city."

"Unless he has a brother."

"True. I suppose we'll have to check." Kathy looked at the photo of Flossie and the president again. "In any case, Flossie apparently worked for him for a year before running off again last winter. At least, that's what Honoria said. She went to Dr. Rothmayer for the croup last month."

"He must have helped. She was in a very nasty state, wasn't she?"

"She was." Kathy yawned, then looked at her watch. "You haven't planned anything for dinner tonight, have you?"

"No. I am getting rather hungry, though."

"I'm not. There was quite the spread at Aunt Marian's earlier. I think I'm still full. And I do have Lowell's manuscript to read."

"I'll have Mrs. Wyman whip up a small snack, then, and leave you to it." Freddie sighed. "I do have some troublesome characters to wrestle into submission, myself. As for Honoria's problem, what do you think we should do next?"

Kathy thought. "Perhaps we should see Dr. Rothmayer. I wonder if I can get to it during my luncheon tomorrow."

"Why don't I do that?" Freddie said. "It will be better than sitting around here all day until you get back from work."

"That will be quite acceptable. I wonder if I should send a message to Honoria asking where her letters are. No, I think not. She does deserve her secrets."

Freddie sighed. "As long as they don't get her killed."

Chapter Five

The next morning, after Kathy had gone to work, Freddie made a point of calling Dr. Arnold Rothmayer, the lung specialist. The woman answering the phone confirmed that he was the only Dr. Rothmayer in New York City, but his schedule for the day was completely filled with patients trying to see him before he left for California at the end of the week.

"I'm not a patient," Freddie said. "I just wanted to talk to him about a nurse he had in his employ almost a year ago."

"Would that be Flossie Walsh?" the woman asked. "I heard about her passing. It's so terribly sad."

"Yes, it is," Freddie said. "There could be a complication, however, and I'd like to talk to Dr. Rothmayer as soon as possible in order to clear it up."

"Can you be here right at five o'clock?" the woman asked. "The doctor does not like leaving his office any later than he must and he absolutely refuses to be late for his supper."

"Oh. I don't wish to delay him."

"You won't if you get here right at five," the woman said brightly. "The doctor usually uses that last hour to write his notes for the day, but he often finishes them after supper. I'm his wife and we live right above the office, so it's no trouble for him. I just want to be sure you have plenty of time."

"Thank you, then. It's very kind of you."

"It's no trouble. I was very fond of the girl."

Freddie hung up and went to spend his day wrestling with his characters. But not only were they being terribly wooden and obstreperous, he couldn't focus on the paper long enough to get anything written. Finally, around noon, he gave up and retreated to his bedroom for a long bath, then having dressed, took himself off for an extended walk around Central Park.

As he approached the Plaza Hotel, Arthur Wright hailed him from the street out front and suggested that Freddie join him and his comrades for a late luncheon. Lacking anything better to do, Freddie joined them, but soon tired of the raucous banter about stocks, horses, and mistresses. Wright, a medium-sized man with blond hair and a receding chin, finally nudged Freddie.

"Come now, Little, you've been awfully quiet," Wright said jovially.

"I guess I don't have much to say," Freddie said with a quiet smile.

"What's gotten into you?" Wright continued. "I was remarking to Delia the other night that we didn't see much of you last year, and you've been damned near a recluse since we all got back to town in September. Middleton said you didn't make it out to the Hamptons at all last summer."

"I've had other things to keep me occupied," said Freddie. He pulled his watch from his vest pocket. "And speaking of, I do have an appointment coming up. If you gentlemen will excuse me."

He got up. It wasn't nearly as close to five o'clock as he wished. So he decided to walk to the uptown office of Dr. Rothmayer, taking the meandering pathways of Central Park to further kill time.

It was a fine day, with just enough moisture in the wind to suggest that rain was on its way. The trees had barely started to turn colors and it would be another three weeks before the color change hit its peak. Perhaps sooner if the weather turned cold. Nannies and other nurses chatted amongst themselves as their young charges ran and played. Others walked infants and toddlers in their carriages. A few young mothers were out, as well.

School was out and older children ran through the park, either playing or heading home. Freddie spotted not a few piles of books sitting abandoned by the path. Teenage boys sauntered through in boisterous packs, while their female counterparts walked along giggling and chattering. The occasional young couple walked hand-in-hand, blissfully unaware of the world around them. A few men around Freddie's age hurried through the park, intent on their destinations, while elderly men and women walked slowly as if to savor the day.

Freddie felt his worry lift for a brief while, although Wright's observation niggled at the back of his mind. It was true that Freddie had been not avoiding, but not particularly seeking out his former haunts. It hadn't even been a year since he'd met Kathy, but since then, it felt as if his life had undergone a deep and profound change. He'd never been fond of going to the opera and only had out of the obligation to be seen. It was expected of people of his social position. But Kathy was passionate about music, and her enjoyment was contagious. And because she had no social position, being a mere working girl, when Freddie took her to the opera, he did so incognito. The seats were up in the balcony, no one noticed he was there and it was pure bliss to go and simply enjoy the opera.

Since they'd been married, going out evenings to loud speakeasies or formal galas was simply not nearly as attractive as it had been before. Freddie wondered if he'd ever really liked such things. Now that he had an excuse to stay in evenings, he found sitting quietly in the study with Kathy so much more enjoyable. Or taking her to a play or concert to actually see a play or a concert. If they went to dinner, it was usually to spend the evening with Lowell Winters. Sometimes Honoria would come. Mrs. Parker might be there. Or Mr. Kaufman, or the rest of that circle. Sometimes the humor would be more brittle wit than not, but it was certainly more interesting than polite small talk about people Freddie found decidedly boring.

Freddie had even invited his fellow authors from Healcroft House to a party at his apartment one evening early in September. What a delightful evening that had been! Honoria played hostess, and the conversation had been stimulating and challenging and the laughter real and full. It had been a pity that he and Kathy had to keep their marriage a secret, but Freddie found himself hoping they could continue as they were. He did not want to go back to "being seen" at the opera, or at formal galas or his old way of life.

Perhaps that was what had been driving Honoria all along. Kathy had probably been very right when she pointed out that Honoria's closest friends were not from their set. If only she hadn't chosen such a radical group to follow. Well, socialists weren't that dangerous, but they were awfully close to the anarchists, and there was good reason to be worried about them. And now, with that body in Honoria's foyer, Freddie was that much more worried.

Fortunately, he'd arrived at the doctor's office off of Amsterdam Avenue. The apartment building was just a block above St. Luke's Hospital and the first few floors were given over to several physicians' practices, with many of the doctors living in the apartments above that. As Freddie looked at the list of doctors, he noticed a Dr. Patrick Callaghan, located on the third floor. He tried to remember if Kathy had mentioned an Uncle Patrick. It didn't matter. The time was close to five o'clock and Freddie didn't want to miss Dr. Rothmayer.

He rode the elevator up to the fourth floor and went to the office listed in the building's foyer. The door was half-glassed, with "Dr. Arnold Rothmayer, Diseases of the Lungs," painted in gold lettering on the top. The door opened and a man with a ragged cough came out. He nodded at Freddie, who entered the office.

The antechamber was a small room with a window facing the back of the building. The electric light bathed the whitewashed walls in pale yellow. There was an oak desk covered with files and papers near the side wall, and behind the desk was another door. File cabinets stood behind the desk.

Freddie went to the inside door and knocked.

A thin, sallow woman opened it. Her graying brown hair was long and pinned up in back and she wore an apron with a bib, tied at her waist, over her straight dark blue dress.

"Are you Mr. Little?" she asked, her voice sounding very much like the woman on the phone earlier.

"Yes. I'm here to see Dr. Rothmayer."

"About Flossie." The woman beckoned Freddie through the door.

The room's most prominent feature was an examining table covered by a rumpled white sheet. Cabinets painted white with glass doors covered the walls and there was a steel sink under the room's back window. Against the far wall was another desk, at which a heavy-set man with dark gray hair and a thick mustache, sat writing. He wore spectacles with thin wire rims, a dark suit and a slightly annoyed look on his face.

"I'm Mrs. Rothmayer," the woman said. "I help with the office work. Our nurse has already gone home for the day. This is Dr. Rothmayer. Doctor? This is Mr. Little. He's come to ask about Flossie."

"Flossie who?" grumbled the doctor without looking up.

"Nurse Walsh, dear. She left us late last November."

"I know when she left," Rothmayer snarled, finally looking up from his desk. He glared at his wife, then looked at Freddie. "Left us high and dry, she did."

Mrs. Rothmayer continued tidying up the already clean room. "She had good reason to, may I remind you. Poor thing."

"She was a good nurse," Rothmayer grumbled, straightening his vest. "But flighty and nervous."

"As I said, she had good reason to be," Mrs. Rothmayer said. She turned to Freddie. "Right before she left, a couple of strange men came to the office. They demanded to see her. Well, Flossie was having none of that. She came back to our apartment later that night in tears. She said her apartment had been searched and her roommate beaten up. Can you believe that? She said the men were after her and she had to leave and never come back. So I gave her a good reference, her wages and a little something extra..."

Rothmayer harrumphed loudly.

"She deserved it," Mrs. Rothmayer growled back at him. "The doctor took her to the train station and let her off there. Then when the men came back and got nasty, he was able to say he had no idea where she'd gone. I was so sorry to hear she'd been murdered."

"By a burglar," grumbled Rothmayer. "It was simply bad luck."

"I seriously doubt that," said Mrs. Rothmayer. "Poor Flossie. She did confess when she first came to us that she was hiding from somebody. I thought it was just a brutal husband. But those two men. They acted like they were from the government."

"Bah!" snarled Rothmayer again. "You think everyone is from the government."

"I most certainly do not."

"Did you ever find out where she went?" Freddie asked quickly before Mrs. Rothmayer could get started again.

"Why do you want to know?" Rothmayer demanded loudly and Mrs. Rothmayer glared at Freddie.

Freddie stepped back. "She was killed in my sister's apartment. And it was not a burglary. I'm trying to find out who might have killed Miss Walsh to help protect my sister."

"Oh, my goodness!" Mrs. Rothmayer said.

Rothmayer burst out of his chair. "You should be leaving this to the police. Damn it, I pay good money in taxes, let those bastards earn it for a change."

"Doctor Rothmayer, such language!" gasped Mrs. Rothmayer. She grabbed Freddie by the arm and pushed him out the inner door and into the antechamber. "I am so sorry for his behavior. It's been a terribly difficult day, what with trying to get everything ready to go to California. We winter there. The doctor has a consulting position with a sanitarium north of Los Angeles."

Freddie lowered his voice. "Did you ever hear from Miss Walsh again?"

Mrs. Rothmayer shook her head. "No. I'm afraid not. I feel so sad, too. She really was a very good nurse. Even saved a patient when the doctor accidentally grabbed the wrong syringe."

"Did not!" bellowed the doctor from the other side of the door.

"She did." Mrs. Rothmayer patted Freddie's arm. "He so hates admitting it when he's made a mistake."

"And no idea where she went?" Freddie asked.

"None at all. I do wish we could be more helpful, for your sister's sake. But we know nothing." Mrs. Rothmayer shivered. "I do hope you don't run into those two men. They were very frightening and I don't doubt they were the ones who killed Flossie. I have no idea where they were from or what their names were, but they're the ones you should be looking for. Rather average-looking, I'm afraid, and very well-dressed. One had a scar across his nose, from a knife fight, it looked like. He was a real dandy, I must say, and it seemed at odds with his fancy clothes." She thought harder, then shook her head. "That's all I can say about them."

"I see. Well, thank you for your time."

"You're very welcome. And keep a close watch on your sister."

"I will. Thank you."

Freddie smiled and nodded, then left the building. It was almost six and full on dark by that point. He debated walking home but decided a taxi would make more sense. Traffic, however, was so dense that walking would have been quicker.

As Kathy trudged up the stairwell from the subway

stop nearest home, she was in no mood to deal with any more idiots. It had been a long day, made longer by the demands of a boss who didn't care that she was doing more work than anyone else at the firm. And office mates who thought this was funny. And contractors who couldn't understand that she was not a secretary.

She looked up at the tall building where she lived with Freddie and once again, it occurred to her that, as Freddie's wife, she didn't have to put up with the people at her office. She didn't have to work there or anywhere if she didn't want to. She sighed. The problem was she very much wanted to do the work. She just got tired of dealing with the people.

It didn't help that Mr. James Ryland was waiting in the building vestibule as she came in.

"Miss Briscow, what a pleasure seeing you here," Ryland said. His smile seemed genuine.

"Good evening, Mr. Ryland," Kathy replied. "Can I help you with something?"

"Oh, just waiting for Mrs. Wentworth to come home." Ryland actually sighed.

Kathy debated telling him it was going to be a very long wait. "Oh, I expect she's out visiting. I believe she said something about staying with an aunt of hers for a while."

"She didn't say which one?"

"I can't say," Kathy said.

Ryland's eyebrow lifted just a hair. Kathy realized he was trying to decide if she was hiding something.

"How is your injury?" Kathy asked, hoping to distract him.

Ryland touched the back of his head. "Much better. Thank you. Um, say, would you like to come out to dinner with me tonight?"

"I'm afraid I can't," Kathy said with a weak smile. "I've got a ton of work from the office to do. But thank you for asking."

"Some other time, then?"

"I'm afraid that won't be possible. Now, if you'll

excuse me, Mr. Ryland, I would very much like to get home."

"Of course." He tipped his hat. "We'll catch up again soon."

Kathy smiled and went straight to the elevator.

"Evening, Miz Briscow," said the operator.

"Evening, Mr. Ellroy," Kathy said and sighed as Mr. Ellroy closed the gate. "What an odious man."

"That Mr. Ryland? I know what you mean. He don't act so bad, but I always get that feeling. Know what I mean?"

"Yes, I think I do."

The elevator stopped on Honoria's floor and Mr. Ellroy opened the gate.

"Thanks again, Mr. Ellroy," Kathy said, hurrying out of the elevator into the vestibule and then into the apartment. She hurried even faster downstairs to Freddie's apartment. Well, hers, too. She was still having problems remembering that she actually lived there. It was her apartment, too.

She was utterly deflated when Roberts took her hat and coat and told her that Freddie wasn't home yet.

"Did he have plans for dinner that he forgot to tell me about?" Kathy groaned.

"I don't believe so, Ma'am. He left this afternoon and said he expected to be back before you got home."

There was a ding outside the foyer door.

"There's the elevator now," Kathy said.

A second later, Freddie walked in. Roberts took his hat.

"Roberts, a second," Freddie asked, then turned to Kathy. "When do you want dinner?"

"Oh, not so late, please," Kathy sighed. "I'm afraid I'm starving now."

Freddie nodded at Roberts, who withdrew into the servants' quarters. Freddie finally embraced Kathy, then wandered into the study.

"Would you like a whiskey and soda?" he asked, going to the credenza.

"After the day I've had, I'll take a straight whiskey."

"I think I will join you." Freddie poured the drinks and handed one to Kathy. "That bad?"

"Not that bad." Kathy took a sip of her drink. "Just people being tiresome is all. Mr. Dillbeck, my senior editor, has decided to punish me for getting Lowell's book to edit and he's doing it by dumping all sorts of menial tasks in my lap. The others have done nothing but tease and joke and it's really not funny. Then Mr. Trimble, the printer? He still refuses to talk to me and, naturally, there was a complication with Mr. Mennerly's print run." Kathy slid onto the couch. "I know I don't have to put up with it. But I do love the work otherwise. Frankly, my darling, it's days like today that make me wish I could ask you to buy the company for me."

Freddie laughed. "You wouldn't like it if I did."

"No, I wouldn't." Kathy sighed and took another sip of her drink. "I'm not even sure you could. It would have to cost a tremendous amount of money."

"Perhaps." Freddie sat down next to her. "Would you like to hear about my day?"

"Oh. Yes, of course. Please tell me."

Freddie did not say much about his luncheon or his thoughts while walking about the park, but he gave her a fairly accurate account of his discussion with Dr. and Mrs. Rothmayer.

"That doesn't sound terribly useful," Kathy sighed.

"I think it's interesting that there were two men searching for Miss Walsh. According to that one servant, there was only the one man seen in the building, getting on the servants' elevator, I believe."

Kathy shrugged. "I have no idea what to make of it."

She got up, and putting the drink on the credenza, went into the hall.

"What are you doing?" Freddie asked.

"I need to get some stomach powders from my

purse," Kathy said. "I had to eat my luncheon at my desk and you know how that upsets my stomach."

She picked the purse up from the hall table and instead of pulling out her stomach powders, she pulled out the cufflink she'd found in Honoria's bedroom.

"Freddie, is there any way to find out who owns this?" she asked suddenly. "Maybe a jeweler would have some record?"

"It's possible, I suppose." Freddie took the cufflink and looked at it closely. "It may even be probable. It looks like there's some sort of jeweler's stamp on here. It's tiny, but look."

Kathy bent close to his fingers. "I think you're right. Would that be like an artist's signature?"

"It could be." Freddie flipped the cufflink over. "It certainly is a handsome piece. I wouldn't mind owning a pair of these, myself."

"Oh, dear. Does this mean you didn't like your birthday gift?" Kathy asked.

"It's quite special," Freddie said, patting his trouser pocket. "However, I specifically requested that you not get me one, and I still mean it." Freddie's glare was not in the least menacing, but it was clear he meant what he said. He pulled her close to him. "Having you here with me is the best present I could ever get, and that's all I want from you."

"No, it isn't by a long shot," said Kathy, with her happy wicked gleam. "But can we at least eat dinner, first?"

"Of course, my darling."

Freddie offered her a warm kiss, which was interrupted by Roberts summoning them to dinner.

Chapter Six

It was with no little irritation that Kathy got herself out of the office by eleven-thirty the next day so that she could get to her luncheon with Edward Roundhouse on time. Fortunately, she had almost caught up on her extra work, then managed to convince Mr. Trimble that he should discuss the print run on Mr. Mennerly's book with her and escaped Mr. Dillbeck's latest request. It had rained the night before, and while the skies still threatened, the day remained dry.

The restaurant was crowded, but Edward was already at the table he'd reserved for himself and Kathy. He stood as she approached and waited until the waiter had seated her to sit down himself. Kathy had barely found a place for her purse when she realized Edward had already ordered for the two of them. At least the swelling around his nose had gone down and the bruising had turned to almost normal coloring.

"They do a corking roast chicken here," Edward said as the waiter returned and placed small bowls of tomato aspic in front of them.

"I have been here before," said Kathy. She nibbled around the edge of the aspic, which she loathed.

"Oh. Of course. How silly of me to assume," Edward said, looking properly abashed. "I appreciate you coming."

"You did offer me luncheon." Kathy put on a fresh smile. "Is there something I can help you with?"

Edward smiled affably. "I just wanted to get to know you. You're quite close to Honoria, you know. And I like her a great deal. There's no reason I shouldn't like you, as well."

"I suppose not," Kathy said, pushing aside the bowl with the aspic. "However, I do have a beau already and I'm not looking for another one."

"Oh! No. This is purely social," Edward protested.

He paused as the waiter removed the aspic bowls and placed plates filled with chicken and stuffing in front of them.

"Purely social," Kathy repeated, trying not to sound too skeptical.

"Yes. I'm widening my circle of friends. That can't hurt, can it?" Again, the affable hapless charm popped out.

"I suppose it can't. And what are your interests, Mr. Roundhouse?"

"Interests?" Edward sat back in surprise.

"Yes. What do you like to do for relaxation? What books do you like to read? What kind of music do you like to listen to? I know you enjoy following the college football teams."

"Oh, yes. And I don't mind a round of tennis every now and again. I also play golf. Do you?"

"No," said Kathy. "I've managed to avoid it so far. Although I had some girlfriends in college who were very keen on it."

"Lots of folks I know are, too. I enjoy it, but I'm not quite so keen on it. I'm not very good at it, either."

"As I understand it, you have to be very keen on it to be any good."

There was another awkward pause.

"Do you go to films much?" Edward asked.

"Sometimes."

"Have you seen The Lost World? Good heavens, it's amazing. You'd almost think the dinosaurs were real."

"So I've heard."

"I've got some friends who are in the movie business. I even went out to Hollywood and saw them making one. It was fascinating."

"I would imagine so."

"So, I've missed Honoria the past few days." Edward toyed with his chicken, his expression more studied even as he affected casual interest.

"She's visiting an aunt, I understand," Kathy said.

"Do you know when she'll be back?"

"Not really."

"She's a corking girl. Well, not a girl, I suppose."

"Not at all." Kathy suddenly realized what Edward was up to. "Are you looking for me to put in a good word for you?"

"Oh, would you?" Edward leaned forward, looking like an eager puppy. "I do like her a great deal."

"I'll see what I can do," Kathy said,

The waiter approached and whispered in Edward's ear.

Edward flushed, then waved at him. "Just put it on my tab."

"I'm afraid we can't, sir."

Kathy pretended not to notice what was going on. Edward sighed and pulled a billfold from his inside jacket pocket. He removed some bills and handed them to the waiter, who left.

"Silly mistake," Edward said.

"It always is," Kathy said, then looked at her watch. "I'm afraid I must head back to the office. Thank you very much for lunch."

Edward popped up as she stood. "And thank you so much for coming. And for talking to Honoria. That would be absolutely corking."

Kathy smiled and headed to the front of the restaurant where she retrieved her hat and coat from the coat check. Out on the sidewalk, she started for the subway, then turned back to check something in a store window. A man in a dark suit with white pinstripes and his hat pulled down over his eyes stopped short and slipped into a doorway. Kathy pretended to ignore him but was not happy when he appeared not far from her on the subway car. She acted as if she was about to get off the train a stop before she needed to, and he began to go to the car door as the train slid into the station. The doors opened and Kathy stepped back into the train car and noticed the man doing the same.

Cursing under her breath, she missed her actual stop, then at the next stop, she scurried off the train at the last second. Moving quickly, she pushed through the crowd. She didn't know if the man was still following her as she entered the building at Fifth Avenue and Broadway where the publisher's office was, but later, as she left the office for the day, she decided she'd rather not take the chance. Leaving the building on the side away from the subway stop, she crossed the street and hailed a taxi.

There was no doubt that Fifth Avenue boasted more than the usual share of fine jewelry stores, many of which catered to Freddie and his peers. Still, he preferred another small shop, located at Park and 53rd. The jeweler was a young Dutchman with ties to the great diamond cutting center in Antwerp. Nils Van Rijn had wheat blond hair, bright blue eyes and was already getting a bit of a stoop in his back, thanks to bending over close work all the time. He wore a green visor and black sleeve covers over his shirt, and a black bibbed apron.

"Good day, Mr. Van Rijn," Freddie said as he entered.

"Good day, Mr. Little," Van Rijn's English had the merest trace of an accent. "It's been a good while since I've seen you. Early last summer, I think. I hope all went well."

Freddie smiled. The last time he'd been in the shop had been to buy Kathy's engagement and wedding rings.

"It went very well, Mr. Van Rijn," he replied. "We're merely keeping it quiet for the time being. It's a long story."

"Ah. That's good to know." Van Rijn couldn't help

grinning. "When you didn't return, I began to worry that you'd been refused."

"There was that danger, but no. We're quite happy." Freddie dug into his pocket. "I do have a puzzle that maybe you can help me with. We found this cufflink and want to return it to its owner. But we have no idea to whom it might belong. We did find what looks like a jeweler's mark on the back and thought maybe you could identify it."

Van Rijn took the cufflink and turned it over and over in his hand. "It's a very fine piece. Let me put a light on it."

He pulled the table lamp onto the glass case bearing several rings and necklaces and got out a magnifying glass.

"Ah." He adjusted the lamp and pulled out a loupe and set it in his eye socket. "These are beautiful diamonds. It's not easy to cut them so well when they're this small." He removed the loupe and studied the back of the link under the magnifying glass and lamplight. "Yes. I've seen this mark before. I don't know whose it is, but I would guess he's in Los Angeles. I've seen it on several pieces from a couple of different film stars."

"Film stars?"

Van Rijn nodded. "They come to New York every so often. And I have built a clientele among the wealthier actors on Broadway. They, like you, appreciate the art of jewelry making."

"You do excellent work," Freddie said. "Would you be able to make inquiries for me?"

"I could write a couple letters. Would you allow me to make a sketch of the piece?"

"Certainly. And I appreciate your checking. Thank you."

And to show his gratitude, Freddie bought a small, discreet pair of earrings for Kathy. The problem, he decided after getting the cufflink back, would be finding an excuse to give them to her. As he left the store, he pondered. Kathy had made it clear on her birthday in

May that she did not want Freddie buying her anything. He already paid for their activities together and even paid for any evening wear she needed, even though they pretended that Honoria loaned Kathy the clothes. He had likewise insisted that she not buy anything for him on his birthday because anything he didn't have, he didn't particularly want, never mind that she had gone out and gotten him something he might, indeed, find useful.

The earrings were pretty and Kathy deserved a small token of his love for her. He went back to the apartment to put a plan together. He did nearly get caught when Kathy arrived home a good fifteen minutes earlier than usual.

"This is a nice surprise," Freddie said, giving her a warm kiss, then straightening his dinner jacket.

"You won't think so when I tell you why I'm early." Kathy dropped a couple letters on the hall table. She turned and faced him. "I was followed this afternoon."

"What?"

"I had that luncheon with Edward Roundhouse and as I left the restaurant, a man followed me onto the subway and when I almost got off, he almost did, too." Kathy paced. "So when I left the office today, I didn't take any chances and took a taxi home."

"I'm glad you did." Freddie pulled her close and held her. "It couldn't have been Edward."

"I doubt he did the following part," Kathy said. She slipped out of Freddie's arms. "But he may have paid the man to follow me. He's up to something."

"That's not surprising."

"Oh?"

Freddie waved her off. "I'll tell you in a minute. What do you think he's up to?"

"He wants Honoria. He was trying to befriend me as a way to get to her. He even asked me to put in a good word for him."

Freddie laughed. "I can't see that doing a bit of good. Honoria can't stand him."

"I believe that. He does have a kind of lost puppy charm, but he's not very interesting, nor is he interested in anyone but himself." Kathy began pacing again. "But I can't think he's so dense as to think Honoria would be interested in him. And then, as I left the restaurant, that's when the man started following me. If it was Edward who paid him, I can't imagine why he'd want to follow me, unless he thinks I'll lead him to Honoria. And I don't know why Edward's so interested in Honoria, but I don't think it's because he's that fond of her."

"I think I know what he wants." Freddie tapped his fingers against his leg. "Honoria's money."

"Doesn't he have money?"

"His parents have money. But the rumor is his father is cutting him off. I'm not sure whether it's his drinking or what. The story varies with the telling. The only constant is that he's being cut off."

Kathy nodded. "That would make sense. The waiter at the restaurant had a problem with the bill and when Edward said to put it on his tab, the waiter said he couldn't. So Edward got out some cash."

"His father must be giving him something, then," said Freddie. "As for the cufflink, my jeweler believes it came from Los Angeles. He recognized the jeweler's mark, but he doesn't know whose it is."

"That's interesting. Edward said he'd been to Hollywood and that he has friends there."

Freddie's eyebrows rose. "Hm. Well. Why don't you get dressed for dinner? We'll eat somewhat early, but I thought it would be nice to be a touch more formal."

"Oh, all right."

She disappeared into the bedroom, then re-emerged. "You said a touch more formal. What does that mean? My Sunday best or a gown and gloves?"

Freddie held out the jeweler's small box. "It means something that will go with this."

"Freddie, what did you do?" Kathy almost glared as she took the box.

"I wanted to buy something from Mr. Van Rijn to encourage his help." Freddie paused. "And I thought a small token of my esteem and love for you would be appropriate. You certainly deserve it."

"That's very sweet, my darling." Kathy opened the box and gasped. "Oh, these are wonderful! Freddie, thank you so much. They're beautiful."

The earrings were not terribly ornate, merely small rectangles of white, rose and yellow gold layered on top of each other with dark black engraved lines.

"It's the least I could do," Freddie said.

"I just feel that I should reciprocate in the same way."

"You're going to buy me earrings?" Freddie said with a naughty grin.

Kathy laughed. "You know what I mean."

"Darling, what's the point of buying me cufflinks or pens or lighters? I have far more than I need. The few presents you've given me were all the more special because they were so unusual. And ultimately, you give me so much more just by being here and giving me hell when I need it."

Kathy's eyes misted a little. "And you don't give me anything? For heaven's sake, Freddie. You treat me like your equal."

"You are my equal and in some ways, my better."

"Not your better. But I do like being your equal. Sometimes I do wish we could talk about our marriage just so I could let people know that a marriage between equals is possible. Even desirable."

"It is, at that. Now, why don't you put your new earrings on and we can have dinner."

"Yes, let's."

They spent the evening going around in circles, trying to make sense of what they had regarding Flossie Walsh and not coming to any real conclusions about anything.

Finally, over coffee in the study, Freddie made a decision.

"I suppose the best thing we could do is find out as much about Miss Walsh as possible," he said, putting down his cup and getting up.

"I'm inclined to agree," Kathy said. "And probably the best place to start would be to go to Caledonia and speak to her family."

"You and I are once again of the same mind." Freddie tapped his fingers against the credenza. "You realize that unless you can get some time off from your job, I shall have to go."

Kathy sighed deeply and profoundly. "I can't possibly take any time off. It's bad enough I'll never make senior editor. I can't give Thaddeus Healcroft even the least excuse to fire me."

"I'm so sorry, darling."

Kathy shrugged. "It's the way it is. At least I can do meaningful work that I enjoy. Now, when do you propose to leave?"

"I could leave as early as first thing tomorrow, but I'd rather not," Freddie said. "It's always better to find out if there's an airfield and where, wire ahead for a hotel and perhaps a car, things like that. But I should be able to take off the day after tomorrow."

"So you're going to fly." Kathy pursed her lips.

Freddie's passion for all things mechanical meant that he not only knew how to fly, but also had his own custom-built Curtiss biplane. He had taken Kathy in the plane the summer before, first to her family in Kansas, where they'd gotten married, and then all over the western half of the country as a honeymoon. Kathy had enjoyed seeing the Grand Canyon and Yellowstone Park and other sites, but she hated flying and refused to do any more if she could avoid it. And any time Freddie went up in his plane, she was only marginally convinced he would return to earth in one piece.

"Of course," Freddie said. "I'll be able to return that much sooner."

"There is that," Kathy conceded unwillingly. "You'll wire me as soon as you land, won't you?"

"Yes, my darling. I'll even give you a flight plan, so if I'm overdue, you can send the search parties out."

"Don't say that." Kathy shuddered. "The last thing you need to do is tempt fate."

"I'll be fine. Now, if you'll excuse me, I'll get my atlas with the airfields listed on it and start plotting my path now."

Kathy felt completely annoyed but had to concede that Freddie was right about it being much faster for him to fly.

The next morning, she left for work before he woke, wondering how late he'd stayed up with his atlas. She didn't notice anyone following her, which was a tremendous relief, and became an even greater relief when she was sent on an errand to the printing plant on the lower East Side. It was more harassment. An errand boy could have picked up the galleys as easily as not. But then Kathy noticed that the address of the printing plant was remarkably close to the address for Ellen May, the woman in the note that Flossie had among her letters. And Mr. Dillbeck had been so spiteful that morning that Kathy had come very close to telling him off. Instead, she took a short detour to the address for Ellen May.

It was on the second floor of a brownstone that, like others in the neighborhood, had a shop on the ground floor, offices on the second, and apartments, or rather, tenements above. Kathy pushed her way up the neat staircase to the number listed in the letter. It was a typical office door, with opaque glass filling the top half.

"The People's Weekly" read the black letters arcing over the office number on the glass pane.

Kathy opened the door into an antechamber crowded with desks covered in papers, some filing cabinets and a lone clerk wearing sleeve covers and a visor hunched over a newspaper and eating a thin sandwich.

"Yeah?" he asked, barely flicking his eyes in

Kathy's direction.

"I'd like to see Ellen May," Kathy said.

"In the back." The clerk nodded at the door behind him.

Kathy turned the knob to the door and stepped into another similar office with only one desk, but more filing cabinets, a credenza under the window, and a tall, slender woman pacing the worn carpet on the floor. Her hair was blonde and pinned up and she wore a dark blue work dress, black stockings, and sensible black oxfords.

"I'm looking for Ellen May," Kathy said slowly.

"That's me," the woman groaned in a familiar voice.

She turned and glared at Kathy, who stepped back, then looked again. The woman's dress was plain and long enough to be a couple years old. She wore no make-up. Yet her eyes were a more than familiar hazel and her other facial features bore an uncanny resemblance to Freddie.

"Hon-," Kathy stammered. "Um. You're Ellen May."

"Yes. I'm Ellen May," she said crossly. "What are you doing down here?"

"I was going to pick up some galleys," Kathy said.

The woman huffed. "I don't doubt you want an explanation."

"It would be nice."

"Let's go get some lunch." She grabbed a purse, a battered felt hat with a large brim and a coat from a hat tree next to the door and pushed Kathy out and through the antechamber.

Once on the street, Kathy scrambled to keep up with the woman's long, angry strides as she headed toward Greenwich Village.

"It's simply hard to imagine how this day could have gotten any worse," she grumbled.

"I'm sorry, Honoria," Kathy gasped. "I had no idea."

"You weren't supposed to," Honoria said. "Oh, it's not your fault. I should have known you'd have found me out eventually. Do you mind delicatessen?"

"I love it," said Kathy. "Are you all right? You sound very distressed."

"Oh, I am. But it's not murderous thugs." Honoria paused and checked behind her to be sure. "It's merely my conviction that if your cause is honorable, it should be honorable enough to pay the bills, for heaven's sakes. Especially when your landlord is actually a rather decent fellow who's merely trying to do well for himself and his family without gouging people unnecessarily."

Honoria paused in front of a delicatessen boasting a lunch counter and several tables inside. The tables were mostly filled with local office workers, but there was an empty one. Kathy nodded and the two went inside. After a short conference, Kathy went to the counter and ordered sandwiches and egg creams.

After a few minutes, the sandwiches were delivered to the table and Kathy could no longer hold in her questions.

"What happened to Madame Kri-what-sky?" she asked.

"She's my other persona," Honoria said. "I couldn't have imagined how convenient it would be to have multiple identities."

"How many do you have?"

"Just Madame and Ellen." Honoria picked up a bit of corned beef that had fallen on the table and ate it. "And myself. Except that each persona is part of me. How did you find me?"

"I found Flossie's letters and there was this note." Kathy dug into her purse and pulled out the envelope and gave to Honoria.

"Oh, good lord," Honoria groaned. "I knew I should have thrown that away. It pains me to speak ill of the dead, but that Flossie was a complete idiot!"

"So you did know her."

"No. I still don't know anything about her, except

that she couldn't keep her stupid mouth shut. That's why I was hiding her at my apartment uptown. I had her down here at my apartment above the newspaper, but she kept coming down and asking questions about me, where I was and all that." Honoria sighed. "I thought she was going to give the game away and I had enough troubles as it was."

"What do you mean?" Kathy asked around a mouthful of pastrami on rye.

"The paper." Honoria sniffed. "I wanted to run a quality newspaper that would help the average worker. Help people get jobs and make a good living for themselves and their families. I wanted women to stand up for themselves. Unfortunately, people don't want to read that sort of thing. And advertisers don't want to be associated with that cause and the ones that do expect to get their space for free because it's for The Cause. Maybe I was wrong to assume that paying rent and wages were honorable pursuits."

"Sounds honorable to me."

"We're being evicted. I just got the notice this morning." Honoria glared at her sandwich, then took a sip of her egg cream. "It was a good newspaper. Freddie isn't the only person in my family who can write. It just didn't pay for itself and I couldn't keep pouring money into it. I suppose I'm more of a capitalist than I thought."

"That's not an entirely bad thing. But how did you get to be Ellen May?"

Honoria smiled at the memory. "My friend, the one who sent Flossie to me. We met during the War. I was volunteering and that's how we got to know each other. In fact, she's the one who introduced me to Henry Wentworth. We used to come down here to listen to the radicals. I think she may have been spying for the war effort, but I couldn't prove it. Because we were both working for the War Office, we decided to make up names for ourselves so we didn't get into trouble. I became Ellen May. And after I got my own money,

I kept it up and eventually started the newspaper. I also started playing Madame Krichevsky. It was just a lark, but it was fun. And I finally felt as though I had a purpose for my life."

Kathy put her hand on Honoria's. "You still do. Just because this newspaper didn't succeed doesn't mean the next one won't."

"That's so kind of you, Kathy." Honoria looked at her. "Do you really believe that or are you just saying that to make me feel better?"

Kathy snorted. "I thought you'd know me better than that by now. If I merely wanted you to feel better, I'd have found something else soothing to say."

"Thank you."

"But this still doesn't answer who killed Flossie Walsh and whether or not that same person wants to kill you."

"What a calming way you have of putting things." Honoria grimaced. "And there might be someone out there trying to kill me. As me, I mean. I've heard that some strange men have been looking for me. The odd thing is that they're asking after Honoria Wentworth."

"How do you mean?"

"I'm guessing they don't know I'm also Madame and Ellen. But people do know that Honoria has friends among the bohemians in the Village, and if I have bohemian friends in the Village, then it might stand to reason I have socialist friends in the Lower East Side."

Kathy nodded. "That makes sense."

"Only I don't, as myself. Well, a few theater folk, but they don't really spend much time around here." Honoria sighed and looked down at her sandwich.

"Still, it seems odd that someone would be looking for you. Unless..." Kathy set her sandwich down, her appetite suddenly dulled.

"Unless whoever was in my apartment was trying to kill me and only killed Flossie by mistake." Honoria looked at her sandwich and took a huge bite, then talked around it. "I've been thinking about that a lot.

Fortunately, I have the paper to worry about as well. And it seems no one knows who Ellen May really is. At least I hope they don't."

"Maybe we need to find a safer place for you to stay," Kathy said, thinking furiously. "Do you remember my old boarding house?"

"Mrs. Lynne's, in the Village, right?"

"If you went there as Ellen May, do you think whoever this is would connect it to me and through me to you?"

Honoria shrugged. "It should be safe. Mrs. Lynne can be a bit of a battleax, as I recall. Would she have room?"

"I don't know." Kathy dug through her purse to find a pen and a memo pad. "Here. I'll write a quick letter recommending you and if she doesn't have room, then maybe she'll know someone who does."

"Or I could find my own place." Honoria grimaced. "Then how do I contact you?"

"Through Miles Yeager's speak, as we agreed."

Kathy sighed. "All right. But something worries me about that."

"There's not much else we can do."

The two finished lunch almost in silence, frustrated by the situation.

"Kathy," Honoria said slowly as she swallowed the last bit of her sandwich. "You won't tell Freddie about me, as Ellen May, will you?"

Kathy bit her lip. "I'll try not to. He does worry about you. He loves you very much and if anything happened to you, I'm sure he'd feel as though he didn't do enough to protect you, never mind that he couldn't have. It's driving him crazy that he can't do more as it is."

"I suppose that's the best you can do." Honoria took a deep breath. "I suppose we'd better get back to whatever we were doing before lunch."

"I do have those galleys to pick up." Kathy gathered her things together as Honoria stood and made ready to leave.

As the two stepped outside of the delicatessen, Kathy almost ran straight into an average-sized man. She recognized the pin-striped suit from the day before, then gasped as she saw the white lumpy scar across the bridge of his nose. Honoria faded back into the doorway as the man grabbed Kathy.

"Well, nice to meet you down on the Lower East Side, Miss Briscow," the man snarled, pushing Kathy back against the window. "Where is Honoria Wentworth?"

Kathy gasped but somehow managed not to look behind her. "I don't know!"

The man's grip tightened painfully around her arms. "Are you sure about that?"

"She- she went to visit an aunt. At least. that's what she said. If she didn't, I have no idea where she went."

"Which aunt?"

"I don't know!" Kathy shrieked. "I don't know her aunts."

"Why not?" the man yelled back.

"I'm her roommate. I don't pry into her life."

"You're useless!' The man banged her into the glass.

All of a sudden, he crumpled and fell unconscious. Honoria stood behind him, breathing heavily, both hands on her purse as if she'd just hit him in the head with it. Which she had.

"You've got to teach me some more of those tricks," Kathy said weakly as she picked her way around the man on the sidewalk.

"Let's get out of here." Honoria hurried back to her office.

Kathy ran after, checking behind her all the way.

The two ran inside the brownstone and hurried up the stairs. Instead of going to the newspaper, however, Honoria led Kathy up two more flights to a small apartment there. Kathy looked around the small sitting room and kitchen and couldn't help smiling.

"It's so charming," she said.

The tiny flat was furnished simply, with a sofa, two overstuffed chairs and a tiny table near the kitchen, which was basically a stove, a sink, and an icebox along one short wall. There was some extraordinary art on the walls, however.

"Is that a Picasso?" Kathy gasped, pointing to a cubist painting above the flowered sofa.

Honoria blushed. "Yes. It's not my favorite, though. I much prefer his blue period."

She went into the small bedroom at the back and Kathy followed her.

"We've got to get you out of here," Kathy said. "I must have led that jackass straight to you. I just don't know how."

"They use more than one fellow to follow you," Honoria said. "That way, you're less likely to notice, since the same person isn't always behind you."

Kathy cursed. "So how do I spot them?"

"Don't worry about it." Honoria went to the closet and pulled out two valises. "Would you do me a favor, though, and get that Picasso off the wall in the living room? And the Gauguin. And the two Mary Cassatts."

"And how much art do you have here?" Kathy all but shrieked.

"I love art. You know that."

"No, I didn't! Why don't you have these paintings at home?"

Honoria choked. "Because no one would understand."

"Of course, they would." Kathy suddenly stopped, because she realized that it was probable most of her set wouldn't. "They'd at least appreciate the price tags."

"Which is exactly why I have them," Honoria snarled.

"Well, I'd appreciate them as art," Kathy said and hurried into the living room.

Not knowing which paintings were which, except

for the Picasso, Kathy grabbed anything hanging on the walls and brought them in to Honoria, who promptly sorted everything out and got the ones she wanted into the larger of the two valises. The other was already almost full of clothes, but a wig with long black hair lay on top.

Honoria looked over the room. "I think that's everything. I just need some paper to sign everything over to Homer."

"Homer?"

"The clerk downstairs. He's not as useless as he looks."

Honoria snapped the two valises shut. Kathy took the larger one and Honoria the other, and the two went downstairs to the newspaper office. Leaving the two valises in the antechamber but taking her purse, Honoria called the clerk into her inner office and spent several minutes with him. He was not happy when he emerged and gave Honoria quite the dirty look as she left the office. Honoria ignored him, picking up both valises and carrying her purse under her arm.

As she and Kathy landed on the sidewalk, Honoria sent Kathy off on her original errand.

"Look, they didn't recognize me," Honoria said softly. "There are decent odds I'm safe. But they clearly know you."

"Wait," Kathy said, then moved closer to Honoria. "I just realized. This is connected to Miss Walsh. The man who attacked me? He had a scar across his nose. The Rothmayers said that a man with that description tried to attack Miss Walsh right before she left them, about a year ago."

"But why would they be looking for me?" Honoria asked. "I mean, as myself?"

"I don't know," Kathy said. She glanced around, but the street was empty. "I'll call on you at Mrs. Lynne's tomorrow after work. Maybe I'll find something out by then. Freddie is going to fly to Ohio tomorrow and talk to Miss Walsh's family."

"All right," Honoria said. "I'll try to keep you abreast of what I'm doing. But it's going to be tricky."

"It will. But we'll manage." Kathy smiled. "We have before."

Honoria reached over and kissed Kathy's cheek. "We have. And we will again. To victory, my sister."

Kathy couldn't help chuckling as Honoria headed up the street, even though it was not in the direction of Greenwich Village. In short order, Kathy hurried toward the printing shop, her original destination, and got the requested galleys.

Later, after she got home from the office, Freddie proved to be so consumed by his upcoming trip, Kathy didn't have the heart to tell him about her encounter with Honoria. The next morning proved to be considerably more difficult for both of them than either anticipated.

"Now, you'll be careful, won't you?" Freddie asked as the two ate breakfast.

"Of course. At least you won't have to worry about me falling out of the sky," Kathy snorted.

"I'm not going to fall out of the sky," Freddie said, wearily.

"Of course," grumbled Kathy. "There's no chance in hell of that happening. You only read about it every other day."

"And you also read about people being attacked on the street," said Freddie, equally annoyed. "We both have plenty to worry about. Are you happy now?"

Kathy merely glared at him. However, some minutes later as he left to go to the airfield, she held him in an exceptionally tight grip, which he reciprocated. There had been passion the night before and it carried over as they kissed each other goodbye.

Kathy spent the rest of the day trying to focus on her work and not worry about Freddie. It didn't work entirely, but she managed to get out of the office at the usual time and didn't see anyone suspicious behind her as she took the subway home. But any sense of calm deserted her as she entered Honoria's apartment.

The first sign that all was not as it should have been was the broken vase in the vestibule. Pictures were knocked askew and every drawer in every table was open. Kathy gasped in horror. She waited until she was reasonably sure she was alone in the apartment, then went through, room by room. Destruction and disarray were everywhere, even in the servants' quarters. Somewhere in the back of Kathy's mind, she remembered that she'd told Virginia to take a holiday, although Roberts had asked the young woman to stay on and care for Kathy downstairs.

The destruction had a pattern, Kathy realized. Pictures were askew as if someone had been looking behind them. Drawers had been upended as if someone had been looking through them. Boxes had been pulled from Honoria's wardrobe as if someone was trying to find something that might have been hidden in them. Even the mattress on her bed was shifted - another sign that someone was looking for something that might have been hidden.

Kathy held her breath and hoped that the person hadn't found what he was looking for. She went downstairs to Freddie's apartment and all was normal. She went back upstairs and called her Uncle Dan.

He arrived within half an hour and shook his head at the mess.

"I think you're right, Katie-girl," he said sadly. "Someone was looking for something. But do you have any idea what?"

"Not really," said Kathy. "I remember thinking last week, when we first found that body, that someone had been looking for something. But I have no idea what that could be. I did find some letters that Honoria had saved and took them downstairs. But when Freddie and I went through them, there wasn't anything curious. We did find a few things in Miss Walsh's room. I think Freddie said he'd called you about them."

"He did, but said there wasn't much to be made

of it."

"We talked to the doctor that she'd worked for some time last year, but that didn't get us much information, except that one fellow I told you about on the phone."

"The one that attacked you yesterday?"

"Yes. Does the description ring any bells for you?"

"It does." Dan shook his head as if trying to erase a bad memory. "We pulled a fellow meeting that description out of the East River this morning."

"What?"

"He'd had his neck broken, Katie-girl, much like your Miss Walsh."

"Are you sure?"

"Yes. I got a good look at Miss Walsh before they shipped her to her family. And I was called for the stiff in the river."

"Do you know who he was?"

"We've got a tentative identification for him - an Elmer Rightman. He seems to have done some time with the Secret Service, but nowadays, he's mostly pulling con games, pretending to be some famous investigator. At least, that's if we've got the right fellow. That scar on his nose is pretty distinctive, though."

Kathy frowned. "Do you want me to look at him?"

"I shouldn't be asking you." Dan sighed. "I'll let you know if we don't get a better identification. But my bones are saying it's Rightman. I'd like to talk to that fellow downstairs. Freddie's man. Roberts, is it?"

"Sure. Come on."

Kathy led the way downstairs to the apartment below. Roberts was waiting for Kathy as she came through the stairwell. If he was surprised to see Dan, he didn't show it.

"Roberts, I'm so glad you're here," Kathy said. "This is my Uncle Dan. He's a sergeant on the police force. I called him because Mrs. Wentworth's apartment upstairs was broken into and searched. He'd like to ask you a few questions."

"Certainly, sir." Roberts didn't even blink an eye,

although Kathy suspected he was not happy.

"Why don't we go into the living room," Kathy said.

Roberts gestured for her to take the lead, which she did. Uncle Dan followed with Roberts right behind. Dan and Kathy settled themselves on the couch and offered Roberts a seat, but the valet preferred to stand.

"Now, Mr. Roberts, the reason I wanted to talk to you is I'm hoping you may have seen or heard something that will help us with what happened upstairs."

"And may I ask exactly what happened?" Roberts said.

"Mrs. Wentworth's apartment was ransacked," Kathy said. "It was fine when I left this morning and now it's a complete wreck."

"We're wondering if you heard anything or saw someone strange in the building."

"I'm afraid not," Roberts said. "The building staff has been much stricter about who comes and goes, even in the servants' quarters. It's been very difficult getting regular orders. I heard Mrs. Wyman, she's the cook for Mr. and Mrs. Little and Mrs. Wentworth, complain about getting groceries delivered. The regular staff doesn't have as many problems getting in and out, fortunately."

"And where were you today?"

Roberts glanced away. "It is my day off, sir. I went to visit with friends. We met for luncheon and then went to see a movie."

"And you had no idea about what had happened upstairs?" Dan pressed.

"As I have almost no reason to go up there, no."

"What about Virginia?" Kathy asked. "Did she take her holiday?"

At this, Roberts shifted awkwardly. "No, ma'am. She has been seeing to your needs."

"I don't have any needs," Kathy said, bewildered.

"You do have laundry to take care of and various parts of the apartment require tidying. And apparently, you are rather hard on your clothes. Virginia has reported replacing several buttons and mending more than a few small tears."

Kathy thought it over. "And I thought I had just gotten lucky. I mean, I knew somebody was collecting the laundry, but I thought that was you, Roberts."

"No, ma'am. That is Virginia's job. However, she's been out since yesterday. I did give her leave to visit her family in New Jersey, I believe. She should return tomorrow."

Dan sighed. "Well, that explains why no one heard anything down here. I'll have to question the people above Mrs. Wentworth's."

"I'm afraid, sir," said Roberts, "that won't do any good. The apartment has been vacant for the past three weeks while the owners are in Europe, I believe. They took their personal servants with them and dismissed the rest of the staff. Mrs. Wyman told me at length about how angry their cook was."

Kathy got up and started pacing. "Roberts, didn't you say that the building staff is being very strict about who gets in, even on the servant side?"

"Yes, ma'am."

"Then how did our villain get up here to ransack Mrs. Wentworth's apartment? Somebody must have seen him."

Roberts rose onto his toes, then settled back on his heels. "There is actually an answer for that. While it has been more difficult for shop boys and the like to make deliveries, it isn't all that hard to sneak past the downstairs guard. One does run the risk of being seen, but I have heard that at least one... gentleman, eager to avoid detection, manages to come and go relatively easily."

"I'm afraid I don't understand," Dan said, sounding more puzzled than annoyed.

"One of the tenants on the ninth floor is a lady who finds herself rather lonely."

Dan laughed. "Oh, I understand that one, now."

"Which doesn't really help us," Kathy said. "Except

for proving that if one is daring enough and has enough reason, one can get into the building without being seen."

"That was my point, ma'am," Roberts said.

"Great." Dan slapped his thigh. "I don't suppose I can convince you to come stay with me and Aunt Beth, Katie-girl."

"Mrs. Little, I do have a suggestion if you would like to hear it. Something Mr. Little suggested, but I agreed there was no immediate need to do."

"What, Roberts?" Kathy asked.

"Mr. Little has given me permission to hire extra footmen to provide security if you see fit."

"How do you mean?" Kathy stopped pacing.

"I can engage a couple of sturdy and well-trained young men to serve here and upstairs. They could provide a physical deterrent to anyone attempting to enter the apartments while giving you freedom to come and go as you need."

"I like that idea," said Dan.

Kathy shot him a glare then turned back to Roberts. "You know what? It is a good idea. Then maybe Honoria could come home without worrying about being attacked."

"Where's she been?" Dan asked suspiciously.

"In hiding," Kathy told him, insinuating that she wasn't going to tell him. "Thank you, Roberts. Please hire as many footmen as you see fit. Is there anything else, Uncle Dan?"

He got up. "That should about do it for now, Katie-girl."

Kathy escorted her uncle out of the apartment. There was a telegram addressed to Freddie on the hall table.

"When did this arrive?" Kathy asked, picking up the telegram.

"Late this afternoon." Roberts gave the barest flicker of a frown. "It must be urgent, but it is addressed to Mr. Little."

Kathy looked at the return address and tore it open. "It's actually for me. See? It's from Columbus, Ohio, where Mr. Little was flying to first. Mrs. Wentworth's mail has been watched, so Mr. Little said he'd send me letters and such addressed to himself."

"I understand," Roberts said.

Kathy smiled briefly. "He landed safely and will spend the night in Columbus, then drive to Caledonia. It's only an hour or so away, apparently." She put the telegram down. "Well, I do have one errand I'd better run. Where are my coat and hat?"

Roberts fetched both items and Kathy's purse. Putting them on, she went upstairs and left through Honoria's apartment.

She wasn't terribly happy about leaving just then, especially since she hadn't had her supper yet, but she needed to let Honoria know what was going on. Kathy went first to Mrs. Lynne's boarding house, only to find that Honoria, in whatever guise, had never been there. Disgusted, Kathy freed herself from Mrs. Lynne and hurried toward the speakeasy in the Village where she'd first found Honoria, but stopped short a block away. Two Paddy wagons were parked outside the small shop that fronted for the speak, but it wasn't the local police who were dragging the patrons outside. A heavy voice cursed the G-Men as he ran past Kathy, which meant the men raiding the speak were Federal Agents. Not that unusual, per se, but usually there were at least some police officers on hand.

Two of the agents pulled one man down the street and into an alley across from where Kathy hid. It was Miles Yeager, the bartender and friend of Honoria's. Kathy couldn't hear what the G-men were asking him, but they got progressively rougher as Yeager either wouldn't or couldn't answer. Kathy backed away and hurried back home.

Across the street, Honoria watched Kathy leave with relief. She wasn't sure what was happening to

Miles, but there wasn't anything she could do about it. Biting her lip, Honoria sank back against the doorway she was hiding in. No doubt Kathy had been trying to let her know what had happened in her apartment. Honoria sighed. Kathy had probably not been down to Freddie's study and found Honoria's paintings and the note hiding there. Honoria would have to find some other way to let Kathy know that she was safe for the time being. Assuming she was safe.

Chapter Seven

Honoria woke up the next morning feeling decidedly uncomfortable thanks to an exceptionally lumpy bed in a small hotel off Broadway and 42nd Street. The place clearly catered to sweet young women fresh off the train from Podunk, Iowa, ready to become Broadway's next big star. Honoria was perfectly willing to eschew the comforts of her Park Avenue apartment. Still, there were limits and the hotel definitely passed them several times over. At least the matron at the front desk was a surly old battle-ax who made it clear that men were absolutely not allowed in the hotel. Honoria wondered if the fact that a man was the last thing Honoria wanted to see at that moment would have reassured the old broad.

Honoria shook the last of the sleep from her eyes. She had a lot to do and little time to do it in. The first thing would be to risk sending a telegram. Then she needed to get a message to Kathy. And then she had to get out of town as quickly and as unobtrusively as she could. Given that there were so many G-men raiding the speak the night before, Honoria had to conclude that whoever was behind these attacks had some significant resources. Unless the raid was a coincidence. But the way the two agents had been questioning and beating up Miles, Honoria doubted that.

That meant it was possible that the train stations were being watched. If Honoria knew how to fly, she might borrow Freddie's plane, but a woman flying was hardly unobtrusive. A woman driving alone was somewhat remarkable, but not unheard of. It wasn't likely that the roads were being watched and there were a lot more roads out of New York than there were train stations. Honoria didn't think it would be that hard to buy a motorcar and she knew enough about them to not get skinned on the price.

She got dressed and washed up and ate with the rest of the girls in the hotel. Something about a couple of them suggested that they'd found a way to get their beaus in for the evening. Honoria left her valise with the desk clerk, an even grumpier version of the matron, and left.

She sent the telegram first, then went to 11th and 39th. There was a candy shop there, but it was clearly closed. Frustrated, Honoria walked around the block, wondering what to do. There was a church nearby, St. Sebastian, the Martyr. Honoria would have paid it no mind, but through the corner of her eye, the pastor's name on the front sign leapt out at her: Father James Callaghan.

There had to be more than one Callaghan family in New York, but Kathy did often say that she had aunts and uncles all over the city. Honoria found the parish office and knocked.

Father Callaghan was not terribly tall, but he had a good-sized stomach and dark hair flecked with gray. He wore wire-rimmed glasses, a full-length black cassock and a rather sour expression on his face.

"You wanted to see me?" he asked, settling into his desk chair and placing his hands across his belly.

"I'm looking for Kathy Briscow's uncle," Honoria said, debating whether to mention Thomas or not.

"She's my niece," Father Callaghan said.

"I need to get a message to her," Honoria said. "It's an emergency. Kathy told me her uncle would see to it that she gets it."

"I'm not an errand boy."

"Of course not, Father. I wouldn't be asking if it weren't the only way. There's something terrible going on. Her Uncle Dan knows about it. I can't telephone her at work and I must leave town today."

"I suppose I could. What's the message?"

Honoria handed him the note. "You can tell her it's from Honoria. I'm her friend."

"You that fancy rich lady she took up with?"

"She shares my apartment, yes."

"I see. Well, I'll do my best."

"Thank you so much, Father."

Honoria left not at all sure his best would be worth anything, but there was no help for it. The car was next. It didn't take much haggling to buy the Model T brand new. The man selling it was slightly amazed, but Honoria smiled and wiggled her behind a little and he gave her everything she wanted, including several road atlases. Honoria collected her valise from the seedy hotel and was on her way to Wisconsin before noon.

Freddie thanked the garageman in Columbus, Ohio, then looked at the Buick he'd just rented with some trepidation. But the car proved hardy and took him to Caledonia in good time. Once there, Freddie found the names of Flossie's sisters at the local newspaper office, where he looked up Miss Walsh's funeral notice. The funeral had been the day before.

Apparently, there were only two sisters left in Ohio, a Mrs. James Carson and a Mrs. Walter Fairmont. Mrs. Carson lived with her husband in Columbus but had come to stay with her sister for the time being. There was a brother, Christopher Walsh, a widower who lived in Caledonia but was away on an extended trip. Freddie wondered what that meant. Another sister, Mrs. Abby Hecker, had moved to California with her three children.

Freddie got the address for the Fairmont family and walked down the street to the tall white Victorian house set in the middle of a large lawn and surrounded by several large trees. The leaves on the trees were beginning to turn, and there were flashes of bright orange among the yellow and fading green. There was a large black wreath on the front door, but nearby, five boys were playing a loud and rowdy game of football. They should have been in school. Freddie guessed they were still mourning the loss of their aunt. At least three were wearing black jackets and knickers.

Freddie went to the front door and knocked. A thin wisp of a woman with Flossie's dark hair and round face answered. She was wearing a black dress covered by a full blue apron.

"Pray forgive me for intruding at this time," he said. "I'm looking for the family of Miss Flossie Walsh."

"And who are you?" the woman asked cautiously.

"My name is Freddie Little. I'm afraid there's no pleasant way to say this. But Flossie Walsh was found in my sister's apartment. We believe my sister could now be in danger, so I'm trying to find out as much as I can about Miss Walsh so that maybe I can protect my sister."

"I'm Mrs. Carson," said the woman. "Flossie was my little sister. It's all been so dreadful."

"Arlene?" demanded an older female voice from within the house. "Who's there?"

"A Mr. Little, Mavis. He wants to know about Flossie."

Mavis, or presumably Mrs. Walter Fairmont, came to the door. She, too, was dressed in black, but on her, it looked as severe as her face. She glared at Freddie.

"Get out of here or I'll call the police on you," she said.

"But, Mavis, Flossie was found in his sister's apartment."

"That's what he says," Mavis snarled, her eyes never leaving Freddie. "And we don't know anything, anyway. Flossie never told us a thing."

"My apologies," Freddie said. "Again, please forgive me for intruding."

The door slammed shut.

"At least he was more polite than those other

fellows," Arlene Carson said on the other side.

Freddie couldn't hear Mavis' response and didn't linger. The family didn't seem frightened, but they definitely seemed to have good reason not to trust strangers. As Freddie returned to the street, he noticed a woman across the street, leaning on the gate of her white picket fence and watching him closely. The house behind her was a small bungalow painted gray with peeling green trim.

He tipped his fedora. "Good day, ma'am."

"You won't get much out of them," the woman cackled.

She looked just old enough to have a couple of young grandchildren, with graying hair and a front tooth missing. Her work dress had a waist and she had a white apron over it with a bib pinned to her top.

"I didn't," said Freddie.

The woman smirked. "They're close, but they've good reason to be. Too many strangers coming around asking questions. That's why Miss Flossie went to Chicago. She used to be a nurse for President Harding, you know."

"She did?" Freddie walked across the street to the woman.

"Well, 'til he died. That's when all the trouble started. You know, strangers asking questions about where Miss Flossie was and all. Then Mr. Hecker. His wife, Abby, was Miss Flossie's sister. Well, Mr. Hecker went for a drive in Miss Flossie's car and was killed. The car was sabotaged. So you know it was meant for Miss Flossie. Well, she took off after that. Not sure where. But about a year ago, I heard she was in Chicago, but then moved to Los Angeles to take care of her brother, Mr. Christopher Walsh."

"I understand he's away."

"And not likely to come back, I'll tell you." The woman picked between another of her teeth. "Got the consumption. He went to California to stay at one of the sanitariums there. In Los Angeles or near there, I think. He's a widower, you know. The two never were blessed with children. I wasn't either, sadly."

"Quite sad. But you seem healthy." Freddie rapped his finger against the fence. "Did you hear from Miss Walsh after that?"

"Oh, no. Was a shock that she was in New York." The woman's rancid breath spewed over Freddie as she beckoned him closer. "You know what it's all about, don't you?"

"That's what I'm trying to find out." Freddie tried not to gasp.

The woman beckoned him still closer. "They murdered President Harding, you know."

"What?"

"President Harding. He was murdered, you know. The tainted crab meat giving him food poisoning that was in all the papers? Pure nonsense, I tell you. It was cold-blooded murder. By his wife. She killed him. Flossie must have known about it or had some proof. She was his nurse, you know."

"So you said." Freddie pulled back, looking for a quick way out of the conversation.

"Mark my words, that's what's behind this."

"I'll take that under advisement." Freddie tipped his hat again. "Thank you for the information."

Smiling, he started back toward the town's center. He was about to return to his car when he saw a window lettered with "Chas. Kling, Photographer." He had the photo from Miss Walsh's room in his pocket, so he tried the door to the shop and found it open.

"Can I help you?" asked a man in shirtsleeves sitting at a desk. Behind him, the sitting area waited, a curtain at the back wall, and various chairs and props scattered about.

"I understand you took this picture," Freddie said, showing him the photo.

"Huh," said the man. He was on the smallish side, with quick, birdlike movements. "The Walsh family. Sad bit of business there. Took this right after the parents died, about four years ago."

"Indeed. I've met Mrs. Carson and Mrs. Fairmont."

Kling looked Freddie over. "Didn't get much out of them, did you? Small wonder. It's been pretty grim over there, what with Miss Flossie getting killed. That's her, right there."

Freddie pulled the other photo out of his pocket. "Did you take this one, as well?"

Kling looked at the photo and flipped it over. "Nah. That's a news photo, that is. Probably some young buck took it and tried to make time with Miss Flossie by giving it to her."

"Too bad. I was hoping you'd know who the other woman is. I mean, besides Mrs. Harding."

Kling looked again. "Nope. Don't know her." He suddenly chuckled. "Mrs. Lennox didn't get a hold of you, did she?"

"Mrs. Lennox?"

"Lives across from Mrs. Fairmont. Show her that picture with the president and she'll give you an earful." Kling laughed.

"I believe I got it already. If it's the same woman, she believes the president was murdered."

"Yep. That's the one." Kling shook his head. "I'll admit, Miss Flossie's trouble started soon after the president died, so of course, Mrs. Lennox believes that's proof positive that he was murdered."

"That's ridiculous," Freddie groaned. "It's impossible that anyone could get away with something like that."

"And there's no reason to," said Kling. "It's just a silly rumor cooked up by Mrs. Lennox and her pals to make Miss Walsh's family feel better."

"I wonder how much of what she told me was true." Freddie frowned. "I know one of Miss Walsh's sisters is a widow. And Mrs. Lennox said that he was killed while driving Miss Walsh's car."

"That is true enough. But the car being sabotaged?" Kling shook his head. "The wheel bolts came off and you know as well as I do that happens all the time. And killing someone that way is hardly a sure thing. It was bad luck, is all."

"Quite possibly," said Freddie. "But we do have reason to believe that Miss Walsh was hiding from someone who was trying to do her serious harm."

"No kidding." Kling thought it over. "That might be. But dollars to donuts, she got herself mixed up with some masher. She was kind of a flighty thing. Flirty, you know? The boys liked her a lot. She probably just caught the eye of the wrong one."

"One who can impersonate a government agent and watch people's mail."

"No kidding. She was running in some pretty swank circles, taking care of the president and all."

"What about the brother?"

"Mr. Walsh?" Kling's chuckle changed from pure amusement to disdain. "Truth be told, that entire family is a bit of work. They say he went on an extended trip out West, but dollars to donuts, he's in one of them fancy sanitariums out by Los Angeles."

"That's what Mrs. Lennox said." Freddie took both of the photos and put them back in his pocket. "She thought he had tuberculosis."

"Gotta give her credit for that one," Kling said. "He was coughing awful fierce before he went. That was back in June. Now, Mrs. Fairmont is collecting the rents and making darned few friends. Not that Mr. Walsh was much better. Put more than one family on the streets here in town, he did. Took after the old man. That whole family is mighty close to the bone, I'll tell you. Frankly, if anybody did sabotage Miss Flossie's car, it probably was Mr. Walsh trying to get rid of Mr. Hecker just so he could get his hands on Hecker's acreage. Not that he got it. Mrs. Abby made sure of that. She sold it a couple months ago and moved out West, too."

"Hm. That's very interesting."

"Maybe. But not that strange," Kling said with a

shrug. "Lots of folks been moving West. Like the song goes, 'How do you keep 'em down on the farm when they've seen gay Paree?' Not much to keep folks here these days, especially if you're a farmer. I'm even thinking of moving to Los Angeles, myself."

"Indeed. Well, I appreciate your help, Mr. Kling."

"You're welcome, sir. Good luck."

Freddie left the shop thinking less about Flossie Walsh and more about whether he could get to Columbus in time to fly to New York before dark. He decided to wait until he returned to the state capitol, which was about fifty miles south of Caledonia. And in spite of some rain, Freddie did indeed get back in time to return his car, change into his flying gear and take off.

As Kathy got off the elevator and went into Honoria's apartment, her jaw dropped almost as far as it had the previous afternoon. The apartment was almost completely back to what it had been before. The two vases that had been broken (the first when Flossie had been killed and the second when the apartment had been searched) were still missing from the tables flanking the foyer door. But order had not only been restored, the place shone as if it had been buffed to a fare thee well. Kathy peeked into all of the rooms. Nothing was out of place. All was perfect.

"Criminy," Kathy gasped.

She went downstairs, the weight of her day at work sinking back onto her shoulders. Roberts was waiting, as usual.

"Roberts," Kathy asked. "How did everything upstairs get cleaned up so fast? It looks as if nothing had happened."

"That is the idea, ma'am," Roberts said with the barest glimmer of a smile.

Kathy handed him her purse, coat, and hat. "It's amazing. Please tell your staff they did an incredible job."

"I'll be sure to, ma'am."

"Roberts…"

He turned. "Yes, ma'am?"

"Look. This may not make a lot of sense to you, but I'm doing the best I can here. My mother never had a servant. She had me if you know what I mean."

"Mrs. Little, you make Mr. Little very happy. That is all that concerns me." Roberts nodded and disappeared.

Kathy looked through the mail on the hall table next to the telephone. There was no telegram, and just letters from her mother and a friend from college, and several letters addressed to Freddie. Kathy looked more closely at the letter from her college friend. It wasn't obvious, but there were traces of having been steamed open.

"Roberts," Kathy suddenly called.

"Yes, ma'am," Robert appeared as if by magic.

"What are you doing with Honoria's mail?" Kathy asked.

"Virginia takes care of that."

"Has she gotten back from visiting her family?"

"Yes, ma'am."

"I'd like to see all of the mail that Honoria has accumulated since last week."

Roberts paused. "I'm afraid there is only today's. The accumulation was taken yesterday, presumably by the miscreants. As I recall, Mrs. Wentworth hadn't received any letters beyond the usual invitations. You could check with Virginia."

"I'd like to."

Roberts started and looked back at the servants' quarters. "If you'll excuse me, ma'am. I believe the front desk is ringing."

Kathy hadn't heard anything, but not only did Roberts disappear, he reappeared and faced the foyer door.

"What's going on?" Kathy asked.

The sound of the elevator stopping filtered through

the foyer door. A second later, Freddie walked in.

"Freddie!" Kathy shrieked in spite of herself.

"Hello, my darling!" Freddie gave her a quick peck on the cheek, then handed his hat and coat to Roberts. "The rest is in the car, Roberts."

"I'll see to it, sir," Roberts said and disappeared again.

Freddie grabbed Kathy and spun her around. "Oh, it is so good to see you!"

Kathy responded with a deep and passionate kiss. "How? What happened?"

"I got what little information there was and came home as fast as I could," Freddie said.

"I'm so glad!" Kathy said. "Oh, good lord. Look at me. Acting like a silly school girl."

Freddie kissed her again. "And I'm acting like a silly school boy. Kathy, all I could think about for that past five hours is how fast can I get home to my beloved wife."

There was more breathless kissing, then Kathy pulled away.

"Oh, no," she sighed. "Mrs.Wyman thinks I'm the only one here eating tonight. I should probably tell her you'll be here. Wait. I think it's a roast pork loin tonight. You can have my share if there isn't enough."

"There will be enough," said Freddie, not quite releasing her even though Roberts had returned. "Oh, Roberts. Have you let Mrs. Wyman know that I'll be here for dinner?"

"Yes, sir."

"But will there be enough?" asked Kathy. "She was only cooking for me tonight and I don't want any of you to go without."

"There will be sufficient, ma'am," said Roberts. "I'll fetch some hors d'oeuvres."

He disappeared again. Freddie squeezed Kathy.

"And you know what's for dinner already?" he asked.

"I'm trying, Freddie," Kathy said. "About a month

ago, Roberts started consulting me on the menu, and I thought I'd better at least try to show some interest. And I do like to eat, so it's been more interesting than I thought it would be. Mrs. Wyman seems happy. She's actually getting to work since we're eating here most of the time. So how was your trip? What did you find out?"

"Not a lot, I'm afraid," he said, then led her into the study, where he mixed two whiskey and sodas for them.

He told her what he had learned from Miss Walsh's family and the photographer but somehow forgot to mention the neighbor's theory.

"So Miss Walsh's brother is in Los Angeles," Kathy said. "The maker of the cufflink is in Los Angeles."

"And if you want to count all possible connections, Dr. Rothmayer is headed there," Freddie added.

"Oh, good heavens. I hope this doesn't mean we shall have to go there."

Freddie grinned. "What? You don't want to go to the City of the Angels?"

"Angels, my backside," grumbled Kathy. "What it means is that you'll have to go since I have to work. Although, I think it is close enough that you'll at least be able to visit my brother."

Kathy's brother, Joshua Briscow and his wife, Betty, lived somewhere near Los Angeles growing orange trees. While Kathy was the eldest of the seven Briscow offspring, Joshua was her next oldest sibling, followed by Abraham, their sister Teresa, then Gideon, Isaac, and Gamaliel.

"That would be nice," said Freddie, who genuinely liked Joshua and Betty.

"Well, maybe we can find out what we need to with letters or telegrams," Kathy said, then looked up.

Roberts was in the door to the study. "Dinner is served, ma'am."

Kathy smiled. "Thank you, Roberts. We're on our way."

The next day, a Saturday, was Kathy's half day at the office. She wasn't looking forward to it. The atmosphere there was getting worse and worse. Even her office mates Fisk and Norbert were starting to snub her when they weren't teasing her. Kathy did her best to ignore them and focus on her work. Which was probably why she was so cross when the phone on her desk rang right before noon.

"Miss Briscow," she said into the mouthpiece of the stand-up phone, as she held the earpiece to her ear.

Other desks in the office had the phones with the ear and speaker both in the same handset. Only secretaries had the older two-piece speaker and ear piece set up.

"Hello, Kathy. It's Freddie here," said the voice on the other end.

"Yes, sir," Kathy replied, mindful that her office mates were probably listening to her. "How can I help you?"

"An errand boy just arrived with a message that your uncle, Father James Callaghan, would like you to stop by the rectory office as soon as possible," Freddie said.

Kathy bit back a swear word. Her eyes flicked up to the three other men at their desks, all of whom were studiously avoiding looking at her. "Thank you, sir. I'll come by after work."

She hung up. Several minutes later, when her work at the office was done for the day, she headed crosstown to Hell's Kitchen and St. Sebastian, Martyr, church. She was admitted to the pastor's office, but her uncle took his time meeting her there. Kathy had often wondered why everyone else in her mother's family seemed largely jovial and friendly, but Uncle James never had. Even Aunt Mary, who was a nun, was a delight compared to the sour priest.

Uncle James finally slid into his over-sized leather desk chair and laid his hands across his belly.

"Your friend asked me to give you a message," he

said after they had greeted each other.

"My friend?" Kathy asked.

"That rich lady you've been living with."

"Mrs. Wentworth? When did she come here?"

"Yesterday. I told her I was not an errand boy."

"She was probably looking for Uncle Thomas," Kathy said, remembering that her other uncle's speakeasy was not far from the church.

"For all the good it did her." Uncle James sat up enough to look over his desk. He delicately picked up a folded piece of paper. "Here is her message."

Kathy all but grabbed the paper. "Thank you, Uncle James. It was very kind of you to take it for her."

"You're welcome. Now, I must get ready to hear confessions." Uncle James eyed her as if she had more than a few sins to confess.

Kathy was reasonably sure that she did, but not having been raised as a Catholic, she wasn't terribly worried about it. She left the office and ran for the subway.

She read the note on the subway train, then when she arrived back at Honoria's apartment, she read the note again.

Honoria's handwriting had always been challenging to read. The note, while clearly in her hand, was more challenging than normal. Kathy realized that Honoria had been writing in a hurry. Worse yet, the note had been written by Madame Krichevsky, and the essential elements were the cards scattered throughout the text.

"Going to L.A. Have to get i-" The two cards spelling the rest of the word were smudged beyond recognition, assuming that there there were two cards and not one or three cards.

"Oh, hell," grumbled Kathy.

She was going to have to share the note with Freddie and possibly share more of Honoria's life with him than Honoria would have liked. But there was no help for it.

Freddie, however, was remarkably stoic on seeing the note.

"It's not terribly clear, is it?" he asked Kathy.

"Well, except for going to Los Angeles," Kathy said.

"That, I'm afraid, is true." Freddie sighed. "I suppose that means I'm going to have to go now."

Kathy sighed even more deeply. "I suppose it does, damn it."

"I should probably leave tomorrow," Freddie said. "Damn. I hate flying on Sundays. You never know where you're going to find a gas station open."

"You could leave on Monday," Kathy said.

"I'd rather leave sooner so that I can come back sooner if you know what I mean."

Kathy did. Sadly, she left him to his atlas and sulked over another manuscript.

Chapter Eight

Freddie didn't usually mind flying cross-country. But, he reflected somewhere over Missouri late on his first day out, his previous flights had been for the sheer joy of flying rather than trying to get somewhere to make sure his sister was safe while leaving behind the woman he loved.

He did stop in Hays, Kansas, where Kathy's family lived, and while he couldn't stay long, he did make a point of visiting with the Briscows while re-fueling. He sent a telegram to Joshua Briscow late that evening after finally stopping in Salt Lake City. The next day's flight was relatively short, and he landed at an airfield in Fullerton, California, shortly after noon.

He went to the flight office to see about hangar space for his plane.

"Do you mind leaving it on the field?" the office man asked. He was a tall and extremely fat man, wearing a beard and glasses.

"I'd prefer to leave it in a hangar," Freddie said. "I do have the money."

The man shrugged. "I suppose. Three dollars a day."

Freddie tried not to sigh. "That will be acceptable. I'll pay for the first week up front."

"You Freddie Little?" the man asked suddenly.

"Yes."

"Your brother-in-law called a while ago. He said for me to call him when you landed so he could come get you."

"That would be very kind of you," Freddie said,

digging out the dollar bills he needed.

After getting his plane settled, Freddie returned to the office to find that Joshua had already arrived in his Packard 120.

Joshua was of average size and took strongly after Kathy, his older sister by a couple years, with brown hair and bright eyes. Joshua also had a rocking limp, thanks to having broken his leg as a boy. Before Freddie could even point it out, Joshua had grabbed his trunk and loaded it into the back seat of the car.

"Betty is looking forward to seeing you," Joshua said. "And you should see Jakie. You know, we used to call him Little J. Only now we're calling him Jake. He's a whole six months old, now. Sitting up on his own and damned near crawling. You and Kathy got one on the way yet?"

"Uh, no," said Freddie. He'd forgotten about the easy intimacy that happened among Kathy's family members. Nor did he wish to explain that Kathy didn't really want to be pregnant just yet, what with trying to advance at her job.

"Odds are it'll happen when you least want it," said Joshua with a grin.

"These things always seem to," said Freddie.

The car was bumping along a dirt road. The air was bone dry and rather warm. Freddie could see a strong breeze bending the trees toward the west. There were a few eucalyptus trees by the side of the road, but on either side, endless groves of dark green orange trees stretched as far as the eye could see. That Freddie expected. What startled him where all the oil wells interspersed among the trees.

"I had no idea this was such good oil land," he said.

"Good enough," Joshua said. "I probably should be drilling more, myself. But I don't know that I've got any oil. My neighbors probably drained off what little I have. One of the reasons I got the spread I did is that the fellow I bought the place from couldn't find any oil on the property. Like I told you, I'm doing pretty well, but it costs to drill for oil and I ain't doing that well."

"It could be a good investment."

"That it could. And it could be a flop. I think the odds are decent. I'm just not sure I want to go to the trouble."

"Have you had a survey done?"

"Not yet," said Joshua. "And what do you know? Here we are."

He pulled up in front of a large white square-shaped two-story house decorated with half columns pressed against the front wall. A large oil derrick loomed over the place, even though it was some yards away. Orange trees surrounded the small yard, and there was a white plaster fountain in the middle of a front lawn that was bordered by the half-circle driveway.

"Got five acres of lemon trees over that way," Joshua said, pointing even as he got out of the car and opened the back door to get Freddie's trunk. "The rest of it's oranges. Valencias. It's the native variety here. Great eating and even better juice."

"I thought you said you weren't drilling for oil," said Freddie nodding at the derrick.

"I ain't," said Joshua with a laugh. "That derrick's dead. The fellow I bought this place put it up and didn't get anything out of it."

The front door opened and Betty Briscow, a young blonde with fair skin, came outside. She was followed by a stocky dark-skinned older woman with black hair pulled back into a bun. The woman was carrying an infant who looked to be about six months old.

"There's my boy!" crowed Joshua, going over and taking the infant from the woman. "Thank you, Isabella."

"Hello, Freddie," Betty came over and gave him a familial peck on the cheek. "It's so good to see you."

"Good to see you as well, Betty." Freddie was glad that Joshua had Baby Jake and Freddie didn't have to hold him.

"Please come on in," Betty said. "We've been so

excited since we got your telegram. I know you have to go on to Los Angeles, but I do hope we'll get some time to visit."

"I hope so, too," said Freddie.

"Well, what do you think?" Joshua asked as they walked inside.

It wasn't as devious a question as Freddie would have usually thought. For one thing, Joshua was simply not capable of that kind of disingenuous behavior. For another, Joshua had no understanding of what Freddie's kind of wealth really looked like.

"It's very nice," Freddie said.

And it was. The floors were parquet, the walls whitewashed. The furniture was new and in the new Art Deco style. A wide, sweeping staircase led to the second floor, where Isabella was taking the baby. The living room stood open and ready, still, Joshua and Betty led Freddie to the kitchen, where another dark-skinned woman tended something on the stove.

"Maria," said Betty to the woman. Betty broke into quick Spanish and the woman answered back. Betty turned back to Freddie. "Looks like a good dinner tonight. Do you like Spanish food?'

"I suppose," said Freddie.

"Would you like something to drink?" Betty asked. "I've got lemonade, water, and orange juice, of course."

"Lemonade would be nice," Freddie answered.

"Tell you what," Betty said. "Let's go talk in the living room. It's a special occasion, isn't it? I'll bring the lemonade in there."

"Good enough," Joshua said. "Come on, Freddie."

As soon as they were out of earshot of the kitchen, Joshua leaned close to Freddie.

"You got any of that really good New York hootch?" Joshua asked softly.

"I brought a bottle for you," Freddie said, smiling.

"Thank you! Just don't let Betty see it." Joshua glanced back at the kitchen. "She's gotten real strict about any liquor in the house. Can't really blame her, either. Her pa was a drunk and abandoned her and her mom and brothers and sisters when Betty was still pretty young. Betty had to take care of the kids while her mother worked herself to death. That's why she knows Spanish so good. They lived on the poor end of town with the Mexicans. She used to work in the packing house. That's how I met her. She'd gotten to be in charge of the packing girls because she could talk to both the Mexican girls and the white foremen."

"I had no idea."

"Betty's something else," said Joshua with a proud grin, then he checked the hallway again. "But she's death on liquor."

"Then I will exercise caution in the transfer of the goods," Freddie said.

The living room was a large room with large windows on two walls, letting in the bright California sunshine. A fireplace surrounded by white sculpted plasterwork stood in the middle of the back wall. The room was filled with new sofas and tables. Movie magazines, plus issues of Life, National Geographic, and even The New Yorker, covered almost every surface. Betty came in with the glasses of lemonade on a tray. She shoved some magazines aside on a credenza next to the fireplace and set the tray down.

"The lemonade is from Josh's trees," she announced, handing a glass to Freddie.

"How nice." He sipped and smiled. "It's very good."

"Thank you," said Joshua. "Have a seat."

"I will, thank you." Freddie looked for a place to set his glass down before settling onto the overstuffed couch.

"Here," said Betty. "Just use the magazine as a coaster."

"I see you're quite the movie fan," Freddie said, seating himself.

Betty giggled. "I am. It's a good thing Joshua treats me like a movie star or I'd be running off to Hollywood to be in the movies."

"She reads all the magazines and the gossip columns," said Joshua. "Who's your big fave now?"

"Ivy St. James," Betty said. "She's a woman of mystery. She's not a big star yet. Mostly plays the sister or the friend of Clara Bow or Thelma Todd or Mary Pickford. She's in a lot of the big costume dramas."

Freddie smiled indulgently as Betty's chatter washed over him. The late afternoon sun slid past the windows and the room slowly darkened. Betty suddenly jumped up and turned on the lights, then hurried into the kitchen.

While Betty got the dining room table set and the last bits of dinner ready, Joshua and Freddie chatted about the oil business and from there, the scandals in Washington.

"We're right in the thick of it here, what with Mr. Doheny living in Beverly Hills and all," Joshua said as they sat down to dinner.

"That's right. I'd heard that," Freddie said.

"You know him at all?" Betty asked, placing a tureen of soup on the table.

"We've met once or twice," Freddie said as Betty served him a bowl of the red broth studded with bits of meat and pieces of corn.

"This is one of Maria's specialties," Betty said. "It's called posole. It's one of our favorites."

"Smells delicious," Freddie said. He took a spoonful and sipped. "As for Mr. Doheny - Oh my God!"

His mouth suddenly on fire, Freddie grabbed the nearest glass he could find. Fortunately, it was the lemonade. The cool, sweet drink soothed the fire quickly.

"I'm so sorry, Freddie!" Betty gasped. "I completely forgot about the chiles."

"Me, too, Freddie," Joshua said, grinning somewhat. "Since Betty and I got married, I've been eating fire so much, it's like my mouth is made of asbestos anymore."

"It's quite all right," Freddie said, clearing his

throat. "It was merely unexpected. I'm actually rather fond of spicy food. I have a friend in London who was raised in India, and he had a servant who would make some of the specialties of her region. They were quite hot but very delicious. And one of my favorite speakeasies in New York is down in Chinatown. The proprietor there will sometimes tease the lads by serving dishes with tiny, very hot peppers. They're wonderful and I've won more than a few wagers eating there."

"Anyway, you were talking about Mr. Doheny," Betty said.

"Him." Freddie mused. "He's not a friend, and... How do I explain this? It's terribly snobbish, but wealth in my circles is defined not only by having a lot of money but also by how long your family has had it. Mr. Doheny is what we would refer to as nouveau, or new in French. It's rather silly, actually, but I sometimes fall prey to the attitude. So when I met Mr. Doheny and was not impressed by him, I didn't go out of my way to befriend him."

"So, how are all your circle taking the scandals?" Joshua asked.

"They're outraged, of course," Freddie said. "Although they'd never say so, I suspect that they're secretly annoyed that Mr. Fall got himself caught. It will make it harder for them to do business with the government."

"I don't understand," said Betty.

"It will be harder to bribe officials and politicians to get what they want," Freddie said.

"So you're saying what Mr. Doheny and Mr. Sinclair did goes on all the time?" Joshua asked, only slightly amazed.

"That doesn't seem very fair," Betty said.

"It isn't," Freddie said with a sigh. "But it's considered the cost of doing business."

"Well, I've had to grease a few palms, myself," Joshua said, shaking his head. "I guess it's the way of the world."

"It's no wonder poor people can't possibly get ahead," Betty said. "My mother tried to start a laundry business, but because she couldn't pay off the man from the county, she couldn't get a license. She had the license fee. The man said that there were already three laundries in town, which there weren't. But he said he'd okay the license anyway if she'd pay him an extra fifty dollars. She didn't have it. So she had to take in laundry privately and hope she didn't get cited for running a business without a license. She only got caught a couple times, and the one time, the officer said he'd look the other way if she could give him twenty dollars. She had to pay it or go to jail."

"How awful," Freddie said.

He decided not to mention the other option her mother had probably had, although he suspected that Betty was well aware of it. Freddie briefly wondered if that was how Betty had attracted Joshua. But she seemed to be genuinely fond of him.

"Fortunately, Joshua never put me in that position," Betty said, as if in answer to Freddie's thoughts. "He was a perfect gentleman. By the time he started courting me, I was so used to pushing off mashers, I didn't know what hit me." She suddenly giggled. "Until the morning sickness started. I would never have thought it, but Joshua made it right. And we were already engaged by then."

"Aw, Betty," Joshua said. "Any man would be lucky to have you. And I'm just lucky those other mashers were too stupid to keep up with you."

Betty blushed becomingly. "Thank you, dearest. I'm incredibly lucky to have met you." She looked over at Freddie. "Joshua is going to pay for a correspondence course so I can learn accounting and help keep track of the packing plant receipts. I already keep track of the payroll. We caught a couple of the foremen trying to cheat the Mexican girls, so Joshua asked me to help out."

"I never was any good at numbers," Joshua said.

"Book learning, all that. That was Pa and Kathy and Abraham. I'm more like Ma that way."

Freddie smiled. Joshua might not be a student in the conventional sense, but he was no idiot, either, and was quite an astute businessman. As was Betty, Freddie discovered. The three spent the evening pleasantly discussing all manner of business issues, including being fair to the labor. Freddie found himself pleasantly challenged by the couple and even decided he needed to re-think several things he'd taken for granted.

The next day was spent touring the ranch and going over the possibilities for drilling oil wells. Joshua was still reluctant, but Freddie decided he didn't mind fronting the money for the operation. That evening, he started a letter to Kathy but decided to wait to post it until the next day when he would be settled at a hotel in Los Angeles and could send that address, as well. He'd already wired that he'd arrived safely at her brother's. It had been an exceedingly satisfactory visit.

Earlier that same day, Honoria knocked at the door of the third orphanage she'd been to in the city of Milwaukee, Wisconsin. According to the information she'd gotten at the Milwaukee library, it was run by the Sisters of the Good Shepherd, and there was also a home for wayward girls there, as well. Honoria sniffed in annoyance. Given all the assumptions that had been made about her the past several days, she didn't doubt there were plenty of folk who believed she belonged there.

It had been a grueling trip. The looks at the various hotels where she'd stayed were bad enough. She'd had trouble getting service at restaurants and cafes. More than one gas station attendant had groped her. Or had tried to. Honoria's friend had taught her well how to defend herself. So far, none of the attendants had thought to call the police on her after she'd hit them.

Honoria had thought long and hard about whether

she should be digging up her friend's past. The trouble was, Mary had learned during the War how to keep secrets and had learned the hard way why they needed to be kept. It wouldn't matter what Honoria said when she showed up on Mary's doorstep, Mary would not tell her what was going on. Only if Honoria could convince Mary that she already had a good idea would Mary spill. And until Mary spilled, Honoria wouldn't know who was after her and whether Freddie and Kathy were safe.

The orphanage was located in a huge stone building built to look like a gothic castle. It was on the outskirts of the city, sitting in the middle of a park, surrounded by trees and grass. The leaves had already gone flame orange, and the dying grass was strewn with the leaves that had already fallen. It was a gray day, the air heavy with coming rain and mist. The heavy oak paneled door had a pointed peak at the top and a black iron grate over a small opening near the top. Honoria half expected the opening to pop open first, but the door was answered by a sister in a black habit and beads, her white wimple and collar framing a youngish face.

"May I help you?" the nun said.

"Yes. I'm trying to find out if my friend was raised here," Honoria said. "Her name is Mary Snow."

"Mary," said the nun with a frown.

But she admitted Honoria and led her to a small, but comfortable sitting room near the front. The walls were covered in a dark wallpaper and the drapes were heavy and dark. The sofa and chairs featured frames of engraved and polished wood, with dark green velvet upholstery. A table carried an old lamp that once may have been lit by kerosene but was now re-wired for electricity. Heavy dark wood framed a fireplace that held a small, but cheerful fire.

"I'll have to speak to Reverend Mother," the young nun said. "Please wait here."

Honoria remained standing and looked at all the

bric-a-brac on the fireplace mantel and on the end tables against the walls. Most of it was framed photos, presumably of the children that had been raised there. More photos covered the walls, in between prints of Jesus and Virgin Mary and a couple of other saints that Honoria didn't recognize.

A short round nun with a lined face whooshed into the room like a strong wind.

"Good day," she said with a strong German accent. "I am Mutter Helen."

"My name is Honoria Wentworth," she said, wondering if she should curtsy.

"Sit, sit. Please." Reverend Mother Helen waved at one of the chairs, then sank onto the couch. "So you vant to know about Mary Snow, ja?"

"Yes, ma'am. She's my friend."

Mother Helen sat back and chuckled. "Ah, Madchen. She vas such a sveet little ting. Vell, I tought so. She could be trouble, too. Alvays into te mischief. But a good girl. Had a lot of spirit. I taught her German, und she learned French und Spanish, too. Fery schmart girl. I know. It doesn't do to haf favorites, but Mary vas vone of mine. She vas such a curious child and zat red hair she had!"

"When she did speak of her past, she mentioned this place fondly," Honoria said, pushing the truth. In truth, Mary had only said that she'd been raised in an orphanage in Milwaukee and that it had been a nice orphanage. "Did she write to you at all?"

"Mary? She is awful about ze letters," Mother said, laughing again. "Even ven she vas here, she vouldn't send tem. Ve vere lucky if ve heard from her more tan vonce a mont. And den two years ago, nuttink." Mother sniffed sadly.

"I know," said Honoria. "There was some trouble. I don't know what. She went into hiding. Do you have any idea what she was doing right before the letters stopped?"

"Just nursink. She vas a fery gut nurse." Mother

Helen's accent grew stronger with her worry. "You say tere trouble vas. Mary okay is?"

"Yes. I believe so. But I have to find her."

"She vas spy durink te Var. Could tat be te trouble?"

"Possibly." Honoria thought it over.

Mother sniffed again. "If tere vas trouble, vy didn't she to us come?"

"I don't know, but I suspect she didn't want to risk getting you hurt. She only came to me because she had no choice. I was the only one who knew her other name."

"Vat oter name?"

"I can't say," said Honoria. "Have there been others asking after her?"

"No. You are te first."

"Well, that's good to know. Thank you, Reverend Mother. I'd best be getting on. I'm going to see her. I'll tell her you said hello."

"Gif her my love." Mother Helen stood and waited for Honoria to rise as well.

Suddenly, Honoria found herself enveloped in the smaller woman's arms and held tightly. Mother Helen released her and went to the door.

"Und tell her to write. Ja?"

"Yes, Reverend Mother."

The small nun disappeared into the orphanage and was shortly replaced by the younger nun who had opened the door.

"I couldn't help but overhear," she said to Honoria.

"Did you know Mary?" Honoria asked.

"We were in the same class," the nun said. "Mary could be difficult as a friend. Reverend Mother always seems to like the difficult ones."

"I got that impression," Honoria said with a small smile. "And I know how spirited Mary was. We used to get into trouble together."

"She had a temper, too. That red hair of hers, I suppose. Anyway, it near broke Reverend Mother's heart when the letters stopped."

"She had no choice," Honoria said. "But I'll let her know. No one's come asking after her, have they?"

"No. You're the first."

"Any evidence that letters have been steamed open?"

The young nun thought about it. "No. I'll look, but I don't think so."

"Well, I'll write you when I can get to a safe place to write back." Honoria dug through her purse and pulled out a small memo book and pen. "And your name is?"

"I'm Sister Theresa," the nun said. "Mary will remember me as Ada Wilkes.'

"And I've got your address. Thanks." Honoria smiled at the young woman. "We'll get to the bottom of this. I promise."

"It will make Reverend Mother very happy." The young nun led Honoria to the door and let her out.

Honoria blew out her breath and pondered her next move.

Chapter Nine

The next day, Joshua insisted on driving Freddie into Los Angeles. Joshua had a tenant in Hollywood he needed to speak to, so it was no trouble to first bring Freddie to the Ambassador Hotel, in the middle of the city. Freddie had decided to stay there because his friend Lowell Winters was staying there.

"It is the place to be," Joshua assured Freddie as they drove through the east side of the city. "All the movie people go there. And I took Betty to the Coconut Grove there about a month ago to see the floor show. We saw Pola Negri in the hall. I'm told she lives there."

"Pola Negri. Imagine that," said Freddie, who hadn't the faintest idea who the person was. The name sounded vaguely familiar and given Betty's interests, Freddie assumed this Negri person was a film star.

As soon as Freddie had gotten himself a room and engaged the services of the hotel valet to get his clothes pressed and hung, he left a message for Lowell, then requested and got a directory of sanitariums in the area. There were quite a few. Freddie changed a dollar bill into nickels and lodged himself in one of the lobby's telephone booths. He spent the better part of the afternoon and another dollar feeding nickels into the telephone, calling the institutions in search of Christopher Walsh.

Finally, a rather grumpy woman at a sanitarium in a town called La Crescenta confirmed that Christopher Walsh was, indeed, a patient there, but he could not come to the phone.

"Is there any message," she asked in a tone that

somehow managed to sound as bored as it was annoyed.

"I'd like to come visit," Freddie said. "Do you know a good time for me to come by?"

"I can make an appointment. One o'clock tomorrow?"

"That would be quite satisfactory."

"Name?"

"Mr. Freddie Little."

"One o'clock tomorrow, Christopher Walsh. Good-bye."

Freddie returned to the hotel desk and consulted a map. The Pacific Electric Line didn't go that far north, but there was a bus line that he could connect to. Freddie decided he would be better off hiring a car and made arrangements with the hotel concierge to do so the next day.

There was a message from Lowell, inviting Freddie to dine with him at the Coconut Grove that evening. Freddie wrote a quick acceptance note and tipped the bellboy one of his few remaining nickels to deliver it.

It had been a busy day, but a reasonably satisfying one. Freddie took a comfortable drag on his cigarette, adjusted his bow tie and checked his dinner jacket in the mirror of the dressing room of his suite. The hotel valet had done an excellent job. White tie and tails might have been more appropriate, but the hotel concierge had assured Freddie that black tie and a dinner jacket was sufficiently formal for the Grove.

Freddie found Lowell in the hotel lobby, chatting with two other men. The taller of the two was thin and stooped over, with red hair and a large hooked nose. His companion was swarthier, shorter and rotund.

Lowell Winters was a large man. Though shorter than Freddie, he was still a touch above average height. But what most people noticed first about him were his prodigious belly and his very thick, very dark mustache. The second thing most people noticed were his incredibly bad manners. Or, more accurately, the fact that author and playwright Lowell Winters was a man utterly without pretense, and as such, a man of great appetites and humor and one prone to voicing his opinion on everything.

The second Lowell saw Freddie, he let out a whoop that startled his companions. Lowell rushed over to Freddie and shook his hand with a great deal of enthusiasm.

"Thank God, you're here!" Lowell gushed somewhat under his breath. "I was about ready to start wringing necks."

"Oh?' asked Freddie.

"These movie people are crazy!" Lowell hissed, then looked up at his companions. "Ah, Mr. Little, let me present to you Mr. Schulman and Mr. Loesch, of RiverWind Pictures. Gentlemen, my good friend, Mr. Frederick G. Little."

Schulman was the taller, red-haired man.

"Oh! I do believe I've heard of you," he said in a slightly reedy voice as he shook Freddie's hand. "You wrote that book about the rich kids gone bad… The, uh, Money something or other."

"The Old Money Story," Freddie said, indulgently.

"Mr. Little, it's a real pleasure to meet you," Loesch said. "We've always had a deep affection for our literary stars."

"Indeed?" said Freddie blandly.

But as he shook Loesch's hand, he noticed something else.

"Mr. Loesch, pray forgive me if I'm being too familiar," Freddie said slowly. "But your cufflinks. They are quite distinctive."

"Aren't they?' Loesch shot his sleeves so that the cufflinks were even more prominent.

They were gold squares surrounded by tiny diamonds. The letter was different than the cufflink Freddie had in his kit upstairs, but it was of a similar design.

"Would you mind if I asked where you got them?" Freddie asked. "I might like to have a similar pair."

"I wouldn't mind if I could tell you," said Loesch with a chuckle. "But my wife bought them for me and I have no idea where they came from. Well, I see the maitre d' is looking at us. Perhaps we should claim our table."

The opulence of the Coconut Grove was such that even Freddie was impressed. Real palm trees studded the room filled with tables covered with snowy white tablecloths. There was no saloon bar but the waiters made it clear that any libation one wanted was available. Loesch ordered martinis all around, along with caviar and water crackers. These were followed by a sumptuous meal, accompanied by Champagne and other wines. Dessert was served just before an exceptionally good floor show.

The only problem was that Freddie wasn't sure what the men wanted from him and Lowell.

"The cachet of our names, I would imagine," Lowell said, back in Freddie's suite, where the two were sharing a nightcap of whiskey in the spacious sitting room. "Even then, I can't imagine why. Most of the writers out here get very short shrift on their work. Still, one of the Warners wanted me, which is why I came out."

"So how do these other fellows come in?' Freddie asked, comfortably ensconced in a white leather easy chair.

"I let Warner know he wasn't the only bidder for my services." Lowell took a deep drink. He was seated on the end of the white velvet sofa, with his feet on the coffee table in front. "Bastard said that was okay, he didn't need me that badly."

"Hm." Freddie blew a couple smoke rings from his latest cigarette. "I will say this much. It was rather refreshing to have someone asking me to work for them, rather than trying to get me to invest in something."

"Do not, under any circumstances, let them know you have money beyond what you make with your book," Lowell said. "Or they will insist that you invest and in large quantities, too. Seriously, Freddie, they're all snakes out here. Movies are little more than a product and half these bastards are making more money off their real estate than their films. Most of them have never read a book, let alone yours. Or my articles or my play. The directors and the actors all think they're making great art, but the moguls only care about money. It's utter hell."

"Then why are you still here?" Freddie asked, with a mischievous glint in his eyes.

"There is money to be made. Quite a bit of it, actually. Even though the actors are paid comparatively poorly, they're still making a mint. Especially the big ones. I can make more writing a script for these illiterates than I can by writing an article or a play. And they are willing to pick up my tab more often than not. So I might as well stick around and see what I can scrape up. That being said, what brings you here? I can't see you trying to seek your fortune in the movie biz."

Freddie laughed and told Lowell about the murder and Honoria's disappearance.

"Have you tried looking up Ellen May?" Lowell asked cautiously.

"I don't recall," Freddie said. "Who is she?"

"Your sister."

"What?"

Lowell took another long sip from his drink. "Ellen May is Honoria's other name. I stumbled upon it quite accidentally a couple years ago doing research on socialists. Ellen May runs a newspaper called The People's Weekly. It's mostly about where to find jobs and women's rights and that sort of thing." Lowell paused. "Honoria swore me to secrecy about it, which is why I didn't tell you."

Freddie got up and started pacing. "I'll have to wire Kathy as soon as possible. If that's where Honoria is. But wait. She's coming out here. Her note said she had to get something. Or help somebody or get to somebody. The damned thing was impossible to read." Freddie paused and looked at Lowell. "You don't know any more of her secrets, do you?"

"None, actually." Lowell caught Freddie's glower and held up his hand. "Nor have I laid a hand on her. She's almost as much my little sister as she is yours." Lowell shuddered in distaste.

"Well, I guess I shall have to start inquiring at hotels." Freddie returned to pacing. "I wonder if Honoria has any friends out here."

"I don't know. Is she friendly with Edward Roundhouse?"

"Not really. Is he out here?"

"Staying right here in this very hotel, as a matter of fact," Lowell said. "We shared a luncheon the other day. I expect you'll run into him sooner rather than later. He's been hanging about in the lobby quite a bit."

"Thank you for the warning," Freddie, thinking about something else, resumed pacing. "I should probably wire my jeweler in New York."

"Jeweler?" Lowell laid his hands across his belly. "Ah. The cufflinks. You wanted a pair."

"Actually, no." Freddie went over to the bedroom and came out with the small gold piece. "I'm looking for the mate to this. Kathy found it in Honoria's bedroom the night of the murder."

"If you'll excuse me for possibly impugning Honoria's character, are you sure some friend of hers didn't leave it earlier?"

Freddie glared at him, then looked abashed. "Actually, we did think of that possibility. The cleaning staff had been in that day and they are pretty thorough."

Lowell took the cufflink and looked at it closely. "It's a nicer piece than I thought."

"We're trying to figure out which letter it is."

"Yes, it's a little hard to tell, but..." Lowell looked at it again, then closed his eyes. "I do believe it's an R. This is based on what I remember of Loesch's set. After you pointed them out, I began to get envious. They are quite handsome."

"R. That doesn't narrow things down that much," Freddie growled. He took the cufflink back and put it in his pocket. "But thank you. I'll make a point of letting Kathy know when I wire her tomorrow."

The two men continued chatting as the evening wore on and Lowell eventually stumbled off to his room around two in the morning. Freddie went to bed right after but found it hard to sleep. Kathy had been sharing his bed for only a few months, and it was odd how fast he'd become accustomed to having her there. It was miserable when she wasn't.

Freddie slept late the next morning but still managed to be on the road to La Crescenta by noon, in spite of the incredibly bad traffic in the neighborhood around the hotel. He arrived at the sanitarium just before one p.m.

It was a huge white building, with two wings extending toward the back, built at the top of a good-sized hill. Dark green trees, including lots of eucalyptus, were planted in spots on the huge, bright green lawn that surrounded the building. It was in stark contrast to the brown, rolling hills, dotted with spots of dark green bushes or trees, and the occasional house and lawn. The day was warm, but not terribly so, and the sky a brilliant blue with the occasional wisp of cloud here and there. Freddie decided that if the rest of the region was like this, it was no wonder there were so many sanitariums in the area.

He looked back toward the city of Los Angeles and saw a light orange haze over the city. Turning to the west, he thought he saw the ocean on the horizon. Leaving the hired Packard in the front of the driveway, he went to the door of the sanitarium and rang the bell.

A rather severe-looking matron opened the door.

"My name is Freddie Little," he said. "I'm here to visit Mr. Christopher Walsh."

"Did you make an appointment?"

"Yes, I did. For one o'clock."

The matron let him into the foyer, then went to a desk and checked a book.

"Freddie Little, right?" she asked.

"Yes."

"Here you are. Mr. Walsh is in the solarium this afternoon." The matron almost smiled. "I'm Mrs. Parsons. Please come this way."

The solarium was a glassed-in addition to the back of the building and looked out on the hills and the back lawn, where a few other patients were walking, some attended by nurses, some not. The room, itself, was filled with potted palm trees and white wicker furniture, comfortably padded in light-colored chintz. Walsh, swaddled in a thick cotton robe in spite of the heat, sat by himself near the back window. He looked deflated, as if he'd been a rather heavy man in his health. His hair had gone white and he wore a set of pince-nez glasses on his nose as he read the movie magazine in his lap.

"Mr. Walsh?" Freddie asked.

The man looked up and smiled. "And you are?"

"My name is Freddie Little." Freddie sat down in a chair that was close enough to talk, but not too close. "I'm so sorry to impose at this time, with your health and all."

Walsh coughed and Freddie shrunk back.

"It's not tuberculosis," Walsh grumbled. "Not that what I have is any better, but it's not contagious. It's lung cancer."

"I'm so very sorry."

Walsh shrugged. "We all have to go some way. But what brings you here?"

"I'm afraid it's not any more pleasant. My sister is in grave danger. Your sister was found in my sister's apartment, and I'm trying to find out why to try and save my sister."

Walsh coughed again. "Terrible business. I can't say what exactly happened, but I suspect you know that Flossie was being hunted."

"Yes. We don't know by whom. We found out from the doctor that Flossie worked for in New York, a Dr. Rothmayer, that a man with a scar on his nose had tried to attack her there, and this same man tried to attack my wife, looking for information about my sister."

"The man with the scar on his nose." Walsh nodded and coughed again. "I never learned his name. But Flossie did say he was working for the real culprit. After New York, she changed her name and went to Chicago. That way, we could still see each other. Then when I got sick last spring, she suggested I come here. She had a great regard for Dr. Rothmayer, and he winters here. He just got here a couple days ago."

"Really?" Freddie mused.

"I got here in June, then Flossie arrived to help take care of me. She'd changed her name, of course. We called her Eileen Benson." Walsh coughed again. "But then the man with the scar, he showed up. Flossie had a friend in Los Angeles, and the friend sent her back to New York, presumably to your sister."

"That's what we think happened. Only, it appears someone was watching my sister and found Flossie in her place." Freddie paused. "The man with the scar, the police identified him as Elmer Rightman. He was found in the East River about a week ago with a broken neck. Just like Flossie."

Walsh coughed. "Seems he got what he had coming to him. Not that it does any good for Flossie."

"No, it doesn't." Freddie fished in his pocket and pulled out the cufflink. "Does this look familiar?"

Walsh looked at it, was about to respond, then began coughing quite hard. One of the matrons, a short woman with graying blond hair, scurried up. She smiled kindly, waited until Walsh had finished, then gave him a glass of water.

"All better?" she asked.

Walsh sipped. "Thank you, Mrs. Fuller."

She smiled then looked at the cufflink. "Oh, very nice."

"Thank you," said Freddie. "I'm trying to find its owner."

Mrs. Fuller shook her head and scuttled off.

"I've never seen it before, either," Walsh said, still breathing heavily.

Freddie slipped the cufflink back into his pocket. "I understand you have another sister out here."

Walsh sighed. "She is, but I'm not saying where. Better you don't know. Me, you can't do anything to. I'm already a dead man. Her, she has three little kids to take care of."

"Then I won't pry. I happened to find out that Flossie worked for President Harding."

"Not directly," Walsh said and coughed again, this time very hard. "Excuse me. She worked for the Hardings' doctor, Dr. Sawyer. My sister was so proud, too."

"So how did she come to work for Dr. Sawyer?"

"Not sure, entirely, but she got out of nursing school and went to work for him. He must have been looking for a second nurse and hired her. She was a good nurse."

"I don't doubt." Freddie looked down at his hat. "Well, Mr. Walsh, I can take my leave now. Or I can stay and we can talk about other things. Or perhaps I can return and bring you something from town?"

"You can stick around for a bit if you like. It would be nice to have a little company." Walsh coughed.

It lasted longer than the other coughs and Freddie wasn't sure Walsh hadn't stopped breathing. But the man recovered himself, and the two chatted about Los Angeles. Or Freddie did most of the talking, since the more Mr. Walsh talked, the more he coughed. After another hour, Mrs. Parsons returned and sent Freddie on his way.

Chapter Ten

It was Kathy's half day again, but it looked like she'd be working for the entire weekend. Not that it mattered. What with Freddie gone, there wasn't much else to do. So she packed as many manuscripts as she could into the large leather bag she'd brought and left the office, carrying two more manuscripts in boxes in her hands. It seemed to take forever to get home through the pouring rain. Roberts, as usual, was waiting as she emerged from the servants' stairs. She waved him off.

"I'm going to set this stuff in the study first," she explained. "It'll be easier."

"Yes, ma'am. Can I take some of it?"

"I wish you could," Kathy moved ahead of him toward the study, with him closely on her heels. "I'm afraid that if I let go of any of it, it's going to go flying all over the place."

In the study, she carefully let the two boxes onto her desk and dropped her bag next to it.

"Now," she sighed, taking off her coat and shaking it a little to get the raindrops off.

Roberts had it in a second and her hat, as well. "I have news, ma'am. The long distance operator called. She's going to try to put through a call from Los Angeles at two p.m."

"Mr. Little is telephoning?" Kathy looked up from wiping the rain off her manuscript boxes.

"I would presume so, ma'am."

"How incredibly extravagant!" Still, Kathy couldn't help smiling. It had been miserable enough the past few days with the awfulness at work. But missing Freddie had left her depressed and grumpy, as well. "Thank heavens I didn't decide to go see a movie this afternoon."

"Indeed. Your luncheon is ready."

"Oh, thank you, Roberts. Please tell Mrs. Wyman that I'll be right there."

At two o'clock, the telephone rang and Kathy answered it before Roberts could. The phone was situated on a small table in the apartment foyer, but the cord was long enough for Kathy to pace as she waited for the operators to finish connecting the call.

"Go ahead, Mrs. Little," the operator told her.

"Kathy?" Freddie's voice asked, sounding very distant and scratchy.

"I'm here. Freddie, is that you?"

"Yes, darling, and missing you terribly."

"I miss you, too."

"Work going well?"

"Well enough," Kathy lied. "So why are you calling?"

"I need you to try to find out more about Mr. Rightman. I think he may have been the owner of the cufflink. Lowell and I looked at it again and we think the letter on it might be an R."

Kathy closed her eyes and tried to see the cufflink in her mind. "Yes, I do believe you're right. It could be an A or a P, too."

"Well, we need to find out if Mr. Rightman had the mate."

"All right. Have you found Honoria?"

"No. Not yet. Did you ever get a chance to visit Ellen May, the woman on the letter Miss Walsh had?"

"Uh, yes." Kathy bit her lip wondering what to tell him.

"Did you see her?"

"Why are you asking?"

"Because Lowell told me she's Honoria."

"Yes, well, I couldn't really tell you because

Honoria swore me to secrecy more or less. Please don't be angry. I was going to tell you. It's only that so many other things were happening, what with her apartment getting broken into and all that."

"I understand."

"Have you talked to Miss Walsh's brother yet?"

"Yes. He didn't say a lot that we didn't already know. Flossie sent him to the same sanitarium where Dr. Rothmayer winters. And their sister, Abby, lives in Los Angeles somewhere, but Walsh didn't want to say where."

"If I find that other cufflink, does that mean you'll get to come home?"

"I'd rather find Honoria, first." Freddie's sigh came through all the static. "You'll wire me with whatever you find out about the cufflink, won't you? I'm at the Ambassador."

"I know. I got your last two wires."

"You can wire back and I'm quite happy to pay for it. You don't need to be so brief."

Kathy laughed. "I'll try to remember that. But this call is costing you a small fortune, isn't it?"

"Aren't I lucky I have one then?"

They chatted for a few minutes longer, then reluctantly hung up.

Kathy sighed loudly, then called her Uncle Dan. He was not at the police station, so she called his home, chatted briefly with Aunt Beth, then got her uncle.

"Hello, Katie-girl," he said, coming on the line.

"Hello, Uncle Dan," Kathy said. "I told you about the cufflink we found in Honoria's bedroom the night of the murder, didn't I?"

"I don't recall as you did," Dan grumbled.

"I'm so sorry. It must have slipped my mind. Worse yet, Freddie has it with him in Los Angeles. We think it probably belonged to the murderer since the cleaning staff had been in earlier that day. It's not the sort of thing they'd be likely to miss."

"Well, what do you want me to do about it?"

"Would it be possible to look among Mr. Rightman's effects to see if there's a missing cufflink? It's a gold cufflink with real diamonds. I can't imagine he'd throw it away just because he'd lost one."

Dan harrumphed a couple times, then cleared his throat. "I could again, but it won't do any good."

"What do you mean?"

"We found his apartment and searched it." Dan snorted. "He was a dandy, all right. He didn't have much, but what he did have was all top of the line. And there were no single cufflinks."

"Oh, bother."

"I wish you would have told me about the cufflink sooner, Katie-girl. I could have gotten a sketch of it."

"You know, I think there might be one, Uncle Dan," Kathy said. "Freddie asked a jeweler here in New York to make inquiries. I'll see if I can get a copy."

"You do that, Katie-girl and have it sent to me, do you hear?"

"Yes, Uncle Dan. I promise."

She hung up shortly after, then looked at the study.

"Roberts!" she called suddenly.

He appeared in a moment. "Yes, ma'am?"

"Do you have the address for Freddie's jeweler? He said he goes to the same one most of the time."

"Yes, ma'am. Van Rijn Jewelry, at Park and 53rd."

"Thanks. I'd better get my hat and coat." Kathy paused. "Uh, Roberts, would it be too much trouble for Mrs. Wyman if I went out to a movie this evening instead of coming straight home for dinner?"

"No, ma'am."

Kathy tried, but couldn't entirely believe Roberts. Nonetheless, she hurried to the jeweler's, where Mr. Van Rijn agreed to make two more sketches of the cufflink, one for Kathy and one for her uncle. While he worked, Kathy looked around the store. The problem was, Freddie had more than enough of everything in the jeweler's cases. No wonder he didn't want presents.

She sighed. She did want to do something nice for him, nicer than a badly knitted sweater. She just couldn't think what.

In Los Angeles, Freddie was wondering why he was still there. He had called several hotels looking for Honoria as herself and as Ellen May. Neither had checked in anywhere he could find. Which didn't mean Honoria wasn't in the city. He could have missed the hotel. Honoria could have used another name. Or Honoria could be staying with some unknown friend. Or it was possible she had changed her mind about going to Los Angeles and was either in New York or someplace completely different.

Freddie had wired his jeweler the previous day, but Mr. Van Rijn had not gotten a response yet, which wasn't surprising. Freddie looked at the city directory and discovered there were quite a few jewelers in the city. He supposed he could check each one, but that would make it difficult to stay undetected by whomever had left the cufflink in the first place.

Edward Roundhouse had also found out that Freddie was at the hotel and had invited him to go out that evening. Freddie didn't particularly want to go, but dinner and a visit to a nightclub would at least fill time.

Freddie spent the rest of the afternoon working on his latest novel and was pleased to discover he'd made excellent headway through a rather difficult scene. He took one long drag on his cigarette, put his papers down and went to get dressed for the evening.

Seeing the cufflink on the bureau top, Freddie put it in his pocket again. There had been too many other searches for him to feel completely safe leaving it in the room, although he had no reason to believe that his room had been searched or would be.

He joined Edward in the lobby and offered to drive for the evening. Although once he got the car on Wilshire Boulevard, he began to doubt the wisdom of driving.

The boulevard was filled with cars fighting each other for space around the streetcars and pedestrians.

"Reminds you of New York, doesn't it?" Edward asked jovially.

"Not entirely," Freddie said. "I think this is worse than New York."

Still, he fought his way through the traffic northwards towards Hollywood Boulevard and the restaurant Edward had suggested.

"Lots of the movie people eat here," Edward said as they entered the cafe.

"Oh," said Freddie.

The room was paneled with dark wood, and matching booths crowded the white-tiled floor. The menu featured all manner of items, including steaks and Welsh rarebit, and the waiter implied, but didn't say, that one could get a martini or a whiskey if one desired.

Freddie ordered a martini and Edward chose a whiskey sour. The steaks were well-made and while Freddie fought to find something interesting to say, it turned out Edward had plenty to say for both of them, although nothing interesting. Until Edward brought up Honoria.

"I'm sorry?" Freddie said, who hadn't been listening.

"Your sister, Honoria," Edward said. "I've been looking for her."

"You have?"

"Yes. I was hoping to take her out. Spend some time with her. If we were Victorians, I'd say court her."

Freddie chuckled. "I'd like to see that happen."

"And why not?" Edward asked. "We both come from good families. We're of an age. We have lots in common."

Freddie thought about Honoria's secret newspaper. "Do you?"

"Well, yes. We know lots of the same people. We go to a lot of the same places. She's a corking girl, your sister."

"I'm glad you think so, Edward, but," Freddie winced. "I don't think you two would do well together. Not that I can speak for Honoria."

"No, you can't," Edward said a little righteously. "I asked that friend of hers... What's her name? Um, Kathy. I asked her to put in a good word for me. She said she would. Your sister hasn't answered any of my letters and I've been sending them almost daily for two weeks now. Yes. I wrote the first one the day after your birthday party."

The day Honoria had hidden herself away.

"I believe she's visiting one of our aunts," Freddie said.

"Which one? I checked with Mrs. Corning and she hadn't seen your sister since the party, either."

"I'm afraid I don't keep tabs on Honoria's whereabouts," Freddie said. "What is your sister up to these days?"

Edward rolled his eyes. "Dora? Mooning over James Whitby. You know the Whitbys, don't you? James is all right, but I don't think Father's going to go for the deal. He thinks James is a ne'er-do-well because he's not got himself up to his nose in the family business. But to what end, I ask you? It's not as though there's anything for us to do. Father's business runs itself. That's why he spends all his time at the Union Club. Good heavens. The way he wants me to work, you'd think we were nouveau."

"It is a conundrum," Freddie said.

He had more interest in his family's business only because his grandfather had taken him through the textile factories when Freddie was a boy. As Freddie came of age, and into his own money from a couple of different trusts and bequests, his grandfather had helped Freddie invest his money to the point that Freddie was able to support himself independently of his family's business. His grandfather had only stepped away from the business a year or so before in favor of

Freddie's father. Freddie's father had completely shut Freddie out of the business, saying Freddie would have time enough to run things.

Many of Freddie's peers, including Edward, it appeared, simply lived off family funds, doing whatever they wanted. Only Edward had appeared to be in a bit of a tight spot. Freddie debated seeing what would happen when the check for dinner came but decided he was better than that and offered to pay. Edward accepted without argument.

It was well after dark when they got to the hotel overlooking the beach in Santa Monica and found a place to park on the street.

"We could have gone to the Clover Club, I suppose," Edward told Freddie. "But everyone knows about the Clover Club, including the coppers. I thought you'd appreciate someplace a little more discreet. Although Marion Davies lives just down that way."

"Oh." Freddie realized he had heard of actress Marion Davies, but couldn't remember if he'd seen any of her films.

The hotel was a sprawling complex of clapboard, with a large room built over the water, surrounded by a wide plank deck. Tables covered by white cloths were lined up along the outer wall and its open windows, most of the tables filled with people laughing and drinking. More people strolled the deck. Inside was a huge ballroom. At one end, a jazz band made up of negroes played loudly while couples danced on the dance floor. More tables surrounded them, but the rest of the room was given over to gaming tables.

Potted palm trees were everywhere. Long white drapes with gold trim were swagged along every wall and the waiters all wore white jackets with epaulets. As Edward and Freddie made their way into the ballroom, Freddie noticed that the gaming tables continued further into the hotel. Smaller tables featured poker games and Twenty-One, and there were bigger tables for craps and roulette and even a faro table or two. Freddie found himself drawn to the jazz band, but Edward led him to the casino's bank. The two bought about fifty dollars' worth of chips each, and then Edward scurried to a Twenty-One table. Freddie ambled among the tables, then found a seat at the roulette table closest to the dance floor. He ordered a martini, decided the gin wasn't up to par and ordered a Bronx cocktail instead.

The band was hot and playing on a tear. Freddie mostly listened as he played the red space over and over again. But this soon bored him and he went looking for Edward. He found his companion at a craps table. Edward was flush with excitement, making bets right and left as if his life depended on it. Freddie watched for a bit more, then when there was a break in the game, he approached Edward.

"Let's go outside and have a drink," Freddie suggested.

"You go. I'm hot."

"So I see, but you do realize that now is the time to walk away, don't you?"

"Nah." Edward laughed and slapped Freddie's back. "I'm on a roll tonight. I'm playing it out."

"If you insist. I'm going outside and ordering a bottle of Champagne. Come share it with me when you're done."

Sighing, Freddie cashed in his chips at the banker's window, then found a table and ordered his bottle. The waiter promptly brought a glass and the bottle, sweating in an ice bucket held up by a wrought iron stand. The lights over the dance floor and its surrounding tables dimmed and a spot appeared over a microphone on the dance floor. Sure enough, there was a show filled with women bearing huge feathered fans.

Freddie sighed as he sipped. There seemed little point to staying in Los Angeles. If Honoria was there, she was well-hidden. The cufflink seemed a loose connection at best, and if he had to spend any more time watching dancing girls and listening to vapid monologues about people he cared little about, he would go crazy. The bottle was still half full an hour and a half later and Edward was nowhere to be seen.

The woman was tall, with dark black bobbed hair and she wore a gown of shiny black satin with a large bow tied in front just below her waist. Gathered pleats fell from the bow creating a swishing flare in front. Her face was artfully made up with rouge and red lips, and a string of good-sized pearls looped itself once around her neck then fell down her fashionably flat figure. She held a lit cigarette in a longish holder, her hands covered in white kid evening gloves.

"You're alone," she said, in a low, rich voice.

"Alas, I'm not seeking company," Freddie said, getting up, nonetheless.

"Interesting. I noticed you bought a bottle. That usually means you're sharing."

Freddie looked around. "My companion seems to have disappeared. Probably got taken up with the gaming. Tell you what? Why don't you finish this lovely champagne and I will say my good nights."

He held his chair for the woman and she gracefully slid into it.

"Thank you," she said and winked.

Freddie signaled the waiter for a fresh glass, bade the women good night and left. He circled the gambling hall one more time, then gave it up and left the hotel. He would send Edward his apologies and leave for New York in the morning.

The street was dark and mostly empty of people. Freddie had just reached the Packard when he felt the crushing blow against the back of his head. He fell forward onto the ground and while he didn't completely black out, he was too groggy to resist as a pair of hands roughly searched his jacket and then his pants.

"Stop! Police!" a voice yelled.

The thief removed his hand from Freddie's front pants pocket and ran off. One of the officers ran after him, while a second gently helped Freddie sit up against the car.

"Are you all right?" the officer asked. He was a burly man in a dark double-breasted uniform with brass buttons running up each side of his chest.

Freddie blinked. "I think so. I've got a hell of a headache."

"Knocked you on the head, did he?"

"Yes." Freddie watched in a fog as the officer picked up something glittering next to him.

"What's this?" the officer asked, shining his flashlight on it.

It was the cufflink.

"I'm looking for its owner," Freddie said. "It was left in my sister's apartment."

"Oh, that's too bad." said the officer.

"What do you mean?"

"I've seen a pair of cufflinks like these before." The officer flashed his light at Freddie. "They belonged to Rigo Ramirez."

"Who?"

"Rigo Ramirez."

Freddie gently shook his head. "I have no idea who that is."

"Rumrunner and mobster. We think he's holed up somewhere in Vernon. Where's your sister's apartment?"

"New York City."

"Oh. Then I don't think this is his. Must be more than one set out there."

"That is inconvenient." Freddie shifted, trying to get more comfortable as he took the cufflink from the officer. "You wouldn't happen to know which jeweler made them?"

"Nope." The officer looked up. "Simmons, did you catch the bastard?"

"Nah. Ran off too quick." The other officer looked and was built much like the first, although he was much younger and his hair was darker. "You okay, sir?"

Freddie struggled to get up and found he could. "I'll

be all right. He didn't get the car keys or the cufflink, that's the main thing."

The first officer helped him stand. "Simmons, go call headquarters and get someone down here to give this fellow a ride home."

"I can manage," said Freddie.

"We'd rather you didn't. You got a nasty knock on the head there. Do you have anybody at home who can sit with you?"

"I'm at the Ambassador. I suppose I could hire a nurse or something."

"Not with your money gone."

Freddie blinked again. "It's not all gone, by any stretch of the imagination. I seldom carry more on me than I care to lose."

Some minutes later, a third officer showed up. He was small and wiry but dressed in the same dark uniform. He cheerfully drove Freddie back to the hotel in the Packard, chatting about nothing in particular. However, he did walk Freddie into the hotel and had the hotel doctor look Freddie over. Freddie didn't think to get his name or the name of the first officer who had helped him.

The doctor said that Freddie had a mild concussion and prescribed bed rest for the next few days. He also hired a nurse to wake Freddie every so often for the rest of the night. Freddie wired Kathy the next morning, leaving out being robbed the night before, asking her to see what she could find out about Edward Roundhouse getting into trouble.

He received the return telegram from her later that afternoon.

"E arrested gambling stop D thinks owes mobsters," it read.

Freddie sighed and handed it over to Lowell, who was keeping him company.

"Do you want me to translate?" Lowell asked.

"I've figured it out," said Freddie. "Edward has been arrested for gambling before. Whether the charges stuck and what his punishment was, I have no idea. But apparently, Kathy's Uncle Dan thinks that he owes money to mobsters." He took the telegram back from Lowell. "It's positively verbose for her. There's actually a word she didn't absolutely need."

Lowell laughed. "You can take the girl off the farm, but you can't take the farm out of the girl."

"Which is all to the better, I suppose. I was going to leave and go home today, you know."

"You don't want to be flying with that bump on your head. How's it feeling, anyway?"

"I still have a nasty headache, but it's better."

Lowell picked up the telegram and looked at it thoughtfully. "You do realize that Edward Roundhouse's name starts with an R, don't you?"

"The thought had crossed my mind. And I've no idea what happened to him last night."

"What if I happen to know?"

Freddie adjusted himself in the big bed. "How?"

"Well," Lowell shifted. "It's complicated. I have made a friend here in Los Angeles. She's quite a charming creature. An actress. Mr. Schulman and Mr. Loesch have her contract. In any case, I mentioned that you were here and being interested in me, she was interested in my friends. She'd already met Edward and was not impressed."

"Points to her."

"Anyway, I telephoned her yesterday afternoon and happened to mention where you and Edward were going, and she thought she'd like to spend the evening gambling, as well. I told her that was up to her. I really don't care for gambling that much."

"Takes too much time away from your drinking, I know," Freddie grumbled.

"She went to the hotel without me. Edward had dragged us there a week or so ago. It's pleasant enough as a speak, I suppose. I have to re-write an entire column for the magazine on short notice, so I stayed here. I'll be dictating it long distance tomorrow."

"So?"

"So Ivy called this morning. She wanted to know what you looked like. She'd seen you arrive with Edward and she thinks it was you that she spoke with."

Freddie frowned. "Tall woman, slender and black bobbed hair?"

Lowell smiled proudly. "That's Ivy. Quite a dame, isn't she?"

"Yes, I think I did speak to her. Very briefly and left her half a bottle of Champagne."

"For which she thanks you. She also said that Edward was doing well, then lost rather heavily and she thought he'd left the speak. But then he came back with quite a bit of cash. Lost it, too, she thinks."

Freddie's brow creased as much as his headache would allow. "That is worrisome. He could have, indeed, been the one who robbed me. After getting my billfold, the thief also searched my pants pockets. One would think he'd take the billfold and not risk the pants."

"Hard to say," said Lowell. "Why would Edward want to search your pants, as well?"

"Could he be looking for the cufflink?" Freddie asked. "He's been awfully friendly of late. Mostly interested in courting Honoria, and if he's in hock to mobsters, he probably needs her money quite badly. But still, if he's in hock to a mobster or some other person, he could be led to do some rather nasty work just to stay alive. What if he left the cufflink and was looking for it?"

"That's an excellent question, my lad," Lowell said, heaving himself out of his chair. "However, it shall have to wait. You have to recover and I have a column to write for a soggy bastard who can't be bothered to turn his work in on time. I'll come by around dinner time, if you like, and bring some real food. I'm sure your nurse has you eating pablum."

"Not really, but I look forward to dinner," Freddie said with a smile.

Chapter Eleven

Kathy went into work that Monday dreading it. However, all seemed normal. If anything, there was no harassment and Norbert and Fisk were even friendly. The only odd thing was that she thought she'd seen Mr. Ryland leaving Thaddeus Healcroft's office around noon, but that didn't make sense. She'd been seeing all sorts of things out of the corner of her eyes since the murder, including the now deceased Mr. Rightman. That evening she got a note from Mr. Van Rijn, the jeweler, that he'd heard from his colleagues but they didn't know who had made the cufflink. It was frustrating, but not entirely unexpected. Kathy decided she could wire Freddie the news the next day.

The next day went badly very quickly. It started normally, but shortly after ten in the morning, Kathy was called to Thaddeus Healcroft's office.

Unlike his father, Thaddeus' hair was dark blond and where his father looked very much the Victorian gentleman, Thaddeus was as modern as could be. He wore a Yale tie. His hair was parted in the center and slicked down. His face was clean-shaven. He sat behind his large desk in a chair that Kathy suspected was actually raised a bit, since he wasn't all that tall when standing.

"Yes, Mr. Healcroft," Kathy said when she was admitted.

Mr. Dillbeck was standing behind the younger Healcroft's desk and he did not look unhappy.

"Miss Briscow, I've had an unsettling report about you," Thaddeus said, looking not at all unsettled.

"Apparently, your morals are questionable."

"My morals?" Kathy asked. "Excuse me?"

"You, apparently, are living in sin and using your paramour's sister to cover it up."

"What?"

"Are you or are you not Frederick Little's lover?"

"I am not living in sin!" Kathy snarled.

"That doesn't answer the question," said Thaddeus.

"Yes, it does. My relationship with Mr. Little is blameless and I resent it that you would think it is other than it should be." Kathy stood up straight.

That set Thaddeus back a bit. "Still, Miss Briscow, there have been rumors. You know we hold our employees to the highest possible moral standards here at Healcroft House."

"No. You hold me to the highest possible standards, Mr. Healcroft. In fact, I suspect this meeting has nothing to do with Mr. Little, at all."

"It has everything to do with him," Thaddeus said. "As of right now, you are dismissed from employment here at Healcroft House. And don't think you are going to get a good reference from us."

"I don't need your reference," Kathy said, her temper boiling over. "I know things about your father. You call my morals questionable. Ask him about his visits to that whorehouse on East 21st and about his liking for buttonhooks. It's not about his shoes, I assure you."

Thaddeus colored up and both he and Mr. Dillbeck looked guilty.

"So you both know the place," Kathy said. "As I said, you're calling my morals questionable? What hypocrites you are. I don't know why having a woman editor is so terrifying to you idiots, but that's what this is about. Not my morals, which by the way, are perfectly upright. I may be living in Mr. Little's apartment, but I'm there as his wife. We are married. We only kept it quiet because of your narrow-mindedness. Now where are my wages? I'm not leaving until I get them. And if you try taking me out of here, you will regret it."

Thaddeus stammered for a moment. "Go back to your office and start packing. I'll have your wages delivered immediately. Mr. Dillbeck, will you please supervise Miss Briscow's packing?"

It took Kathy barely half an hour to get her belongings into a carton. As she finished, an errand boy showed up with an envelope and she took her time counting the amount inside. Mr. Dillbeck tried to growl, but one look from Kathy quelled it. Fisk, Norbert, and Burton remained very focused on their own work. But Fisk looked up at Kathy and smiled weakly.

In the building's lobby, Kathy arranged for a messenger to take her carton to Freddie's apartment. Then, not knowing what else to do, she went outside to the sidewalk and began walking, not sure where she was going.

Sometime later, she took the stairs down to the apartment she shared with Freddie. The apartment she could now publicly proclaim as her home. In her hands was a brown paper bag with grease stains starting to come through the bottom. She'd needed to down her sorrows badly and most speaks were not open that early in the day. And if there wasn't alcohol, there was delicatessen and pastrami on rye.

Somehow, Roberts was occupied elsewhere when she came in. It didn't matter. Kathy wandered into the foyer and saw that the morning post had arrived. There was a letter from her mother and another from Freddie. It was addressed to him, but in his own sprawling handwriting and the return address was The Ambassador Hotel, Los Angeles, California.

Kathy opened the envelope immediately and began reading, feeling the pang of her loss and her missing husband all the more.

"Excuse me," demanded an imperious voice.

Kathy looked up. Gloria Derby Little, in full righteous indignation, emerged from the drawing room, dressed in a dark green day dress, and strode over to Kathy.

"What are you doing here?" she asked, snatching the envelope. "And reading my son's mail?"

Kathy snatched the envelope back. "That is my letter. That is your son's handwriting on the front, so why would he be sending himself mail unless he had another purpose?" She waved the letter in Gloria's face. "And not only is this meant for me, I have every right to be here reading it. In fact, my presence here is completely blameless and I'll be damned if anyone is going to say otherwise!"

Gloria stepped back, her hand on her chest. "Such language!"

The telephone rang and Roberts got it first.

"Mrs. Little," he began.

"Yes?" both Kathy and Gloria answered.

"A Mr. Pierce Jennings is downstairs," Roberts said.

"Send him away," Gloria said.

"Send him up," Kathy said at the same time.

Gloria glared at her and Kathy glared back.

"Send him up, Roberts," Kathy said again. "He obviously knows I'm here and he may as well come to this apartment." She sniffed. "The jig is up, Roberts. They know about Freddie and me."

"My sympathies, ma'am," Roberts said and spoke into the phone.

Gloria looked at Roberts in surprise, then looked at Kathy.

"What in Heaven's name is going on here?" Gloria asked.

Kathy groaned loudly and looked up at the ceiling for help. "Mrs. Little... I mean Mother Little, Freddie and I are married. This is not the way I wanted to tell you. I know we should have let you in on it sooner, but—"

There was a loud pounding on the foyer door. Roberts glanced at Kathy, who nodded. Roberts opened the door.

Pierce Jennings stormed into the foyer, all fury and bluster.

"Where's Freddie?" he demanded.

"In California," Kathy said.

"How could you do this to me?" Jennings demanded. "I was at the publishers' office today and they said you'd been dismissed for moral turpitude. You're living in sin with Little!"

"I am not living in sin!" Kathy yelled. "We are married!"

"Married?" shrieked Jennings.

"Yes. Married."

"How could you do this to me?" Jennings demanded. "Who is going to edit my books now that you're gone! I can't let anyone else touch them."

"No one else will put up with you," Kathy said.

"Exactly. I'm doomed. And all because you had to marry Little!"

Kathy put her head in her hands. "I can't imagine this getting any worse."

"Mr. Jennings," Gloria's voice cut through the foyer and stopped Jennings' bluster cold. "I think it is time you left. Would you be so good?"

It was not a request. Jennings stammered for a moment, then sniffed and left, but not before getting a good look at the envelope Kathy still held in her hand.

In the quiet that followed, Kathy finally lifted her head and looked at Gloria.

"I suspect you would like an explanation," Kathy said softly.

"I would," Gloria said.

"Um. Okay. We can go in the study." She looked down and saw the brown bag she'd brought in. "Do you like pastrami on rye?"

Several minutes later, Gloria was ensconced in Freddie's favorite overstuffed chair, her feet comfortably up on the matching hassock and Kathy was sitting behind her desk, with her feet propped up on the corner of the desk. Both were munching on the sandwich Kathy had brought home, which Roberts had kindly unpacked and put out on plates and brought napkins and tea to drink with it.

"So you and Freddie are married," Gloria said, after swallowing a dainty bite. "By the way, this is quite tasty."

"I love pastrami on rye," sighed Kathy. "And, yeah. Freddie and I tied the knot. Last summer. We've been trying to keep it a secret so that I could keep working. You know how the papers always seem to cotton onto what he's up to."

"So vulgar, but I'm afraid true." Gloria dabbed at her mouth with her napkin. "But why would you want to continue working?"

Kathy sighed. "I don't know if this would make sense to you, but I really loved my job. I loved making good novels even better. I loved haggling over print runs. I loved choosing titles and making sure that the galleys were corrected and all of that."

"You loved having a purpose."

"I suppose you could say that. Actually, I think it was more than that. I love being able to support myself, earning my own way."

Gloria nodded. "That I understand. I do wish you could have said something to me."

"I had a feeling." Kathy sighed and picked up a loose piece of meat and popped it in her mouth. "I think Freddie was afraid you wouldn't approve of me, and if I'm honest, I was afraid, too."

Gloria sighed, as well, the hand holding her bit of sandwich falling into her lap. "To be honest, I have no idea how I would have reacted last summer. Kathy, if I have been focused on getting Freddie married to someone of our sort, it is mostly because our sort know each other better."

"I think I understand that." Kathy frowned. "This whole being rich business, I have to be honest, I have not been adapting to it well. Poor Roberts. He's been trying so hard, but I still do silly things like eat toast on the way to the subway stop. I'd rather knit than sit quietly. My telegrams are too short. I tell people to come up even when I don't want to see them. And there are things that Freddie does that I just don't understand. Or really want to, when it comes right down to it. Don't get me wrong. I love him desperately. I wouldn't have married him if I didn't. But sleeping until nine or ten in the morning? Good lord, if I did that, I'd have been out of my job faster than I was. I've had to get up and work my entire life. I can't imagine not doing it." Kathy sniffed. "I don't know what I'm going to do now that my job is gone."

"You'll find other things to do," said Gloria.

"They won't be as much fun," grumbled Kathy. "I want my job back. Oh well. It's gone now." She suddenly brightened a little. "But that means I can go to Los Angeles."

"Los Angeles?" asked Gloria.

"That's where Freddie is." Kathy swung her feet off the desk. "And Honoria, too."

"Honoria?" Gloria asked eagerly.

Kathy frowned. "Well, we think she's there. She left us a note and said that's where she was headed. That's one of the reasons Freddie went there." Kathy paused. "It has to do with that girl who was killed in Honoria's apartment."

"I thought the police had taken care of that," Gloria said.

"Nope. We were told they had ended the investigation." Kathy looked at Gloria. "We thought that perhaps you had asked the police commissioner to end it."

"Good heavens, why would I do that?"

"To keep the publicity to a minimum. Freddie said that it made sense. No point in letting it get out how easy it would be to get in here and steal stuff."

Gloria frowned. "I never would have done that. If someone is getting into these apartments, I would have wanted him caught as fast as possible. In addition, whoever that young woman was, she was still a human being and deserves justice. I want the killer caught and as promptly as possible."

"Then who decided to stop the investigation?" Kathy drummed her fingers on the desk. "Something else to figure out. In the meantime, I need to get to Los Angeles as fast as possible. Without flying."

"Oh, heavens! You wouldn't do that."

Kathy suddenly grinned. "Not without a lot of arm-twisting." She laughed. "That's how Freddie got me home last summer and probably how we ended up married. Long story. I'll have to tell you someday." She looked at Gloria. "You don't mind that I married him, do you?"

Gloria smiled. "No, darling. Part of me is simply glad that he got married. That you seem to genuinely love him, that, that is music to my heart."

"I do love him," sighed Kathy. "I don't think I'd put up with all this nonsense if I didn't. Now, I need to call the train station about times so that I can get my ticket."

"Good heavens, my dear. You don't need to do that."

"How else am I going to get my ticket?"

Gloria laughed. "My dear. You are absolutely right. You do not know how to do this at all." She looked around. "Is there a bell or something so we can summon Roberts?"

Kathy grimaced. "I usually holler."

"What?"

"Roberts?" Kathy yelled, then winced, embarrassed. "I still don't know how Freddie gets him. But he always shows up."

Roberts appeared at the study door. "Yes, ma'am?"

Kathy looked at Gloria.

"Roberts," Gloria said. "Mrs. Kathy wants to get to Los Angeles as soon as possible. Without flying."

"Certainly, Mrs. Little," said Roberts. "Eh, it will

take a day or two to get the family car."

"Can I leave sooner than that?' Kathy asked. "I don't need a fancy car or anything."

"I should be able to get you on the Limited tonight," said Roberts.

"With appropriate accommodations," said Gloria.

"Of course, Mrs. Little, I'll have Virginia start packing."

"Virginia?" asked Gloria.

"Mrs. Wentworth's personal maid," said Roberts. "Since Mrs. Wentworth has been gone, Virginia has been seeing to the younger Mrs. Little's needs."

"Not that I have a lot of them," said Kathy.

"Have Virginia join Mrs. Kathy," said Gloria.

"Yes, Mrs. Little." Roberts looked at Kathy, who nodded in confirmation.

Roberts withdrew and Gloria smiled.

"There." The older woman smiled. "That's all you have to do."

"All," grumbled Kathy. "Criminy. I'm never going to be any good at this. Sh— Uh, oh dear. I've got to wire Freddie!"

Kathy ran to the phone in the hallway. She got connected to Western Union and ordered her telegram, not knowing that Roberts would be ordering one in a few short minutes, as well.

Gloria sat back in her chair and continued eating her sandwich. It was very tasty. And while her daughter-in-law could have had better antecedents, she was polite, and most importantly, clearly loved her son. All was right with Gloria's world.

Freddie's head didn't ache. That's what he reminded himself as he left his bed for the tea room at The Ambassador. Lowell had asked if Freddie was up to a luncheon there with Lowell's friend Ivy, and Freddie, being utterly bored with being bedridden, had accepted.

The woman from the gambling boat was sitting

at Lowell's table as Freddie approached. She smiled warmly as Lowell got up to greet Freddie.

"Freddie, I'd like to present to you my new friend, Miss Ivy St. James," Lowell said with unusual pleasure. "Miss St. James, my dearest friend in all the world, Mr. Freddie Little."

"It's a pleasure to officially meet you, Mr. Little," Miss St. James said in that deep, throaty voice of hers.

"Likewise, Miss St. James," Freddie said, sliding into a seat at the table. "So how did you and Mr. Winters meet?"

She chuckled warmly. "My contract with RiverWind Pictures. Mr. Schulman and Mr. Loesch are courting Mr. Winters, so they brought me along in the hopes that I would convince him to sign a contract."

Freddie looked over at Lowell. "I didn't think you were that interested."

"In RiverWind?" asked Lowell. "Not really. But I have to admit I do find Miss St. James interesting enough. She's quite literate."

"I do my best," Miss St. James said. She was wearing an afternoon dress of rich blue, trimmed with matching sheer scarves on her sleeves and around her neck. A matching blue cloche hat almost shielded her face. She flicked one of the scarves out of the way as she fitted a cigarette into a holder significantly shorter than the one she'd been carrying a few nights before.

Both Freddie and Lowell whipped out their lighters. She smiled and let Lowell light her cigarette.

"I did read your book, Mr. Little," she said, blowing out smoke. "I really enjoyed how you played light versus dark in your thematic structure. And poor Ava. What a tragic character. I almost wanted to slap Meaberry when he finally rejected her."

Freddie smiled. "I almost wanted to slap him, as well. But I just couldn't make it work for the two of them, and my editor was most insistent that it would make a stronger book if he ultimately rejected her and regretted it ever after."

"That reminds me," Lowell said, his eyes still on Miss St. James. "Has your editor had a chance to look at my book?"

"I have no idea," said Freddie. "She only mentioned that she had it. She never tells me about anyone else's work."

"Telegram for Mr. Little!" a boy's voice cut through the chatter of the room. "Telegram for Mr. Little!"

Freddie waved and the boy came over. Freddie tipped him a nickel, then looked at the yellow envelope.

"I think it's from New York," he said, unfolding the sheet inside. "Yes. It's from Ka- uh, Miss Briscow." He read it and frowned. "What in heaven's name..?"

"Miss Briscow is famously terse in her telegram writing," Lowell explained to Miss St. James. "Would you like me to try and interpret it?"

Freddie handed the telegram over.

"Everyone knows stop Fired stop Coming L.A." the paper read.

"Oh, dear," said Lowell. "Someone figured it out about you two."

"Figured what out?" Miss St. James asked.

"Miss Briscow is actually my wife," Freddie said. "We've been keeping our marriage a secret so that she could continue in her position as a junior editor at the publishing house where she works. However, as Mr. Winters pointed out, apparently someone has found out about the marriage and she was fired from her job as a result. And she's coming here to Los Angeles, but doesn't say when or how she will arrive."

"Probably the California Limited, I would think," Lowell said.

"She probably expects to wire me as soon as she has the information," Freddie said with a sigh.

Another boy's voice cut through the chatter. "Long distance call for Mr. Little! Long distance call for Mr. Little!"

Freddie waved the boy over and tipped him. Lowell got up with Freddie, who then followed the boy into the hotel lobby and a phone booth there. The boy waved at the switchboard operator across the lobby.

"The operator will connect you now," the boy said.

Freddie waited for the phone to ring, then picked it up. "Little, here."

"I'll connect you to New York now," the operator said. "Go ahead, New York."

There was a bunch of static.

"Little, is that you?" whined the male voice on the other end. "How could you do this to me?"

"May I ask who's calling?" Freddie asked.

"It's Jennings. How could you, Little? They fired her for being married to you and now we don't have an editor. Couldn't you have just let her alone?"

"Who? You mean Miss Briscow?"

"Well, if she's Miss Briscow, then you two are living in sin and it's no wonder they fired her."

"We're not living in sin. I just got the news from Miss- I mean Mrs. Little. So why are you calling?"

"Because this is a disaster of the first order! Who's going to edit our books? Who will do them justice? That idiot Thaddeus? We have to start our own publishing company. You can finance it, Little. We all know you've got pots of money sitting around. I've talked to Mennerly. He's on board. Davidson and Kettner will go along, too."

"What about Mrs. Petrie?" Freddie found himself asking.

"We'll get her on board. You'll have to talk to her. But we need to have a meeting. You must come home immediately."

"I will come as soon as I can," said Freddie. "Now, Mr. Jennings, I am at a luncheon with friends. Why don't you write your proposal down and send it to my apartment in New York, and I'll contact you after I've looked it over."

"No, no. We need to take care of this immediately!"

"Mr. Jennings, I'm afraid I must hang up now. I'm terribly sorry."

Freddie hung up. He went over to the switchboard operator and asked her not to connect any more calls from Mr. Pierce Jennings. She smiled and made a note of it.

"Well?" Lowell asked as Freddie gingerly returned to the table.

"It was Pierce Jennings on the phone," Freddie said.

"You know Pierce Jennings?" Ivy brightened. "Oh, I love his work. So vivid and visceral."

"And he is anything but," sighed Freddie. "My headache was gone and now it's back."

"What did he want?" Lowell asked.

"He heard about Kathy getting fired and wants me to pay for a new publishing company. Apparently, he's already got Mr. Mennerly agreeing to it. At least, that's what he says."

"Even odds it's true," said Lowell. "But the blithering idiot does have a point. With Kathy gone, who's going to edit our books? I don't have to worry about Thaddeus since I made sure that having Kathy do the work was a condition of them getting the book. But what about you?"

Freddie gently shook his head. "My contract was only for The Old Money Story. I more or less let them think they would get the next one as soon as it's written. But there have been no official promises made. Actually, of Kathy's authors, I think Mrs. Petrie is in the worst position, but I don't know the particulars of her contract. Only that she's very unhappy with it. I know I had to do a bit of arm-twisting to get her assigned to Kathy."

"Hm," said Lowell. "As much as I hate giving Jennings his due, I also have to concede his idea of a new publishing company is not a bad one. Not that you should pay for it, Freddie. But it could be like that United Artists film company that Pickford and Fairbanks and that crew started. Only for authors."

Freddie shrugged. "I'll have to think about it." He

turned to Miss St. James. "I apologize for monopolizing the conversation, Miss St. James."

"Oh no. It's fascinating."

"Telegram for Mr. Little!" rang out again. "Telegram for Mr. Little!"

"Oh, dear lord, what now?" Freddie grumbled as he signaled the boy. After tipping the boy, he tore open the envelope and sighed in relief. "Apparently, Roberts wrote this one. Kathy will be arriving on Sunday on the California Limited at La Grande Depot. I guess I'm not going home this week after all."

"But you'll get to see your wife that much sooner," Miss St. James pointed out.

"Sort of," sighed Freddie. He debated explaining about his plane but decided there wasn't any point. Kathy was on her way and that was that.

After that, he mostly enjoyed his luncheon. Miss St. James was clearly very bright and lively. Freddie couldn't help wondering how Kathy would react to her. Lowell was quite taken with her. Still, something niggled at the back of Freddie's brain and he didn't put his finger on it until he was back in his room and ordering dinner from room service.

Honoria's note: "I'm going to get (help? find?) I-something or other." It suddenly occurred to Freddie that Ivy would have fit what Honoria wrote. Iva was a far more common name. Was that the word Honoria wrote? Could it have been Ira? Ivan? Something else that wasn't even a name? Kathy still had the note, so Freddie had no way of knowing.

But he did have one option. He called the kitchen quickly, ascertained that he had several minutes before his dinner would be ready and that it would be okay to go downstairs and make a phone call.

Betty Briscow was a little surprised to get a call from Freddie but happy to speak to him, nonetheless.

"You got to meet Ivy St. James?" Betty gasped. "How utterly exciting!"

"She seems very nice," Freddie said. "And quite

intelligent. She'd even read The Old Money Story."

"Oh, Freddie! I completely forgot to tell you when you were here! I finally got Josh to buy a copy and I read it. It was so wonderful! I wish I could get Josh to read it."

Freddie chuckled. "That's very kind of you, Betty, but completely unnecessary. I know Miss St. James is a particular favorite of yours. Do you know anything about her background?"

It was Betty's turn to chuckle. "Just what the studio publicist puts out and that's not necessarily true. I can't always tell, but it seems like they stay as close to the truth as they can get away with. I sort of figure if I see the same story told different ways in different magazines, then it's probably true. If it's either the exact same story or they keep messing up the important parts, then it's probably something the publicist cooked up."

"I hadn't thought of that," said Freddie. "You're very perceptive, Betty. What seems to ring true regarding Miss St. James?"

"Maybe not the Woman of Mystery, except that she really is," Betty said. "There doesn't seem to be a lot on her background, although she doesn't get a lot of coverage because she's not a big star. What I mostly see about her is that she was an orphan and struggled heroically to become an actress."

"Any idea where she's from?"

"Not really. Some magazines have her coming from Idaho, others from Chicago. Somewhere in the middle of the country, I would imagine."

"How long has she been in Hollywood?"

"That's even harder to say, but I started seeing her on the screen about a year ago. No. A bit longer ago than that. The magazines only started following her since last spring. Like I said, she hasn't really done any starring roles. She mostly plays the friend or the sister, or sometimes the wise servant."

"Hm. I expect I shall have to contact her studio's

publicist then," Freddie said. "Please give Joshua my best."

"I will. Thanks, Freddie. Bye."

Back in New York, Gloria Little made a point of accompanying Kathy and Virginia to the train station to make sure that all was as it should be. Kathy was surprised that she had a compartment all to herself. Virginia quickly unpacked Kathy's suitcase, then disappeared to her berth.

Gloria sniffed. "I do think you would have been more comfortable in the family car."

"Perhaps," said Kathy, who was more than comfortable as it was.

"Now remember, Virginia will see to tipping the train staff, so you don't have to," Gloria said. "She'll also see to keeping your clothes in good order. That Bendel suit you have on is quite charming."

It was the suit Kathy had bought only a few weeks before, a lavender wool, with a pleated skirt and pleats set into the bottom of the long jacket. Gloria had sent Virginia after a cloche hat and purse to match. Kathy had pulled several books from Freddie's library to read on the train, along with a letter from her mother. She'd also brought some yarn and knitting needles.

"Roberts has already seen to all the details," Gloria continued, "so all you have to do is relax and enjoy the trip."

"Yes, ma'am," Kathy said, feeling rather timid.

"He has also seen to arranging your meal sittings, although you can change that with the conductor if you feel the need to. Do you have your ticket?"

Kathy pulled the envelope from her purse. "Right here. Thank you so much, Mother Little." She looked around the compartment. It was the size of a small room, perhaps cramped for two or more people, but more than big enough for a single woman. "You know, I could have done nicely with a berth."

"Nonsense," Gloria said.

Outside, the conductors were calling "All aboard!"

"Well, time for me to leave."

"Thank you again." Kathy reached over and kissed Gloria on the cheek. "I really appreciate all your help."

Gloria blinked and smiled. "You're very welcome, darling."

A whistle blew loudly.

"Now, I really must leave." She bustled away.

Kathy tried to settle herself on the buttery soft leather bench. The compartment was paneled with wood and featured a private toilet. Green velvet curtains framed the window and there was a teak wood table jutting from the wall in front of the bench. It was already dark as the train began to move. Kathy looked out the window and watched as the lights of the city slowly slipped into the distance.

The next day, Freddie met Lowell for a late breakfast in the hotel tea room and asked about Miss St. James.

"What do you want to know?" Lowell asked.

"Where's she from? How long has she been an actress? When was the last time she was in New York?"

"I have no idea," Lowell growled. "Ask her yourself."

"No, seriously. I'm curious."

Lowell sighed. "She hasn't been acting that long but seems to be terribly good at it. I saw her last film and it was quite good. I think it was for Mr. Mayer's studio, um, MGM. She doesn't do that much for RiverWind. Frankly, I think Schulman and Loesch are making more money loaning her out to other studios than they are from any films they're making."

"That's interesting. I wonder if she's been in New York lately."

"Not to the best of my knowledge." Lowell took a big slurp of coffee. "If you want, I'll have Mr. Schulman give you a call today."

"That might be very helpful," Freddie said.

Mr. Schulman called promptly.

"I'm trying to find out about Miss Ivy St. James," Freddie said, once again ensconced in the downstairs telephone booth.

"What about her?" Schulman asked. "Came to Hollywood about two years ago. She was originally my secretary. But I needed a girl for a small role in a film, and she agreed to do it. Did a couple other films and people liked her. I loan her out quite often."

"Do you know where she's from?"

"Somewhere back East. She won't say. Says she was raised an orphan and doesn't want to remember that part of her life. I keep hoping she isn't on the lam from the cops somewhere and I'm going to have a ghastly mess on my hands. I probably shouldn't have hired her, but she is quite fetching and damn quick on the uptake. Not to mention a natural actress."

Freddie silently sighed. "Do you know if she's been in New York recently?"

"That I do know. She's been in Hollywood since she got here. I see her almost every other day."

"Well, thank you, Mr. Schulman. I appreciate the information."

"Say, have you thought about us doing a movie of that book of yours? Those rich kids gone bad would make one hell of a film."

"I'm thinking about it," Freddie said.

"I'm offering some very attractive terms. I think we can even get Woodie Van Dyke to direct. Maybe even Clara Bow for the girl, what's her name."

"Ava."

"Yeah. Ava. Think about it, why don't you?"

"I will. Thank you very much, Mr. Schulman."

In Chicago, Kathy got off the train simply for a change of pace. Hers and a couple other cars were bound for California and it would take a few hours to get the rest of the California train connected. Kathy walked around the Chicago station a couple of times, looking at the shops, debating whether she wanted a bit of chocolate or not. It was somewhat unnerving the way she kept seeing familiar backs everywhere she turned. Mr. Fisk seemed to be everywhere, although Kathy had to concede his profile would remind one of just about anyone. She thought she saw her Uncle Dan at least three times, Mr. Ryland once, Pierce Jennings more than a few times, Mr. Rightman twice.

Kathy put it down to the unnerving sensation of being followed. She was fairly certain no one was at that moment, but it had been happening enough before she left. She walked around the station once more, ate lunch at a lunch counter, then returned to her compartment and tried to read. Even after the train got moving again, she found it hard to concentrate. She hadn't slept well the night before, even though the berth in her compartment was quite comfortable. But then, she hadn't slept well on other trains she'd been on, so perhaps that was it.

More likely it was the sudden upheaval of her life. She was still furious with Thaddeus Healcroft and couldn't stop thinking about all the things she could have said to that worm of a man. Then there was the opulence of the train car and her own compartment. It was unnerving, is what it was. Gloria Little approving of her. Kathy looked at her hands. She'd left her engagement ring at home. The diamond wasn't huge, but it was far larger than she felt comfortable wearing. But she had remembered to put on the matching wedding band.

Being secretly married had been great fun. She'd had the benefits of being married without having to play the public role of being a wife. Kathy wondered if she'd ever accept being rich with the same casual grace that Freddie, Honoria, and their mother did. She also couldn't quite get over the feeling that it was somehow grossly unfair that she had fallen into such good fortune and her sister and her mother hadn't. Her mother was happy enough as she was. Kathy's sister, well, that was a whole other kettle of fish. Still, Kathy wasn't sure that there wasn't someone else out there who deserved what she had more. It was confusing and unnerving. She couldn't wait to see Freddie. At least when she was with him, it all seemed to make sense.

Chapter Twelve

When Honoria's car broke down for the third time in Sacramento, she decided that she'd had enough of driving. She sold the car to a garageman for pennies on the dollar, reflected that it had gotten her that far, and convinced the garageman to give her and her luggage a ride to the train station.

The train line ended in Oakland and Honoria transferred to the ferry that would take her across the bay to San Francisco. She found a hotel off of Union Square, then found a library not far away. The directory there provided a list of nursing registries. Honoria copied down the addresses. Fortunately, there were only five of them. It wouldn't necessarily turn up Mary Snow, but it might help.

After all, San Francisco was the last place Honoria knew Mary had been before whatever it was had happened and Mary felt compelled to go into hiding. And Mary had been a nurse. It was how she and Honoria had met during the Great War. Mary was helping the doctors examine the young draftees, then later helped with the returning wounded. Honoria had volunteered to help because that's what one did during those horrible years.

The two had formed a bond based on both the desire to escape what they were supposed to be and the love of mischief. And when Honoria decided she'd had enough of her parents' supervision and rules, it was Mary who cooked up the scheme to marry Honoria off to one of the young soldiers preparing to go off to war. It was Mary who had found Henry Wentworth.

Honoria wondered if Mary had known that Henry had come from an old moneyed family down in Virginia. All the young men were encouraged to make their wills and Henry had left everything he had to Honoria.

Honoria's father had tried to get the marriage annulled but failed when Honoria made it clear the marriage was valid. Henry's family, after he died, tried to make friends with Honoria, but she'd only been polite. Henry's money had gone to her. Freddie had managed it and made sure that Honoria was more than comfortably well-off. And unknown to everyone, Honoria had kept her friendship with Mary Snow alive, the two sending letters to secret addresses simply for the fun of having a secret.

Except that Mary had had quite a few more secrets than Honoria had initially guessed. During the war, Honoria had wondered if Mary had also been doing some spy work, finding German spies among the returning wounded. Then Mother Helen, at the orphanage, had confirmed it. It certainly explained a great deal about Mary and her love of secrecy.

But how did that play out in San Francisco? Honoria decided that she liked the city, with its quaint cable cars and steep hills. She imagined Mary would have liked it, too. There was a certain brash newness to the city, which Honoria realized was probably because of the horrible earthquake there almost twenty years before. The city had been almost completely levelled, if what she'd heard was true. That so many buildings had sprung up so fast was quite impressive.

Honoria found a small Italian restaurant not far from the wharf and piers where fleets of fishing boats docked and sold fish. The waiter placed a small teapot filled with good red wine on the table. Honoria poured a cupful, and ate heartily. She debated finding a nightclub or speakeasy; the city supposedly was rife with them, but decided instead to go back to her hotel.

The next day, she visited the various nurses' registries. Or would have visited them all, except that

Honoria found what she wanted at the third registry she visited.

It was in a small building not far from the University of San Francisco, near one of the hospitals in the area. The matron wore a blue-striped dress with a white-bibbed apron tied at her natural waist. Her gray-brown hair was pulled into a bun at the top of her head, but stray hairs formed a halo about her head. Her face was narrow and almost came to a sharp edge down the middle.

"I'm Mrs. Amaranth," she said when Honoria came into the office. "What do you need a nurse for? Aging mother?"

"No," said Honoria. "I'm trying to track an old friend of mine. Mary Snow."

"Oh, Mary!" Mrs. Amaranth laughed, showing the gaps in her back teeth. "Good heavens, it's been over two years since I last saw her. A wonderful nurse and quite a looker. I'm guessing some handsome young swain swooped her up and took her away from us."

"I have good reason to believe that did not happen," Honoria said. "She's been missing these past two years. I'm trying to find her and help her."

"Oh, that does sound serious." Mrs. Amaranth turned around and looked over a row of journals on a shelf over a row of filing cabinets. "Let's see. Ah. July nineteen-twenty-three. That would be the last time she worked for us. She worked with a couple other registries, as well. I can give you their addresses. A good nurse doesn't lack for work, you know." She flipped through the pages of the journal she'd pulled from the shelf. "Let's see. Ah. Here she is. She worked through the twentieth of July, caring for an elderly couple. He finally died and the children took the mother home to live with them. What's this? Well, now I remember. See this?"

She showed Honoria the entry, which Honoria couldn't read. Honoria shook her head.

Mrs. Amaranth nodded. "Mary often worked with

Captain Joel Boone, of the Navy. She'd worked with the Army during the Great War and got her training, I understand, just a few years before that, working for the Army in Texas. They had to get involved when Pancho Villa's men started raiding the Texas border towns. Anyway, this note here says that Mary would not be available until further notice because Dr. Boone had called her again to help take care of President Harding. Hm. I wonder if she was on duty when he died."

"She never mentioned it. I had no idea she was caring for the president."

"Well, things did not go well, as you know. Not Mary's fault, I'm sure. Anyway, she never said anything more than Dr. Boone had called. She wouldn't have said that much, but she'd agreed to take on a patient, then had to cancel because of that. We all figured out why when we saw her with the president's party as they came into the Palace Hotel. It was so exciting to have the president here. We were all agog, and then to see Mary with them. You couldn't miss her with that red hair of hers."

"No, you couldn't."

"Well, we never saw or heard from her again. If you find her, I'd love to have her come back to us. She was one of my best nurses."

"I'll tell her that," Honoria said. "Thank you so much."

"You're very welcome, dearie." Mrs. Amaranth smiled as she returned the journal to its place.

As Honoria left the building, an omnibus was just arriving at its stop. Honoria boarded, pondering what to do next. So Mary had been working for President Harding when he died. Honoria wondered if Flossie Walsh had also been caring for the president at that same time. It seemed likely. Flossie had been inordinately proud of that picture of herself with the Hardings, and had made sure Honoria had seen it. Although, as Honoria thought about it, Flossie had never said anything about her work with the president. On the other hand, Honoria had been doing her best to discourage Flossie's confidences.

Mary had sent Flossie to Honoria. Both were in hiding from something terrible. It seemed more than likely that whatever Mary was hiding from, Flossie was as well. Which meant that Flossie's murder was connected to Mary.

The omnibus line ended near the Sutro Park. Honoria wandered through the park surrounding the old, abandoned mansion. The wind whipping off the ocean chilled her to her bones as if it were the dead of winter in New York instead of October in California. It was oddly refreshing.

Honoria pondered simply staying in San Francisco, quietly disappearing like Mary had. Was it possible to live without people expecting things from her? As a young socialite widow, she was expected to behave a certain way, to work with the right charities, to go to the right parties, be friends with the right people, people who had no understanding of who she was and didn't care that they didn't.

But were the socialists and other friends she'd made as Ellen May that different? They, too, expected her to support their cause, go to their parties and events, be friends with their friends. And while Honoria thought she might have more in common with them, they didn't really know her any better than her socialite peers and wouldn't care that they didn't.

Or perhaps it wasn't the expectations that were the problem. Perhaps it was that she had spent so much time trying to be what everyone else had expected of her that she had no idea of what she expected of herself. Perhaps that was what Mary had meant the last time she and Honoria had seen each other.

It was late June nineteen-hundred-and-twenty-two. Honoria had convinced Mary to go to Europe with her and had paid for the trip. The two had laughed their way across the continent, drinking wine with abandon.

Honoria had started her art collection. Thanks to Mary's ability with languages, they had escaped the usual stops for Americans and instead had toured small villages and beaches. Lots of beaches.

Somewhere on the Spanish coast, Honoria had suggested that Mary come live with her as her companion. It was in a small tavern overlooking the Mediterranean. They had been eating olives and skewers of chicken and saffron rice and drinking the rich, deep red wine of the region.

"We could live like two happy old maids off the fat of my late lamented husband's money," Honoria said. "We could even find an Italian villa and make wine or something."

"We'd kill each other inside of a year," Mary said.

Honoria had sighed. "Why do you say that?"

"Honoria, darling, we're both too independent. You'd want to do something and I wouldn't and you'd be upset and hurt. Or the reverse." Mary paused and took a long drink from her glass. "And I'd resent being your pet."

"Mary, how could you?"

"Honoria, my sweet darling, I have to be honest. I was thinking the same thing, about how lovely it would be if we could live like two old maids running all over Europe or New York. And I deeply appreciate this trip. I have had a wonderful time and hope to make the most of the time we have left." Mary paused again and took another long drink of wine. "But, and I really, desperately do not want to hurt your feelings, but it's a little hard when you're paying for everything. I feel like I need to be profoundly grateful or do everything you want to do whether I want to or not simply because it's not my nickel funding this." She held up her hand as Honoria started to protest. "I know you don't mind and you're happy to do it, and I really believe that you are. It's just that... I'm not even sure what it is, but I almost feel like I'm your servant and I can't help wondering if you ever think that I'm being nice to you simply because you have money and I don't."

Honoria sighed. "I never really thought that. Perhaps once or twice when we had a spat. But you've been very careful, and to be truthful, I can generally tell when someone just wants to know me for my money. It's appalling how obvious avarice can be."

"Thank Heavens for that. Still, it's hard to be the poor one."

"It's not easy being the rich one," sighed Honoria, then stopped. "Oh, that must have sounded terribly callous. But damn it, Mary, you're the first person I've ever met who didn't expect me to think or do this, that or the other simply because of who my parents are. And I never seem to please anyone because I don't think or do this, that or the other. I think that's why I love being Ellen May. No expectations."

Mary snorted. "No expectations from the socialists? You must be kidding. They're so wrapped up in their cause, you're either completely for them or completely against them."

"Perhaps."

"Seriously, Honoria. Your problem isn't what other people expect of you. It's what you expect of yourself."

"I don't understand."

Mary put her wineglass down on the bar. "My darling, I've watched you for several years now, and it has always seemed to me that..." She paused, fighting to find the right words. "It's as though you're always trying to make somebody else happy until you just can't any longer and then you explode."

"I do?"

"When you married Henry? That's the perfect example. You came down and volunteered because that was what was expected of you, but then you couldn't take being such a nice little girl and did something outrageous. But once Henry left for Europe, you went right back to being a nice little girl. Then when it got too much for you, you went down to the Lower East Side and became a socialist. But you didn't just give up your old life. You used a false name and created a new persona. The problem is, that persona isn't the real Honoria Little, nor is the nice little girl."

"Then who is the real Honoria Little?"

Mary picked up her glass again. "That, my darling, is the subject of your life's work. Just as mine is to find the real Mary Snow. But neither of us is going to find our true personas gamboling about Europe. We'll find it by finding our true work. I'll tell you a terrible secret. I don't like nursing. I'm good at it because I do care about people. But if I could find some other way to put a roof over my head, I would. You, who don't need to work, need to find your true work as well. That being said, I am quite happy to be gamboling about Europe in the short term. One does need a bit of respite now and again." Mary put the glass down and grabbed Honoria's hand. "But I do mean this seriously, Honoria. You need to find your true work. That much the socialists seem to have right. You'll know it when you find it, I'm sure."

At the time, Honoria had put the speech down to Mary being slightly in her cups. But looking over the Pacific Ocean and watching the gray fog sliding in toward land and eventually embracing her, Honoria wondered again what life would be like if she were anybody other than who she was. As for her true work, she still hadn't found that. The newspaper had been fun and the parts that had annoyed her really had more to do with dealing with the socialist cause than with running a newspaper.

Freddie had found his true work. He was so much happier and peaceful when he was writing. Kathy had found hers, too. She loved working at the publishing house and even though the harassment from her boss and co-workers was annoying, Kathy clearly enjoyed the work itself.

So how did one find one's true work? Honoria strolled the park one more time, then went to find an omnibus back to her hotel. She felt the pull of worry over her friend, not to mention her brother and sister-in-law. Still, it couldn't hurt to spend an extra day or two in San Francisco pondering and trying to make sense of her life.

What Honoria couldn't have known was that Kathy was also desperately trying to make sense of her own life. As the train continued its relentless pace toward the West Coast, Kathy found it harder and harder to stay in her own compartment. She'd tried sitting in the coach section with Virginia, but Virginia was clearly embarrassed by it. Kathy then took to wandering the train corridors, stumbling through the smoking car, trundling through the dining car when there weren't any seatings, pacing the observation car when all else failed.

They were just coming to Colorado, and the white-peaked Rocky Mountains when Kathy stumbled into the observation car for the fourth time that day. She saw someone who looked alarmingly like Pierce Jennings sitting at the far end. The mountains rimmed the horizon and were quite spectacular. But the man who looked like Pierce Jennings sat alone at a table, oblivious to the beauty of the scenery around him.

Kathy looked again. The man was Pierce Jennings. She debated beating a hasty retreat but somehow found herself walking up and sliding into the seat next to the dejected author.

"Mr. Jennings," she said softly.

He looked up and brightened when he saw Kathy. "Miss Briscow! What are you doing here?"

"Going to Los Angeles," Kathy replied. "I might ask you the same thing."

"Me? Oh. I'm going to Los Angeles also. Mr. Little is there."

"Yes, I know. I'm going to meet him."

Jennings nodded. "Of course. So am I. I must convince him to start a new publishing company. He and I and Mennerly and Davidson, we must band together and create a new being out of the ashes of

Healcroft House."

"I think Healcroft House will survive quite nicely," Kathy said, chuckling in spite of the bitterness.

"But not without you. You're the only decent editor they had. If we create this new company, then we can hire you and I'll be all right."

"That's assuming you finish your next manuscript, Mr. Jennings," Kathy said kindly.

"Oh, that." Jennings looked completely dejected.

"Not going well?"

"Of course. It's going to be my best novel yet," he said, utterly unconvinced. He paused and looked at Kathy. "Actually, I have a wonderful idea, but I can't seem to get it down on paper."

"Tell me about it."

"Well, there's this young factory worker. He's been slaving away, year after year. So he becomes a socialist. Only he's betrayed by the cause and loses hope in everything."

"And..?" Kathy asked.

"What do you mean and?" Jennings sat up straight and sniffed in righteous indignation. "It's wonderfully tragic."

"Well, it sounds like a very interesting character and situation, but not a lot happening," Kathy said. "What event inspires him to become a socialist?"

"He's been working like a slave for years and years."

"So he decides out of the blue that he should become a socialist? Couldn't there be something that happens that makes him decide that the factory owners don't care and he needs to take action? Perhaps the love of his life also works in the factory and is... perhaps killed by the machinery and the owners don't care. And perhaps your young worker is drowning his sorrows in a speakeasy and a socialist talks him up and convinces him to join the cause."

"Oh, that's good." Jennings mulled it over. "And we can follow the young worker's fight to get his fellow workers to join the cause and maybe start a strike. Yes. That's it! And the strike goes badly and someone else the young worker has come to love, she gets killed by, by, by the police! Yes!"

Jennings scrambled to his feet.

"That helped?" Kathy asked with a mischievous grin.

"Yes! Yes! Thank you for clarifying my thinking." Jennings turned to leave, then quickly turned back. "We'll set a publication date once we get the new company up and running."

He hurried off.

"Manuscript first, Mr. Jennings," Kathy called after him.

A new publishing company? Kathy shook her head. It had to be more of Jennings' usual delusional thinking. Kathy wondered what Dr. Freud would make of Pierce Jennings.

Still, helping Jennings with his story had been the most interesting thing she'd done since she'd gotten on the train. Freddie had once suggested that if she wanted a job at another publisher's all she had to do was say that he'd take his book there. Perhaps she could hint that Mr. Mennerly and a couple of the others would want to follow her, as well.

That's assuming some other publisher wouldn't object to her taking a job from a married man with a wife and children to support. She snorted. That always seemed to be the rationale for not hiring a woman, even when the woman in question also had children to support. And not only did Kathy not have any children, she did have a husband who could support her beyond her wildest dreams.

But she didn't want to be supported. Nor did she want to make a career of being Mrs. Freddie Little. It was too aggravating.

Kathy went back to her compartment for lack of anything better to do. She tried picking up one of the books she'd brought, but somehow Herman Melville just didn't seem that interesting. Knitting was usually soothing, but the yarn was not cooperating, or more likely, she was too agitated to remember the pattern for the sock, which she'd brought because the sweater was too bulky. Cleaning out her purse would be more interesting. But the lavender purse was brand new and didn't hold any bits of paper or old hard candies or any of the usual detritus that somehow landed in her purses. Kathy suddenly brightened. The purse did have a letter from her mother that she'd completely forgotten to read.

The letter was chatty and full of news about her sister Teresa (recently widowed and now chasing the local newspaperman), about her younger brother Gideon (helping out with the farm and talking about taking a correspondence course in agriculture) and her still younger brother Isaac painting a mural on the side of the barn and having trouble reaching the top bits (he was only fourteen and just starting to grow). But then there was the bad news. Her youngest brother Gamaliel, age eleven, was getting teased and bullied at school. Rumors about her sister Teresa's late husband were starting to circulate and for some reason, the wags had decided that Bill Javits had visited his perverted attentions on Gam.

Sadly, Kathy knew the rumors were true. But even her mother didn't seem to know. Ma was mostly worried about Gam, Isaac and Gideon getting into repeated fights with the other boys and getting painted as troublemakers, never mind it was the other boys who started the fights.

Kathy looked at the letter, her eyes filling with tears. What else could go wrong? What else could make her life look any more miserable than it already did? She tried not to start thinking that way, but as the day went on, and then the night, and the following day, the thoughts plagued her.

Her last night on the train was spent tossing and turning. The few moments when she did sleep, angry, hurt dreams about nothing, in particular, haunted her. She was awake when the conductor knocked on her door and announced that the Los Angeles stop was coming up in less than an hour.

The weak light of a fall dawn eked through the green velvet curtains and when Kathy peeked around them, she saw a brown, arid landscape punctuated by dark green groves of orange trees and oil derricks. She got dressed in her Bendel suit and Virgina showed up and shooed her out of the compartment so she could pack Kathy's things before the train reached the Los Angeles depot.

As the train finally slowed and pulled into the red brick depot topped by a Moorish dome, Kathy felt excitement building within her. She had no reason to believe that Freddie would be on the platform to greet her and yet she firmly believed he would be there. Fortunately, the train car's corridor was on the platform side of the station, and as the platform slowly slid past, Kathy spotted the familiar tall, gangling form topped by strawberry blond hair. Her heart leapt, but then she sighed. Lowell Winters was there, too. She liked Lowell tremendously, but at that particular moment, anybody accompanying Freddie was her sworn enemy. She wanted Freddie all to herself.

Kathy was at the car's door even before the conductor and she shuffled impatiently as he took his ever-loving sweet time getting the car door open and placing a step stool on the ground to help her out. She hurried down the platform toward Freddie, who was walking quickly toward her.

He was there. She bounded into his arms and was about to kiss his mouth when he suddenly pulled back.

"I'm anxious too, my darling," he said. "But..."

He nodded at Lowell, ambling along behind.

"Oh. Damn," Kathy muttered. "I'm just so glad to see you."

"And I am, too," Freddie said with a reassuring smile as he gently put her hand in the crook of his elbow. "I can't tell you how terribly I've missed you."

"Hello, Briscow," Lowell said loudly. For whatever reason, although Kathy's name was pronounced Bris-coe, rhyming with oh, Lowell still said Bris-cow, rhyming with how.

"Hello, Lowell," Kathy said, feigning her pleasure. "How are you doing these days?"

"Well enough," Lowell said.

"My darling," Freddie said. "Will you please excuse me while I arrange for Virginia and the luggage to be sent to the hotel?"

"How did you know that Virginia came?" Kathy asked.

"Mother wired me," Freddie said as he went to talk to the porter and the conductor.

Kathy sighed with some relief. She wasn't going to have to explain about that part of the whole debacle.

At least Lowell had the grace to make himself scarce as soon as they got to the hotel. Kathy again felt completely overwhelmed by the sumptuous decor and the suite of rooms that was Freddie's temporary home. Not that Kathy had much time to think about it.

Another hour or so later, she had rinsed herself out in the ongoing attempt to avoid pregnancy and sat on the edge of their bed wondering why she had bothered. She had no job to save. It wouldn't matter if she got pregnant.

Freddie stirred and got up.

"Kathy, dearest, we do need to get dressed," he said. "I promised your brother that we would go out to his ranch to have dinner with them this evening."

"Oh," said Kathy.

She picked herself up and got her clothes on.

"I asked Virginia to pack a valise for you so we won't have to worry about leaving early," Freddie said, sliding into a fresh union suit and pants.

"Thank you," Kathy said numbly.

She wanted to see Joshua, but it would have been nice if she'd been consulted first.

"Kathy, is everything all right?" Freddie asked.

The dam burst. "No! It's awful. I lost my job, Freddie. And I've been without you for over two weeks and when I tried to hug you on the platform, you pulled away! How could you? I just wanted to hug my husband and you didn't!"

"We were in public, Kathy."

"You were embarrassed by me."

Freddie was flummoxed. "Not by you. But it was unseemly."

"Unseemly?" Kathy's pacing took on an agitated turn. "It was a train station platform. People hug and kiss when they haven't seen each other in forever. It happens all the time."

"Not to me. And you are my wife. There are standards that I expect from you."

Kathy turned and gaped. Freddie knew he had said the worst thing possible. She could see him trying to find a way out, but he had no escape.

He took a deep breath. "We had better get to the car. Your brother is expecting us."

The hour and a half drive to Orange County was cold and silent. Freddie spent it trying to dissect how the reunion had gone so terribly wrong while Kathy fumed. As the hired car pulled up into the circular driveway in front of Joshua and Betty's house, Kathy swallowed her anger.

Joshua and Betty both came out to greet them, with Betty holding Jakie. Kathy smiled and cooed about how big Jakie was getting. She didn't notice Joshua and Betty glancing at each other. Betty nodded and took Kathy inside the house, ostensibly to show it off to her sister-in-law. Outside, Joshua patted Freddie on the back.

"How was the drive out?" Joshua asked casually as Freddie gazed past the front door of the house.

"Hm? Oh. Fine." Freddie forced himself to smile. "And how are you?"

"Better than you are," Joshua said with a grin.

"Come on, Freddie. Let's go look at the new drilling site."

"Of course."

It was a short walk, made in silence. Joshua stopped not far from the dry derrick on his property.

"What the hell is going on with you and Kathy?" Joshua asked. "You two looked like you were driving up to the divorce court."

Freddie sighed deeply. "Oh, God. I hope not." He looked at Joshua. "I have no idea. The thrust of her complaint seems to be that I didn't let her hug me on the platform when she got off the train. I'll admit I was embarrassed, but not by her. Just an unseemly display of affection is all."

"Funny," Joshua said. "I can't see Kathy getting that all het up and bothered by not getting a hug."

"Well, I did say something rather unforgivable," Freddie conceded. "I just don't know how to take it back. Or what to do about it. Is this what they call a marital spat?"

"I'd say it's a full-on fight," Joshua said. "Have you gotten through the yelling yet?"

"Yelling?" Freddie blanched.

"Uh oh," Joshua said. "Haven't you never had a lover's quarrel?"

"I suppose. But I've never yelled at anyone. I just broke it off."

Joshua shook his head. "You ain't gonna break this one off, at least not easily."

"I don't want to break it off."

"Course you don't. You just gotta fight it through is all."

"Fight." Freddie wasn't sure but thought he might be feeling nauseous.

"What are you so worried about?" Joshua asked. "She's worth fighting for, ain't she?"

"Without question. But the only fights I've been in involved punches thrown and that sort of thing. Yelling? Absolutely not."

"You don't want to be throwing punches," Joshua said, kicking at the dirt. "Didn't your parents ever fight?"

"My parents barely spoke to each other in my presence," Freddie said. "If they fought, I would have no knowledge of it."

"Betty was kind of that way, but for different reasons. When her folks fought, somebody got hit and then her pa left. So I had to teach her."

"What do you mean?"

Joshua took a deep breath. There were a couple of hay bales nearby. He settled on one and motioned Freddie to take the other.

"I put the bales down to mark the new drilling spot," Joshua said, then took another breath. "Here's what it is. Now, you seen my family yelling at each other. We get angry. We yell and then all's well. Right?"

"Yes." Freddie settled himself on the bale and took out his cigarette case.

He offered a cigarette to Joshua, who took it. Joshua pulled a match from his pants pocket and Freddie got out his lighter and cigarette holder. The two took a moment to light up and blow smoke.

"Okay," Joshua said finally. "When I was young, my ma and pa had a fight for the newspapers. They were yelling and screaming. It was awful. We all hid, we were so scared. Then the yelling stopped and Pa was holding Ma, and she was crying. And then that stopped. So Kathy and I, we crept downstairs and Ma held us. And I asked Pa what was going on. And he said he and Ma had had a fight and that it was all fine. I said it didn't seem all that fine to me. And you know what Pa said? He said that when two people love each other and live together, they sometimes get really mad at each other. Well, we'd seen plenty of that, what with Pa whooping our backsides and Ma scolding us. But Pa said that when people are married, they will fight sometimes. And you gotta get through the yelling, cuz you're angry, but the sooner you get through that, the sooner you can get to the listening and the sooner you get to the listening, the sooner you can find out what the problem is, 'cuz it ain't always what the yelling is about, and the sooner you can find out what the problem is, the sooner you can get things on track. But you can't skip the yelling or the listening, because if you do, you just stop talking and never find out what the problem is. It took a little bit for Betty to cotton onto that one, but she did, and we've gotten through."

Freddie thought this over. "That's a very interesting philosophy."

"I suppose. And it's messy, I gotta tell you. I know Kathy's temper. But I'll tell you this much. Having her yell at you is lots better than if she's mad and not talking to you." Joshua shuddered. "I got her that mad once. I do not ever want to do that again."

Freddie found himself chuckling in spite of himself. "So what do I do?"

Joshua grinned. "Probably not much. I'll see if Betty and I can give you two some time alone after dinner. If I know Kathy, it won't take much to get her yelling at you."

"Oh, God," Freddie prayed. "I don't doubt it will."

"You'll be fine. You know damn well the only reason Kathy likes you is that you got the cojones to stand up to her."

"The what?"

"Mexican for..." Joshua gestured.

Freddie blushed.

"So what do you think about the new drilling site?" Joshua asked.

In the living room, Betty handed Jakie off to his nurse, then looked at Kathy, who was staring blankly at the fireplace.

"So what happened with you and Freddie?" Betty asked.

Kathy sank onto the couch and sniffed. "I don't know. It was probably my fault. No, it wasn't! Oh,

Betty, it was just awful. Here, we've been apart over two weeks. And then I lost my job and everything is so awkward because being rich like Freddie is, it's not that simple. And all I could think as I was on the train was it will be all right when I get to Freddie. It will be all right. We'll get everything sorted out and it will be fine. So when I saw Freddie on the platform, I couldn't help it. I ran right over and gave him a big hug and tried to kiss him and he pulled away. And I tried not to get mad even though it hurt. But then we didn't get to talk about me losing my job or anything. And he had his damned friend on the platform, too. Why would someone bring his friend along to meet his wife after a two-week absence?"

"Somebody who isn't thinking straight, that's for sure," said Betty.

"And then Freddie said he had standards for his wife that he expected me to keep."

"That was not a smart thing to say."

Kathy pulled a handkerchief from her pocket. "I am so mixed up. I have no idea what I'm going to do about work. It's so uncomfortable telling servants what to do and I'm expected to do it anyway. And, Betty, the last thing I wanted for a career is to be Mrs. Freddie Little. We were supposed to be married our own way. Now he suddenly expects me to be the wife he wants me to be."

"You don't know that. He could have just said it in anger. Men do that, you know?"

"No, I don't."

"Josh says stupid things all the time when he's angry. And I do, too. The important thing is to keep talking and to try and ignore the stupid stuff."

"If Freddie would keep talking."

Betty sat down next to Kathy. "I know. It's hard. But you two really love each other a whole lot. You'll find a way to keep talking."

"Thanks, Betty. It's just been so awful. I mean, I'm glad his mother isn't angry about us. But she was tutoring me all the way to the train station and it was a little embarrassing."

"I expect it would be," Betty said. "And I don't mean to scare you, but getting used to having servants is a little too easy."

"How many do you have?"

"Just the housekeeper, the cook and the nurse. Joshua had already hired the housekeeper and the cook when he bought this place mostly because he needed Elena to keep things in order and Maria to cook for the orchard crews. We hired Isabel to help care for Jake right after we came home from Kansas." Betty reached over the sofa to the end table and tried straightening one of the stacks of magazines. "I have plenty to do, keeping an eye on the packing house payroll and helping out with the bookkeeping. But I also have plenty of time to read and whatever I want to do. It's awfully nice to spend a whole morning doing nothing but reading, I'll tell you. But some days, I just want to scream."

Kathy shuddered. "I can imagine."

"I did one day, not too long ago." Betty giggled. "And thanks be, Joshua understood. That's when we decided I should take my correspondence course in accounting. But it took a little bit of yelling to get to that point."

"Freddie wouldn't yell," Kathy said. "He's too well-bred. I used to think that was so nice."

"It is nice. It's just inconvenient when you both need to get something off your chests." Betty looked up and at the kitchen. "I'm guessing that smell means it's time for dinner. I hope you like enchiladas."

"What are they?"

"Tortillas, which are flat Mexican corn breads, wrapped around cheese and whatever Maria decides to add to them." Betty got up and straightened her dark blue dress. "Then she pours a chili pepper sauce over them. But this one will be really mild. I didn't know if you liked spicy food or not."

"I don't think so," Kathy said hesitantly.

Some minutes later, Joshua had ushered Freddie inside to the dining room. The talk over dinner was rather formal and stiff. But Kathy decided she did like enchiladas. Sometime later, Joshua and Betty showed Freddie and Kathy their room and shut the door on the two of them.

It was a nice room, with pretty white curtains on the windows, small red flowers dancing across the wallpaper, a dark oak bureau, and a brass bed. Freddie and Kathy found themselves staring at each other for several minutes before Freddie sighed.

"I'm not sure what to say," he said.

"'I'm sorry' would be nice," Kathy said, folding her arms across her chest.

Freddie felt his anger rise. "You're not the only person here with a grievance."

"And obviously, your grief counts for more than mine."

"No." Freddie took another deep breath and tried not to pace. "But it would be nice if you'd have let me explain why I found it so embarrassing to be hugged in public. And it would be even nicer if you didn't insist there was something strange or inhuman about my feelings."

"It would be nice if you treated my feelings with some consideration," Kathy snarled. "Maybe even consulted me before deciding when we were going to visit my brother."

Freddie paused. Kathy did have a point.

"Fine. Let us outline our grievances, then," he said. "You go first."

Kathy broke down and sank onto the edge of the bed.

"It's been horrible," she sobbed. "First, I lose my job, then your mother tries to re-make me in her image and is so enormously kind about it, I can't say no. And the entire time on the train, I'm feeling lost and miserable, and all I could think was when I get to Freddie, it will be all right. I just need Freddie and everything will be fine. And then when I finally get to you, you pulled back. And why the hell did you bring that idiot Lowell?”

“He asked,” Freddie said softly. “And I know you like him.”

“Not anymore.” Kathy looked up at him. “Your turn.”

“Oh.” Freddie’s forefinger rapped a quick tattoo on his leg. “I pulled back because I am not used to public displays of affection. You are right that it happens often enough on train platforms. But I am always embarrassed when I see it.”

“You’ve kissed me in public before.”

“I have not.”

“You most certainly did last New Year’s Eve in Times Square.”

“I did not!” Freddie stopped. “I did. I was drunk.”

“Not that drunk.”

Freddie smiled at the memory. “Perhaps not on alcohol, but I was drunk on being with you.”

Kathy suddenly screamed.

“What?” Freddie yelped.

“How am I supposed to stay mad at you when you say sweet shit like that!” Kathy bounced up and started pacing furiously. “Damn it, Freddie. I don’t know what to do. My entire life is gone and it feels like I’m supposed to be this nice socialite wife and I don’t want to be.”

“I don’t want to be a socialite, either,” Freddie said. “And your entire life isn’t gone. Just one part of it.” He went on quickly in the face of Kathy’s glare. “A very important part of it, admittedly. But there’s no reason to believe that you won’t be able to get on with another publisher. You are very good at what you do.”

“And I am also a woman with a very rich husband to support me,” Kathy complained. “Why, in Heaven’s name, would anybody take a job away from a man with a wife and children to support to give it to me?”

"What does that have to do with anything?"

"That's what I'm always hearing. I shouldn't work because I'm taking a job away from a man trying to support his family. Never mind that I was trying to support myself. Never mind that some of my friends were widows with children to support. No. We don't deserve jobs because men need them."

Freddie sighed. "You're right. It is vastly unjust. But there is a possibility of a new venture. A group of authors, including Mennerly, Davidson, Jennings, Lowell and myself, banding together to create a new company."

Kathy gaped. "You mean Jennings wasn't being delusional?"

Freddie frowned. "What do you mean?"

"He was on the train. He said that he needed to convince you to start a new publishing company."

"He'd already proposed the same to me and said I should pay for it."

"Oh, dear lord." Kathy resumed pacing.

"The idea is not entirely without merit," Freddie said. "I mean about we authors banding together. Lowell liked the idea. Which does mean we would need a good editor, and I know both Lowell and I would not mind hiring her even though she has a ridiculously rich husband to support her."

Kathy looked away. She tried snarling at Freddie, but couldn't. "What about your standards for your wife?"

Freddie cringed and looked up at the ceiling. "My darling, you are almost completely perfect. You just have this one little flaw."

"Flaw?" Kathy growled. "Aside from the fact that wanting to hug you after a two-week absence seems hardly flawed at all, you did not even come close to answering my question."

It was Freddie's turn to sink onto the edge of the bed. "That might not have been the best expression I could have used."

"I would say not. It was quite possibly the worst expression you could have used." Kathy began pacing. "I thought we were going to define the terms of our marriage."

"That doesn't mean I can't have standards."

"It would have been nice if I'd known ahead of time what they were!"

"I can't foresee every eventuality."

"Well, neither can I." Kathy stopped suddenly. "What the hell are we talking about?"

"My comment earlier this afternoon." Freddie paused. "Which was not entirely appropriate."

"It was not at all appropriate."

"Perhaps not." He watched her pace. "But I was embarrassed."

"And I was miserable." Kathy looked forlorn.

"Which I had no way of knowing," Freddie said standing. "I suppose I could have guessed you were not happy about losing your job. And, by the way, I do want to hear all about it. But I thought you were merely excited to see me. It didn't occur to me that you were looking to me to save you."

Kathy glared at the floor. "I guess, given the way I've insisted on being so damned independent, it wouldn't occur to you that I'd need you."

Freddie reached out to her and she slowly slid into his arms. "I'm afraid it didn't. Even though I know you need me at least as much as I need you."

Kathy started crying again. "I just wanted to be with you. You're the only thing that makes sense right now."

"I'm beginning to understand that," Freddie said. "I'm sorry I was so hard on you."

"And I'm sorry I got so het up and angry." Kathy laid her head on his shoulder. "I guess I can avoid the public displays of affection."

"And I do want to hear all about your job and what happened afterward," Freddie said.

Kathy nodded and slowly began to tell him.

The next morning, the two arrived in the kitchen well after daybreak to find Betty at the stove and Joshua someplace else.

"He's taking the oranges that got picked on Saturday to the packing house," Betty told them. "Steak and eggs okay for breakfast?"

"That would be delicious," Freddie said. "Kathy?"

"Fine, but not too much steak for me." Kathy looked perplexed. "I don't understand. If it's harvest, won't you be too busy to be feeding us?"

"Well, Maria is busy getting lunch ready for the crews," Betty said, breaking three eggs into a skillet. She threw two small steaks into another. "But we're harvesting oranges all fall. They don't all ripen at the same time, and the crews need daylight to see which ones are ripe and which ones aren't. Joshua's told me about wheat harvest in Kansas."

Kathy shuddered. "I hated harvest. Cooking all day and night and still having to help out bringing the wheat in."

"The nice thing about oranges is that you don't have to rush them anywhere," Betty said. "Although we do try to get them packed and on the rail cars within a day or two of picking. But we can afford to close the packing house on Sundays. I'm guessing that since you two slept in, you got things worked out last night?"

"More or less," Kathy said. "Can I help you with anything?"

"I'm fine. Either of you want coffee?"

"Yes, please," said Freddie.

It was a leisurely day, in spite of Joshua coming in and out. He was busy in the orchards as the orange harvest was reaching its peak. But finally, at six o'clock, with the sun sinking into the horizon, Joshua came in for dinner.

"Kathy, when was the last letter you got from Ma?" he asked.

"Right before I left New York," she said. "There

was some bad news in it."

"Oh?" Freddie asked.

"About Gam and the boys?" Joshua asked.

Kathy nodded and turned to Freddie. "There have been some rumors going around about Bill Javits and Gam."

"Oh, dear," Freddie said. "They didn't say anything about it when I visited on the flight out."

"Yeah, well, Isaac and Gideon have been in several fights," Joshua added. "Along with Gam, of course."

"That is not good news," Freddie said.

"We've got to get those boys away from there," Joshua said.

"Gideon won't go," said Kathy, buttering a roll. "According to Ma, he seems pretty determined to stay on the farm. He and Pa got into a big dust up because his grades were slipping. Pa was worried that Gideon wouldn't get into college and Gideon said it didn't matter because he wasn't going to college. He didn't need it to farm."

"He's got a point," Joshua said. "But what about Isaac and Gam? Betty, you think we could take them?"

"I don't see why not," Betty said.

"Kathy, if you don't mind," Freddie said slowly, "I'd like us to take Gam. We could take Isaac, too."

Kathy caught Freddie's eyes and knew what he was thinking. "I think Gam might be happier with us. I don't know about Isaac, though. He's always been really keen on art and perhaps we could send him to art school."

"You gonna write Ma?" Joshua asked.

"Speaking of," Freddie said. "I was thinking of inviting your whole family to join Kathy and me for Christmas in New York this year." He paused as he noticed Kathy's scowl. "Assuming Kathy likes the idea, as well. I'm sorry, my dear, but I didn't get a chance to ask you earlier."

"That's all right," Kathy said.

Joshua glanced at Betty. "Betty and I won't be

able to go. December is our busiest time."

"But won't you be done with harvest by then?" Kathy asked.

"It ain't harvest. It's that we might get a freeze," Joshua said.

"Here?" Freddie asked.

"Well, it ain't like winter in Kansas," Joshua said. "But it can get below freezing some nights. And those mostly happen in December. If we don't get the smudge pots out and lit to warm up the trees, the oranges freeze and I could lose my next two crops."

"That does sound serious. And I was hoping to reunite your mother with her brothers and sisters," Freddie said.

Kathy grinned. "That's so sweet of you, Freddie."

Joshua shrugged. "Go ahead. I don't have to be there for that. Maybe some other Christmas, you can all come here."

The conversation drifted from the feasibility of getting the entire Briscow clan to either New York or California to other topics that didn't seem to have much to do with each other. Freddie and Kathy eventually made their way to bed, feeling much better about their future. And the next day, as they drove back to Los Angeles, they tried to define the terms of their marriage and found they couldn't.

"We'll have to make it up as we go along, I guess," Freddie said eventually, as they passed through the small town of Whittier.

"Why not?" said Kathy. "It shouldn't be that hard. As long as we keep talking."

"True."

"Have you found out anything new about Flossie Walsh since you last wired me?"

Freddie shook his head and lit a cigarette as he drove. "Not really. Oh, I did meet Lowell's friend Ivy St. James. She's a film actress with no background that I can see and she's quite interested in what I'm doing as well as what Lowell's doing."

"Ivy," Kathy said. "Could Honoria have written Ivy?"

"I thought it might be, which is why I tried to find out what I could about her. Sadly, she was apparently an orphan and refuses to talk about her life before acting. Do you have Honoria's note with you?"

"It's in my purse," Kathy said, pulling it out.

She held the slip of paper tight against the rush of the wind going through the car and looked at the writing.

"It's impossible to say," Kathy finally said as she put the note away. "It could be. This first card should be an I. But the rest is completely smudged."

"Even more interesting, on Saturday, we were at luncheon together with Lowell, and I happened to mention Flossie Walsh. It was subtle, but Miss St. James reacted to the name."

"That is interesting. But I have no idea what it means. Has she been in New York recently?"

"No," said Freddie. "Her producer, a Mr. Schulman, said that she has been in Los Angeles for some time and he sees her almost every day."

"She could have paid somebody to attack Flossie, I suppose. Perhaps she paid Mr. Rightman."

"Perhaps. But how will we prove it?"

Kathy stared out at the road. "I haven't the faintest. Could Lowell help?"

"He's completely infatuated with her."

"Lowell?"

"Yes, Lowell. It's not entirely surprising. He has always had a weakness for beautiful witty women with deep voices."

"Wonderful. Now, what do we do?"

"I haven't the faintest," Freddie said. "We could visit Flossie's brother Christopher Walsh. Perhaps you could make sense of him."

Kathy thought about it. "Oh, why not?"

Freddie looked at the road ahead and re-plotted his way so that they went to La Crescenta instead of

Hollywood. As they eventually pulled into the circular driveway, Kathy had to admit she was impressed.

"That's quite a view," she said, looking south toward Los Angeles. "And the air is so clean up here."

"It is," Freddie said.

He got out of the car and tried to get around front to open the door for Kathy, but found she'd already gotten out of the car.

The front vestibule was deserted when they entered the building.

One of the matrons, a medium-sized woman with graying blond hair and a black dress, came out and started when she saw Freddie and Kathy.

"I'm so sorry," she said, blinking. Her eyes were red from crying. "We're all at sixes and sevens today. We've had a most unfortunate incident here."

"I'm so sorry," Freddie said, recognizing her as the matron who had helped Mr. Walsh with a glass of water on his first visit to the sanitarium. "Mrs. Fuller, right? I'm Mr. Freddie Little and this is my wife, Miss Kathy Briscow. Would we be able to visit Mr. Christopher Walsh, please?"

The matron let out a sob. "No. No. He— He died yesterday."

"Oh, no," Freddie said.

Another matron, much like the first one, appeared from the back. Freddie recognized her rather severe look from his first visit there. She was Mrs. Parsons, he suddenly remembered.

"Mr. Little?"

"Yes?" Freddie asked.

Kathy waited patiently at his side, debating whether to say anything.

"How good of you to come by," Mrs. Parsons said. She turned to Mrs. Fuller. "Margery, go see if Sergeant Gibbs can speak to Mr. Little."

Mrs. Fuller scuttled off.

"Sergeant Gibbs?" Freddie asked.

"Yes. He's an investigator with the Los Angeles

County Sheriff's Department," Mrs. Parsons explained. "Unfortunately, Mr. Walsh was murdered. I found him. Suffocated in his sleep with his pillow."

"How terrible," Freddie said.

"I've never seen the like." Mrs. Parsons sniffed. "And Mr. Walsh was doing so nicely, too. First, you come to visit and that nice Ivy St. James. Although, she's come a few times."

Freddie looked at Kathy, who was still holding her tongue.

"Miss St. James was here?" Freddie asked. "Might I ask if anyone saw Mr. Walsh alive afterward?"

"Of course," said Mrs. Parsons. "We can't have women visiting our male patients in their rooms. And that's where Mr. Walsh was killed. No, Miss St. James met Mr. Walsh in the solarium and spent all yesterday afternoon with him."

"No one saw her leave," said Mrs. Fuller triumphantly, coming back into the vestibule. "Sergeant Gibbs will see you in a minute. And there was that other strange fellow that was seen around the grounds. He could have snuck in here and harmed poor Mr. Walsh."

"Mrs. Fuller! I'll see Little now," hollered a voice from down the hall.

Mrs. Fuller looked up, then smiled at Freddie. "Please come along."

Kathy tagged along after Freddie to a small conference room. Sergeant Leon Gibbs had a squarish build on a tallish frame. His nose was red and had been broken, possibly more than once. He'd kept his bowler hat on, even as he sat at the conference room table. His suit was dark, and the cuffs on the sleeves were just beginning to fray. He glanced at Kathy as if she were a mere annoyance, then motioned for Freddie to sit down.

Kathy slid into the chair next to Freddie.

"Your name?" Gibbs asked, his voice deep and raspy as if he had the croup. He looked down at the small notepad in front of him, then licked his pencil.

"Frederick Little," Freddie said, "and this is my wife, Kathy Briscow."

"Can you tell me where you were yesterday?" Gibbs asked.

"We were visiting my wife's brother and family in Placentia," Freddie said.

"Pla-what?"

"It's in Orange County," Freddie said. "We didn't leave until this morning."

Gibbs glared at Freddie. "So according to Mrs. Parsons, you came out a couple times to visit Mr. Walsh."

"I actually came out three times over the past two weeks," Freddie said.

"Why? Were you friends or something?"

Freddie sighed. "When I first visited, it was to get information about Mr. Walsh's sister, Flossie Walsh. She was murdered in New York earlier this month. I visited again because Mr. Walsh seemed lonely and I enjoyed his company."

"Are you a cop or something?"

"No," said Freddie. "My wife and I are looking into the murder simply because the New York police have been requested not to. We don't know why, merely that the request came from someone highly placed."

Gibbs fidgeted with his notepad. "So what did Walsh tell you?"

"Nothing much. Only that his sister had been hiding from someone and feared for her life. An Elmer Rightman was apparently chasing her at the behest of another, whose name we do not know. However, Rightman was also killed in New York shortly after my wife caught him following her."

"Any reason why someone would kill Mr. Walsh?"

Freddie looked at Kathy.

"There is no reason unless his death is connected to his sister's," Kathy said.

"I didn't ask you," Gibbs growled.

"Nonetheless," Freddie said. "My wife is right. Mr. Walsh was a dying man. Unless he knew his sister's secret and had threatened to share it before he died, there does not seem to be any motive to kill him that we know of. He had property, but his other sister in Ohio was managing that and would most likely inherit it."

"However, we did just learn that Miss Ivy St. James was here visiting the day he died," Kathy added.

"She couldn't have done it," Gibbs snapped.

"Why not?" asked Freddie.

"She didn't. We've interviewed her."

"She could have paid someone," Kathy said.

"And she apparently knew Miss Flossie Walsh," Freddie said. "I had mentioned the name to her and she recognized it. And there seems to be no other connection to Mr. Walsh that I can think of."

"Or Miss St. James was just doing a kind deed," Gibbs said. "Walsh wasn't the only person here she visited."

"You might still want to enquire," Freddie said.

"Listen, pal, don't tell me how to do my job." Gibbs jabbed his pencil at Freddie. "I got just as good a reason to look at you."

Kathy opened her mouth to speak, but Gibbs jabbed his pencil at her.

"And you, keep your mouth shut. I don't need no wild ideas from crazy dames."

Freddie stood. "Sergeant Gibbs, I cannot allow you to insult my wife like this."

"I can insult who I want. And if you don't want me to run you in for obstructing justice, then you'd better keep your nose out of this." Gibbs slapped his notebook shut. "And don't think I'm not gonna check out your alibi. Now, scram."

Freddie and Kathy left the room, shutting the door behind them.

"Odious man," Freddie grumbled.

"And all bluster," Kathy said quietly as they

walked through the vestibule. "He doesn't think we killed Mr. Walsh and probably never did."

"Then why threaten us?"

Kathy smirked. "To show off who's in charge. If he was that serious about us as suspects, he would have asked for my brother's name and he didn't."

"That's true. He didn't." Freddie looked back at the conference room door thoughtfully.

As they approached the door to the outside, Mrs. Fuller shuffled up to them.

"Mr. Little," she said softly, pressing an envelope into his hand. "After your last visit, Mr. Walsh said that if anything should happen to him, I was to give you this note."

"Do you know what's in it?" Freddie asked.

She shook her head. "I have no idea. But you should know, the man that was sneaking around yesterday. I got a good look at his sleeves. He had on one of those cufflinks, like the one you showed Mr. Walsh that day." She sniffed. "Mr. Walsh was such a nice man. We're all going to miss him terribly."

"I will, too," said Freddie. "Thank you."

With Kathy's approval, they waited until they were back in their hotel room to open the envelope. There was a sheet of paper with the sanitorium's address on it and shaky, but clear handwriting.

"President Harding was murdered," it read. "My sister had proof and that's why she was killed. She never said who killed the president, only that she'd seen it done. C. Walsh."

Chapter Thirteen

"It's preposterous! Utter nonsense!" Freddie proclaimed as he paced in the sitting room of his suite. "Poppycock!"

Lowell sat in one of the two easy chairs and across the table, Kathy sat in the other chair, working a sock in fine gray wool on five needles.

"Nonetheless, it is possible," Lowell said, gesturing with a glass full of whiskey.

"Why, in Heaven's name, would anybody kill President Harding?" Freddie demanded.

"According to the rumors I heard," said Kathy, "he was killed by his wife, Florence. He'd been unfaithful to her."

"That doesn't make sense," Freddie protested.

A generous tea, with sandwiches and cakes, sat on the short table in front of the sofa. Freddie had ordered it after he and Kathy had read the letter from Mr. Walsh for a fifth time and could make no more sense of it than after they'd read it the first time. So, they'd decided they could use some extra help and called Lowell to consider the mysterious note, and Freddie called for tea. The revelation was shocking enough that Lowell hadn't touched anything on the table.

"It makes sense to me," Kathy said, showing Freddie a quick grin with a wicked sparkle.

"My darling, you are nothing like Mrs. Harding, nor am I anything like Mr. Harding." Freddie fitted a cigarette into his holder and lit up.

Lowell snorted. "If infidelity were a reason to do away with a president, I assume we'd have had a great many more assassinations than we've had."

"Infidelity has nothing to do with it," Freddie growled, his frustration growing. "Mrs. Harding had no reason to kill her husband, no matter how many mistresses he had. In fact, she lost the most by his death. Once he was dead, she was no longer First Lady."

"It stands to reason," said Lowell.

Kathy saw the angry glint in Freddie's eyes and wondered why Lowell hadn't seen it. Or perhaps he had and that was the point.

Freddie let out a deep, annoyed sigh. "Lowell, you're being utterly obtuse."

"And you are wandering again. As your beloved wife would put it, get to the point."

Kathy had to swallow a giggle, especially as she was about to suggest the same thing.

"Mrs. Harding loved being First Lady," Freddie said. "Her parties at the White House were the talk of Washington. I even went to a few of them, courtesy of Aunt Wilma Smith."

"Aunt Wilma?" Kathy asked.

"My father's sister," Freddie resumed pacing. "She married a decent enough fellow, by all accounts, but then he decided to run for office and became a senator, eventually. Uncle Alfred Smith. Anyway, they moved to Washington. Aunt Wilma got quite taken up with Washington society. Uncle Alfred passed away a few years ago, and Aunt Wilma has more or less drafted several of her nephews to squire her about to various parties and events, including invitations to the White House. I went to three or four parties there during the Harding Administration and I did not need Aunt Wilma to tell me that Mrs. Harding was in her glory as First Lady."

"But Aunt Wilma did tell you," Lowell said.

"Yes," Freddie conceded. "Aunt Wilma being Aunt Wilma, she had quite a lot to say on the subject, including her views of the President's dalliances. It wasn't so much his lack of discretion that bothered Aunt Wilma so much as the fact that one of his mistresses was his wife's best friend."

"Mrs. Harding could have divorced her husband," Kathy pointed out.

Freddie chuckled. "I happened to hear one of Aunt Wilma's friends suggest the same, but Aunt Wilma opined that it would be a very cold day someplace eternally very warm before Florence Harding would let her husband out of her clutches. And having met Mrs. Harding, I have to agree with my aunt's assessment."

"Well, we can't ask Mrs. Harding about it," Lowell said. "She's dead. And come to think of it, so's that doctor that the Hardings made such a fuss over."

"Dr. Sawyer?" Freddie frowned. "That's odd."

"Yes. He died about two months before Mrs. Harding did," Lowell said. "I wrote a column about it suggesting that if he'd been a better doctor, then maybe old Warren would be around to answer for this Teapot Dome nonsense."

"Oh, I remember that," said Freddie. "Not one of your better efforts, Lowell."

Lowell shrugged, then looked at Kathy curiously. "What, in heaven's name, are you doing, Briscow?"

"Turning a heel," Kathy said calmly as she focused on her stitches.

"That seems oddly domesticated," Lowell said.

"It's better than twiddling my thumbs," Kathy said. "And since I don't have anything to edit at the moment, well, it's good that I have knitting to enjoy. But let's stay focused on our discussion. And while I agree, Freddie, that someone murdering the president seems a bit hard to believe, what else have we got to go on?"

"Not much of anything," Freddie said.

"Then why don't we look at this as if the president was murdered and see what we come up with?" Kathy suggested. "And if he was murdered, and it wasn't because he was unfaithful to his wife, it would almost have to be because of scandals in his administration.”

“Why do you say that?” Lowell asked.

“What other reason would there be to kill him?” Kathy said.

“Perhaps the Bolsheviks wanted to take over,” Lowell said.

Freddie snorted.

“Honestly, Lowell,” Kathy cut in quickly to cut Freddie off. “That doesn’t make any sense. If the Bolsheviks wanted to destabilize the government, they wouldn’t have killed the president in a way that most folks would take as a natural death. They’d shoot him in public.”

“Maybe they wanted to create a conspiracy,” said Lowell. “Let people think Harding died naturally, then get enough rumors flying to question it. Meanwhile, a host of others falls dead, including Mrs. Harding and their doctor. Scare the heck out of folks wondering who will be next.”

“Well!” Freddie snapped. “It’s patently obvious why you write fiction.”

“And patently obvious why you don’t,” Lowell snapped back.

“Freddie! Lowell!” Kathy all but hollered. “Fighting with each other is not going to help us figure this out.”

The two men stopped and looked at her in shock.

“We’re not fighting,” Freddie said.

“Not much, at any rate.” Lowell laughed. “Remember that time in White Plains, when you were so damned sure it was the transmission and I knew damned well it was the brakes. Came to blows, didn’t we?”

“We did, as a matter of fact,” Freddie said, chuckling. “And I was right about the transmission.”

“It was the brakes, man!”

“That was Oyster Bay, earlier that year.”

“It was White Plains. Oyster Bay was the carburetor.”

“You’re dead wrong, Lowell.”

"Enough!" This time, Kathy did holler. "It doesn't matter what was what, and who's to say either of you remembers any of those times correctly. Decent odds, both of you were dead drunk."

Lowell looked over at Freddie. "How does she know that?"

"Oh, for Heaven's sakes," Kathy groaned. "Most of Freddie's stories about you involve some sort of public drunkenness. Now, let us attempt to stay focused on who might have had a reason to kill President Harding."

"No one," said Freddie.

"What about someone from his administration?" Kathy asked. "There were so many that were corrupt. In fact, it would almost have to be somebody in the government, because who else would have the resources to watch Honoria's mail? Or hire former government agents? Could it be that the president was about to expose someone? Perhaps Mr. Daughtery, the former attorney general?"

"I suppose that's possible," Freddie said. "Which means it could have been anyone. Wait. Mr. Walsh said that Rightman, the man with the scar on his nose, was actually working for the real culprit. So whoever killed Flossie was probably not the real person behind Harding's murder, if such it was."

"Which means we still don't have any viable suspects," Kathy sighed.

"You do have that blasted cufflink," Lowell pointed out. "Assuming the letter is, indeed, an R, you have several potential suspects, including our dear friend Edward Roundhouse."

"And Elmer Rightman," said Kathy. "But he's dead and supposedly, he had no single cufflinks at his house. I can't imagine him throwing out the mate to that one simply because he'd lost one."

"Nor I," said Lowell.

"I wouldn't throw one like that out," said Freddie.

"So, if the cufflink belonged to Elmer Rightman, he must have lost the mate, as well," said Kathy. "I, for one, am not interested in scouring New York City for a missing cufflink."

"Or Los Angeles," Freddie said, sullenly, then he perked up. "We're forgetting one other person with an R in his name. Dr. Arnold Rothmayer."

"But Flossie liked him and recommended him to her brother and even Honoria," Kathy said.

"All the better to turn against her," Freddie said. "And he is here in Los Angeles and at the sanitarium where Mr. Walsh was murdered. Furthermore, he was in New York when Flossie was killed, and it wasn't until I explained that I was trying to find out about Flossie's murder to protect Honoria that he became angry and stopped answering my questions. He could simply have been cross, but it does seem suspicious."

Kathy frowned. "Any evidence that he might have been recently injured? There was that bloodstain on the sheet, you know."

Freddie shook his head. "None that I could see, but it could have been a head wound."

"Or it could have been a nose-bashing," Lowell said. "Which leads us back to Edward Roundhouse. It seemed to me, his nose had been broken fairly recently when I first saw him here in Los Angeles."

"He needs money and he does have connections," Kathy said, turning back to her knitting. "And a broken nose does cause quite a bit of bleeding. I wonder..."

"What?" asked Freddie.

"Could there have been more than one person involved?" Kathy asked, her fingers moving somewhat more slowly. "I know that only one man was seen in the servants' stairwell the night Flossie was killed, but that doesn't mean there was only one man in Honoria's apartment. Or even if there was, it doesn't mean the cufflink belonged to that person. It seems likely, but it's not technically proof. And there was one other person who was in New York when Flossie was killed and had arrived in Los Angeles in time to kill Mr. Walsh."

"Who?" asked Lowell.

"Pierce Jennings," Kathy said. "I did think it was odd that he was on the same train as me. He said he was coming out to convince Freddie to set up a new publishing house."

Lowell laughed heartily. "I know. He spent a good hour trying to get me to sign on, as well. Finally, in an effort to shut the little pest up, I introduced him to Mr. Mayer."

"Of Metro, Goldwyn, Mayer," Freddie explained in the face of Kathy's puzzled look.

"He's the most illiterate of them all," Lowell chortled. "And irony of ironies, he'd not only heard of Jennings, the two got along famously and now Jennings is happily ensconced in a bungalow near the ocean writing furiously away on Mayer's dime. This business never ceases to amaze me."

"Just because we find Mr. Jennings annoying doesn't mean he's not a good writer," Kathy said. "And his books do sell quite well."

"Nor does it mean he's a cold-blooded killer," Lowell said. "He doesn't appear to be in hock to anyone, which means it's unlikely anyone is trying to control him. So, with all due apologies, Briscow, so much for your suspect."

"There is one other option," Freddie said. Sighing, he turned toward Lowell. "Ivy St. James. We know she wasn't in New York, but she could have paid someone. Honoria was supposed to be looking for her but didn't say why. And Miss St. James was at the sanitarium the day Mr. Walsh was killed."

"Ivy didn't kill anyone," Lowell snorted.

"And how much do you really know about her?" Freddie pressed.

"Enough to know she wasn't paying someone to scatter cufflinks in Honoria's apartment," said Lowell.

"Lowell," said Kathy with a small sigh. "It's entirely possible you're right. But you don't have any proof. And according to Freddie, she did go to some lengths to meet him for no other reason than he was your friend. That seems rather odd to me."

"But you don't have any proof that she did," said Lowell. He let out a loud harrumph, then took a long drink of his whiskey. "However, we should probably look more closely at her. It would appear my luck regarding the fairer sex is holding strong."

"Oh, don't be ridiculous," Freddie said.

"Lowell, we haven't proved anything yet," Kathy added quickly. "We're merely looking at her because we have to look at every possibility. Why don't we invite her to dinner tonight? That way, we can have a long friendly chat and see what comes up."

"That seems reasonable," Lowell said.

He finally bent toward the table in front of the sofa and took a small pastry.

Nonetheless, the three spent their evening musing in circles, especially since Miss St. James sent her regrets for the dinner party with no explanation for her absence.

"Which doesn't mean anything nefarious," Kathy pointed out again to Freddie the next morning as they ate breakfast.

"But it doesn't look good," Freddie pointed out again.

He was spared Kathy's retort by a loud pounding on the suite's door. Freddie looked at Kathy, the two shrugged, and he answered the door.

Edward Roundhouse stumbled into the suite, followed quickly by Lowell, who for once, was wearing a full suit and tie.

"Get in there, you intemperate weasel!" Lowell growled at Edward.

Edward, who had landed on his knees, looked as though he'd been on the wrong side of a nasty brawl. His right eye was swollen and blackening. There was dried blood under his nose, which was also swelling and starting to add new colors to the fading bruises already there. He was in shirt sleeves and didn't even have a collar on his shirt, let alone a tie, and his pants were sporting new holes at the knees.

"What, pray tell, is going on here?" Freddie demanded.

"Edward, what happened?" Kathy gasped, going to him.

"He was beaten up by mobsters," snarled Lowell. "Damned near led the bastards to my door this morning. Thank God for the hotel's concierge. He saw to keeping the mobsters at bay."

Freddie sighed and looked at the sobbing Edward. "Gambling debts?"

"I can get it back," Edward said. "Just one good streak. I swear I can get it. Those last fellows, they were playing with rigged dice. I can't win against that. But I can if the dice are clean. I swear I can."

"Blithering idiot," Lowell growled. "I should have handed him right back to the mobsters."

"No!" wailed Edward.

Kathy looked up from dabbing Edward's nose with a handkerchief. "Lowell, you can't do that. It would be inhuman."

"I can't think of anything else that would change this fool's ways," Lowell growled. "He's worse than a drunk."

"How much do you owe, Edward?" Freddie asked with a tired sigh.

"Close to ten thousand."

Even Freddie winced at the amount. Lowell strode over and made as if to kick Edward, but Kathy prevented it with a solid glare. She turned back to Edward.

"There, there," she said. "We'll find some way to make this right. Although, good heavens, that is an awful lot of money."

"And I don't doubt he owes even more to mobsters in New York," Freddie said, blandly.

Edward groaned.

"Well, we have to do something," said Kathy, getting to her feet.

She caught Freddie's eyes. Freddie, in turn, signaled Lowell, whose eyebrows rose in response, but he refrained from blurting out his next comment.

"Oh, Edward," Kathy said, as if she'd suddenly remembered something. "We found your cufflink."

"Cufflink?" Edward frowned. "I'm not missing a cufflink."

"You mean this isn't yours?" Kathy held up the cufflink that they'd found in Honoria's apartment. The tiny diamonds twinkled in the morning sun.

"No. I mean— Yes, that is mine. I remember now. I lost it the other day." Edward grabbed for it.

Kathy pulled it out of his reach effortlessly. "Really, Edward. You lie so badly."

"But it's mine," he whined unconvincingly.

Lowell looked like he was about to kick Edward again. "Why, in Heaven's name, would you want to claim something that would tie you to a murder?"

"What?" Edward scrambled back and landed heavily on his seat. "I didn't kill anybody. Honest, I didn't."

"In other words, it's not your cufflink," said Kathy.

"No." Edward suddenly perked up. "What if I know whose it is?"

Freddie folded his arms and glared down at the man. "Do you really?"

Edward swallowed. "Sort of. I mean, I've seen cufflinks like that before."

"Where?" Lowell barked.

"Downtown." Edward swallowed and licked his lips. "At a jewelry store on Sixth Street and Broadway, near the movie palaces. Some of my movie friends go there. A Jew owns it. Funny looking fellow with a beard and curls next to his ears. Keeps his hat on indoors and has a funny accent."

"Sixth and Broadway?" Freddie looked over at Kathy, who nodded. "All right. We'll investigate it. But first, we have to figure out what to do about you, Edward."

"I won't gamble anymore," he moaned.

"Hah!" Lowell snorted. "The only way to keep you from gambling would be to put you in a straight-jacket."

Freddie laughed. "Lowell, my dear friend, I think you've hit the nail on the head."

"What?"

"We'll hide Edward in a sanitarium," Freddie said. "There are all kinds of them north of here. Very nice places."

"That's an excellent idea," Kathy said. "They'll be able to keep an eye on him, too."

"But I don't want to go to a looney bin," Edward complained.

"Do you want us to turn you over to the mobsters?" Kathy asked.

"No!" Edward shrieked, then whimpered. "What if they think I really am crazy?"

"I'll see to it they don't," Freddie said. "I know some people who can give me an excellent reference. I think we can find appropriate and kind accommodation for you, Edward. At least until your father can claim you and bring you home."

Freddie was gone less than half an hour, and within another hour, two young men in white uniforms appeared with a straight-jacket in hand. Edward protested, but they got him into the jacket and took him out of the suite in a remarkably short time.

"I think that's quite enough excitement for one morning," Lowell said. "What now?"

"I think we'd better investigate that jewelry store," Kathy said. "Do you want to come with us, Lowell?"

Lowell demurred. "Perhaps Kathy should stay here while Freddie and I go."

Kathy opened her mouth to give Lowell a piece of her mind, but he stopped her quickly.

"Somebody has to stay behind in case there's trouble," he announced.

"I seriously doubt there will be trouble," Freddie said. "We're merely trying to return the cufflink to its owner, and what are the odds that Edward knew what he was talking about in the first place?"

"We'll have to hope that he did," Kathy said, getting her hat, "otherwise it's more aimless searching."

"Admittedly," said Freddie, fetching a hat, himself. "Come along with us, Lowell, and we'll go to luncheon afterward. Besides, I think you know that area better than we do."

"True. However, that does mean I shall have to afflict myself with your driving," Lowell said.

"Oh, not again," Kathy groaned.

"No, not again," said Freddie. He turned to Lowell. "I will be the bigger person and let you drive."

"Can you loan me a hat as well?" Lowell asked. "In the interests of getting going sooner rather than later."

Freddie laughed and went to fetch one. "I'm just lucky that hat size is the only size we share. I shudder to think how many suits I would have lost to you."

The ride to the downtown section of the city was crowded with traffic, as usual. Lowell was able to find the jewelry store on Sixth Street. He was not able to find a parking space anywhere near it.

"This is insane!" he growled as they circled the block a second time.

"Lowell, just let us off near there," Freddie pointed. "Keep looking for a spot and you can meet us at that cafe next door when you find one."

"Assuming I find one," Lowell said.

He stopped the car long enough for Freddie and Kathy to get out to a chorus of horns honking, curses, and several rude gestures.

"Feels like home, doesn't it?" Freddie said to Kathy as they hurried to the sidewalk.

The shop was small and the front window seemed a tad dingy with the words "Kok's Jewelry" etched on the glass. However, once inside, it was clear that Mr. Kok was an exceptional artist. Gems winked from necklaces and earrings in Art Deco patterns. A collar of multi-colored stones looked like an ancient pharaoh might have worn it, but for the clean modern lines in the design. Freddie looked at a case of cufflinks and beckoned Kathy over. She looked and nodded. They had found the jeweler they were looking for.

Mr. Kok was stooped and wore glasses. His glossy black hair was topped by a skull cap and he did have curls at his temples. He wore a black coat that reached his knees.

"May I help you?" he asked in a voice that sounded almost German.

"I hope so," said Freddie. He pulled the cufflink from his pants. "We're trying to find the owner of this cufflink."

Kok took it, looked at it, then quickly pushed it back at Freddie. "You do not vant to find this person."

"We're not looking for Mr. Ramirez," Freddie said. "I was told he has a similar pair. We found it in New York. My jeweler thought it came from here, and since I had business here, my wife and I decided we'd ask around."

"You do not vant to ask around," Kok said.

"But I was told Mr. Ramirez was in Los Angeles when this was lost," Freddie said. "It can't be his."

"One Mr. Ramirez, yes. But there is his brother. He has a pair, too, and you do not vant to ask about him."

"Why on earth not?" Freddie asked.

"Because I don't like it," said a voice behind them.

Kathy gasped as she turned. The man was tallish, with a square face, dark skin, and dark black hair. His suit was dark with pinstripes and diamonds glittered from both of his cuffs. He also had a gun trained on Freddie and Kathy.

"That's Mr. Ramirez," Mr. Kok said. "Mr. Rigo Ramirez."

"Get out of here," Ramirez ordered the jeweler.

Mr. Kok left.

Ramirez glared at Freddie. "I'd like to know why you're so anxious to return my brother's cufflink to him,"

"It's a valuable piece," Freddie said.

"Not that valuable," said Ramirez.

"Nor is it necessarily your brother's," Freddie said.

"Oh, it is." Ramirez chuckled. "He's been complaining all month about losing it. And I know how and where he lost it, and I would be willing to bet, you do, too. That's why you're looking for him."

Kathy slowly began to slip sideways.

"Don't try it, chica," the man said, keeping his gun firmly aimed at Freddie. "I'll kill him first. Or maybe not."

It was a small room and Ramirez quickly grabbed Kathy's arm. Pulling her close, he put his gun in her side.

"I think we need to go see Jaime," he said. "Both of you, come with me, and Mr., if you even think about moving the wrong way, your wife will die. Are we clear?"

Freddie, his heart in his throat, looked at Kathy then nodded. Ramirez pushed them outside to the street.

"You like my building?" he asked Kathy, pointing at the tall, columned sandstone above them. "It's a good thing I own it, you know? Makes it easy to find out who's looking for missing cufflinks. Especially when they're stupid enough to let the cops know they're looking for them."

Freddie gulped. He had done just that when he'd been hit over the head and robbed.

His car was parked on the street. Ramirez nodded and a young blond man, almost as tall as Freddie and twice as wide, slipped out of the car and opened the door. Ramirez nodded at Freddie, who got in the back seat, then Ramirez shoved Kathy in next to Freddie and shut the car's door. Freddie grabbed her hand and held it tight as the car pulled away from the curb, leaving Rigo Ramirez laughing on the sidewalk.

Chapter Fourteen

Honoria stretched, basking in the warmth of the late afternoon October sun. Her feet were bare, which was amazing in October. But that was what California promised.

She was resting in one of the two Adirondack chairs her friend had set up in the backyard of her Hollywood Hills bungalow. It was a charming house, in the Spanish adobe style, with white plaster walls, two floors, a red tile roof and a turret in the front. In the back, a tall hedge along a wooden fence created privacy in the long, narrow back yard. A lush green lawn filled the space dotted with two orange trees, a lemon tree, and a lime tree. Mary had done well for herself.

Honoria had been there almost five days and hadn't learned a thing that she didn't already know. Mary had been quite firm - the less Honoria knew about Flossie's murder, the safer she'd be. Honoria had chosen to take the days as a sort of vacation, but it was getting time to consider contacting Freddie and Kathy at their hotel.

Mary, her dark black bobbed hair swinging, came out of the glassed French doors at the back of the house carrying a tray loaded with a pitcher and two glasses. The pitcher was filled with a deep red wine and slices of oranges, apples, and lemon.

"It's coming on for tea time," Mary said, in her deep throaty voice. "Would you like some sangria?"

"I'm parched," Honoria said, sitting up. "I'd love some."

But as Mary poured the drinks, there was a loud

banging and ringing from the front of the house.

Mary tensed.

"If you like, I'll get it," Honoria said.

"No, I'll go," Mary said, leaving her glass on the small wooden table between the chairs.

Mary went to the front door, and Honoria followed.

There was a small doored peephole on the door, which Mary opened and then shut quickly.

"Damn!" she hissed. "I should never have let Lowell come here."

"Lowell's here?" Honoria asked softly.

"Damn it, Ivy!" Lowell yelled from the other side of the door. "Let me in! I need to speak to you! Now!"

Honoria and Mary looked at each other.

"He's using your other name," Honoria said.

"That's how he knows me."

"Ivy! Damn it! I'll break this door down."

"That's not like Lowell," Honoria said. "It must be something serious."

Mary nodded and slowly opened the door.

Lowell burst through before he could be invited in. He stopped when he saw Honoria.

"Honoria, what are you doing here?" he demanded.

"Mary, I mean, Ivy is my friend," Honoria said.

"More to the point," Mary said. "What are you doing here, Lowell?"

"Mary? Your name is Ivy," Lowell yelped.

Mary sighed. "It's both. I was Mary and that's the name Honoria knows best. But Ivy St. James is my name now."

"You were lying." Lowell began pacing the living room's shiny dark wood floor. "Oh my God, Freddie was right." He turned on her. "Why did you kill Christopher Walsh?"

"I didn't kill Walsh," Mary said calmly. "Did you come here to hurl false accusations at me?"

Lowell found a sofa next to an arched window looking out on the side of the house and sank into it.

"I don't know what to think," he said. "I just know

that Freddie and Kathy have been kidnapped. I saw the gangster take them and put them in a car."

"What?" Honoria yelped.

"We were looking for the cufflink's owner, the one they found in your apartment," Lowell said. "I drove them downtown and they got out while I went to find a parking space. Only I couldn't find one. I was coming around the block for the fourth time when I saw Freddie getting into the back of a car. And a man pushing Kathy into the back, as well. I'm pretty sure he had a gun on them. I tried to follow them, but I lost them."

"What jewelry store and what did the man look like?" Mary asked.

"A place called Kok's, on Sixth and Broadway." Lowell shut his eyes. "The man was tall, though not as tall as Freddie. But a broad-shouldered, swarthy fellow. Looked like a Mexican or some sort of Spaniard, I'd say."

"Rigo Ramirez," Mary said, sinking into a chair. "He must have been watching the store for his brother. It would have been very easy to. Rigo owns the building. Do you remember what the cufflink looked like, Honoria?

"I have no idea. I never saw it."

"It's square, and surrounded by tiny diamonds," Lowell said. "And there's some sort of letter in the middle of a leaf design. We are fairly sure it's an R."

"It is," Mary said. "And I know who it belongs to. I've seen those cufflinks before, and not just on Rigo." She looked at Honoria. "I'm also fairly sure where your brother and his wife are. That's why you were being chased by those government types. They wanted you to get to me."

"That's what I thought," said Honoria, pacing. "And now they've got Freddie and Kathy."

Mary got up and grabbed Honoria by the arms. "There's some good news in this. They probably took your brother and his wife as a way to get to you, and they want you to get to me. And if that's the case, then Freddie and Kathy are probably still alive."

Honoria glared at her friend. "I think it's high time you told us what's really going on here."

"Indeed," growled Lowell from the sofa.

"It's a long story and there is a nice pitcher of sangria in the back," Mary said. "Wait here and I'll get it."

"My brother and his wife have been captured by this monster," Honoria said anxiously.

Mary glanced at her wristwatch. "It won't be dark for another hour or so and I know for a fact that the monster won't do anything until after dark. It would be too easy to alert the neighbors."

"We should call the police then," said Lowell.

"The police are who probably told Rigo that Freddie and his wife were looking for the cufflink," Mary said.

There was tense silence in the room as Honoria paced and Lowell glowered at nothing in particular. When Mary returned, she'd added a glass to the tray with the pitcher and the two filled glasses. She set the tray on a low table in front of the sofa, poured out the extra glass, handed one to Lowell, then nodded at Honoria. Honoria took her glass as Mary took hers and settled into her chair, a large leather overstuffed one. Honoria took the chair's mate across from Mary.

"It is true, Lowell, that I was raised an orphan," Mary said after a sip from her glass. "And leaving the orphanage at age fifteen, I went to join the army fighting Pancho Villa. That's where I got my training as a nurse. I'd lied about my age. But that didn't matter because I had one skill that was even more important than nursing. I could speak Spanish."

Honoria gasped. "You can speak German, too."

"Yes." Mary took a deep breath. "And you'd guessed correctly. I was a spy as much as I was a nurse, especially during the Great War. I uncovered more than a couple of Germans posing as Americans. I enjoyed the work. I suppose it was lonely, but growing up an orphan, I was used to that. And when Dr. Joel Boone, of the Navy, needed someone to keep an eye on President Harding when he returned from Alaska, he turned to me. I was living in San Francisco at the time. It made perfect sense. Flossie and another nurse, Belinda Gibbons, had been with the Hardings and Dr. Sawyer from the beginning of their trip. Flossie was worried because she'd found emptied ampules of digitalin and had talked to Dr. Sawyer and Dr. Boone about it. Dr. Boone had no confidence in Dr. Sawyer, which wasn't surprising. Dr. Sawyer was a homeopath, you know."

"No, I didn't," said Lowell. "I have no idea what a homeopath even is."

"It's a different philosophy of medicine," Mary said. "Not as scientific as standard practice. Some even call it quackery. I know Dr. Boone did. But Mrs. Harding set great store by it, and apparently Dr. Sawyer's tonics had helped cure her of some disease or other. In any case, by the time President Harding arrived in San Francisco and I joined the party, he was quite ill. That story that went around about him getting food poisoning from tainted crab meat? That was something told the press to cover it all up. I can't say for certain, but I do think the president had been given a dose of arsenic. He did have a bad heart, which would explain why, if someone had been trying to poison him with digitalin, it hadn't worked. The digitalin was probably keeping the president alive."

"But why kill him?" Honoria asked.

"Let me tell you what I witnessed and that might explain a little," Mary said. "It was related to the scandals in his administration. There we were, his second night in San Francisco. The president had come around earlier that day and it looked to me like he'd make a full recovery. Mrs. Harding was reading that silly story from the Saturday Evening Post that got all the news, and he fell asleep shortly after that.

"Flossie, Belinda and I were in the next room.

We closed the door once we saw that the president was asleep. Mrs. Harding sat up and read. That is until we heard someone arguing with Mrs. Harding. Mrs. Harding was telling him that she'd changed her mind, but the man she was arguing with told her that the president was threatening to come clean about everything and that what the man was going to do was the only way to save himself and Mrs. Harding.

"I knew something was very wrong then and was trying to get into the room quietly and unseen, but Flossie, that idiot, wrenched the door open. We saw the two arguing over what what I now realize was the President's dead body. Mrs. Harding ran for the doctor, which I guessed was part of the plan. The man looked at us and grinned. He told us he'd killed a president, he'd have no problems killing us."

"Oh my god," gasped Lowell.

"Mary, you poor thing." Honoria put her glass on the table, then slipped over to Mary's side.

Mary took another long drink from her glass and shrugged. "He couldn't kill us then. It would make the president's death even more suspicious and they did not want to risk that. But right after the funeral, I decided to hide. I told Dr. Boone what I'd seen and he agreed that not only would it be impossible to prove, I would be risking my life and the lives of the other nurses, as well, if I said anything. So, he helped me hide. Then Belinda was killed and Flossie's brother-in-law died in her car, which had been tampered with. Dr. Boone knew because he'd been watching all three of us hoping to keep us safe. I decided then not to take any chances. I moved to Los Angeles, cut and dyed my hair and went to work as a secretary for RiverWind Pictures. When Mr. Schulman asked me to act in his film, I thought, why not? I could hide in plain sight. Better yet, I'd learned the murderer's true name, Jaime Ramirez, and discovered that he has a house here in Los Angeles. Dr. Boone took care of knowing where and what Mr. Ramirez was doing when he wasn't in

Los Angeles. Then Flossie, again, acting like an idiot, followed her brother out here when he got sick last summer. She found me through Dr. Boone and after it was clear that Jaime knew Flossie was in Los Angeles, I sent her to you, Honoria. My best guess is that Jaime started looking at you again and found Flossie in your apartment by accident. In any case, Jaime Ramirez has Freddie and Kathy, probably at his house here in the city. They'll probably be the worse for the wear, and I'm sorry about that. But the good news is that I doubt he'll kill them until he can get what he wants from you."

Lowell glared at her. "Are you sure you know where they are?"

"As sure as I can be," Mary answered. "Jaime's not above using his mobster brother's help, but he generally keeps his distance to protect his secret."

"What secret?" Honoria asked.

"That his real name is Jaime Ramirez rather than the name he uses," Mary said, getting up. "He looks enough like a normal Caucasian that he goes by another name. I suspect his real boss knows he's a Mexican and probably uses that against him."

"And you know where he lives," said Lowell.

"Yes." Mary smiled weakly. "I made a point of finding out as much about Mr. Ramirez as possible to protect my own skin." She glanced out the window to the lengthening shadows outside and shuddered slightly. "It's getting close to dark. We should probably make a plan before going over there."

"Why don't we just call the police?" Honoria asked.

Mary shook her head. "As I said, Rigo Ramirez owns them. Besides, I'm tired of hiding, of always checking over my shoulder, waiting for Jaime to find me. I think it's time we simply had it out."

"But he'll kill you," Honoria said.

"Not if we get him first," Mary said, her voice taking on an even grimmer edge.

Kathy had kept her hand tightly in Freddie's

as the car bore them away. It was impossible to tell the direction they were being taken. She looked at Freddie. He'd nodded briefly out the window and Kathy gathered that he'd seen Lowell and that Lowell had an idea of what was going on. As the car chugged up one hill, then coasted down another, Kathy stroked the mother of pearl handle on the pocket knife she'd given Freddie on his birthday. It had been in his hand when he'd grabbed hers.

The car stopped and the two mobsters forced Freddie and Kathy out of the car. Their boss, Rigo Ramirez, was nowhere to be seen. They had pulled up in front of a low clapboard house. One of the mobsters grabbed Freddie's arm and the other grabbed Kathy's. With guns solidly jammed in their ribs, Freddie and Kathy had no choice but to stumble down the concrete steps along the side of the house, which turned out to be much larger than it looked from the front. It had been built onto the side of a hill that sloped sharply downward from the street.

The two mobsters pushed Freddie and Kathy into an unfinished room at the bottom of the house. Wood cases lined the back wall just behind two pier posts that had been painted royal blue. The rest of the room was gray and lit by the large windows that looked out at the descending slope of the house's back yard, including the one window in the lone door to the room. A small window in the side wall overlooked the concrete steps to the street and hung open, letting in the dry, warm air. In the corner farthest away from the steps were two wooden chairs that had seen better days on either side of a crate holding a kerosene lamp.

The mobsters tied Freddie and Kathy to the pier post closest to the door, stopping only to pat Freddie down. Kathy held the pocket knife tight in her hand, hoping the men wouldn't notice it. They didn't. As soon as Freddie and Kathy were tied with the rough hemp rope, the two men settled into the wooden chairs and got out a pack of cards.

"When's he going to get here?" asked the first, a medium-sized man with dark black hair and the darker skin of a Mexican.

The other, the blond that they'd seen earlier, shrugged. "When he wants."

"Well, do me a favor, Squires, and don't go riling him," said the first man.

"I'll do what I want, Manny."

The first man shook his head and dealt the cards.

The October sun slowly filled the room with shadows as it slipped toward the horizon. Kathy tried to open the knife, but couldn't. She was able to nudge it into Freddie's hands. Freddie glanced down at her and she nodded. He got it open and Kathy struggled to stand taller so that the two mobsters couldn't see Freddie's arms move as he slowly and carefully hacked at the rope.

Manny and Squires remained involved in their game, grunting and swearing every so often. Once, Manny jumped up and angrily threw his cards on the table, but Squires slowly got up and slid his hand into his suit jacket. Manny backed off.

Kathy wondered why the two men seemed so uninterested in her and Freddie. Admittedly, it did look pretty hopeless, being tied up and armed with only a small knife in a closed room with two men and their guns. Perhaps that might make them careless and give her and Freddie a chance. She shifted, trying to loosen her hands. The men ignored her.

As dark came on, Squires lit the kerosene lamp, and the card game continued. Kathy wasn't sure how much later it was when there was a loud thump upstairs and dust fell from the bare boards of the ceiling. As Manny and Squires both chuckled, Kathy looked up at Freddie. He frowned and blinked. It was fairly obvious they didn't have much time left, but Kathy couldn't tell if Freddie was trying to say that he had freed himself or that he wasn't going to be able to cut the ropes any time soon.

Several minutes later, it sounded as though a band was tuning up above them. Kathy heard the faint scratching of steps on the concrete stairs outside. She tried to stretch around, but it didn't matter. The door opened and James Ryland, dressed in a dinner suit, came in.

"Squires," he barked without looking at Freddie and Kathy.

"Yes, Mr. Ramirez," Squires said with a mocking grin.

Ryland's glare was truly menacing. "You will not use that name. Now, get upstairs. Clara Bow's just arrived and I need you to keep that nosy little minx distracted. I don't think we want our little 'It Girl' to find out what will be happening down here as soon as the band gets going."

He glanced over at Kathy and Freddie with a smile that said he was looking forward to whatever plans he had. Kathy worked to keep her expression stoic. Obviously, Mr. Ryland was having a party with a band to cover whatever screams might happen when he tortured the pair.

Ryland went back upstairs, presumably to greet the rest of his guests, followed by Squires, who offered Manny a nasty smirk. Manny looked disgusted. He glared at the outside stairs, then settled back into his chair by the crate and began dealing a hand of solitaire.

The band upstairs began blasting out the Charleston.

"There's no accounting for taste," Kathy sighed, in a mostly futile attempt to fight back her fear.

"However tired we may be of that tune, it does get people up and dancing," Freddie replied softly, apparently attempting to ease the tension, as well. "Hence, a very good choice for a band's first number."

Manny glared at them. "What are you talking about?

"The Charleston," said Freddie.

"You're planning something." Manny got up and

started pacing angrily. "You damn White people. You're thinking I'm just a dirty Mexican and I don't speak English, so you can get one past me. Well, you can't. My family has been here longer than your people. And what happens? Your stupid courts steal my family's land. Just because we're Mexicans."

Manny spat at Freddie's feet.

"That's terrible," said Kathy.

"Don't try to make it up to me!" Manny yelled, whirling around and putting his face in hers. "You wouldn't do shit for me if your hands weren't tied to that post. We owned this city once. Now the only jobs we can get are picking crops and cleaning up after you people. And what makes you so much better than us, huh? Nothin'. Absolutamente nada."

He stopped and looked at the small window over the stairs. Kathy caught a brief flash of movement and a minute later, Ryland and Squires came through the door.

"I swear, she left," Squires was saying. "I put her in her car, myself. Wanted to go to some other party Marion Davies is having."

"You better be sure," Ryland snarled before turning to Freddie and Kathy. "Mr. Little, and do I understand correctly, Mrs. Little? How very interesting. I had no idea that was what was afoot when I turned you in to your boss, Miss Briscow. Excuse me, Mrs. Little. This should make things just that much easier." He pulled out a revolver and aimed it at Kathy's forehead. "Now, Mr. Little, I want to know where your sister is."

Freddie swallowed and stood taller. "I'd like to know the same thing."

"Do you honestly think I believe that?" Ryland grinned.

"Sir, you have a gun pointed at my wife's head. Why would I say I don't know if I had any idea where my sister is?"

"Leave them alone, Jaime," said a deep female voice. "We both know it's me you really want."

Ryland turned to the doorway where Mary Snow stood, dressed in a black blouse and riding pants.

Freddie sprang forward and tackled Ryland. The two fell forward onto the cement floor and Ryland's revolver went flying into the wall. Kathy struggled, but her ropes were still tied fast. Mary rolled back outside and away from the door.

Ryland bucked. "Get her!"

Manny ran forward and out the door. Kathy heard a thud, an oomph, and a yell as Manny apparently went rolling down the back hillside. Freddie struggled to keep Ryland down, but Ryland bucked him off just enough to get turned around and reached for Freddie's neck. Squires had his gun out and was trying to get a bead on Freddie without hitting Ryland. Kathy saw the barrel flare from a gun poking in through the side window rather than heard the shot. The bullet went wide and shattered the glass on the back window on the far end of the room. Squires aimed at the small side window but got a bullet through the sleeve on his gun arm for his trouble. He howled and sank into one of the chairs.

Freddie managed to break Ryland's grip on his neck. He punched Ryland once, twice, but then dodged one of Ryland's fists, then fell back as Ryland's other fist connected with his ear. Both men struggled to their feet. Freddie pressed forward, his best prep school boxing form, landing two hits to Ryland's belly before knocking the man backward toward the far corner of the room.

But as Squires had shifted in his chair, it broke underneath him. Squires sprawled, his legs kicking the crate with the kerosene lamp on it. The lamp toppled. Kathy watched as it fell and broke. Seconds later, flames leapt up and the crate began smoldering.

Ryland staggered up and pushed forward toward Freddie, only to get pummeled a second time. He landed one punch in Freddie's belly and grazed Freddie's chin with an uppercut, but Freddie already had a strong left coming along. It landed squarely in the side of Ryland's face and he went down and stayed down.

Honoria and Mary both scurried in and set about trying to untie Kathy. The smoke from the fire mostly blew through the shot-out window, but the crates at the back were not only catching, one of them exploded bits of glass. Squires got to his feet and ran for the door.

"Where's the pocket knife?" Kathy screamed.

"Here!" yelped Honoria, scraping it up from the floor.

"That's not going to cut anything," Mary yelled.

She pulled a heavy hunting knife from the sheath at her waist. The smoke billowed and all three women began choking. Freddie scrambled to a window to catch his breath, then pushed both Honoria and Mary out the door. The contents of another crate boiled over and the bottles exploded. The flames lapped eagerly at the spilled alcohol. Freddie grabbed Mary's knife and staggered over to Kathy.

"Down here," Kathy gasped and coughed.

She'd slid to the floor. Freddie made short work of the ropes and pulled the two of them out of the room.

Mary and Honoria were waiting on the steps. The band had stopped playing and there were loud screams as the party-goers realized the house they were in was on fire.

Freddie coughed loudly and waited to catch his breath.

"Go!' he gasped.

Kathy coughed, then pulled him up the stairs, following on the heels of Mary and Honoria.

As the two stumbled to the top, they saw Squires, who had somehow also gotten to the street, grab Mary and push her toward a car parked across the street. Two other mobsters were waiting with their guns and made it clear that Honoria, Freddie and Kathy should also follow Mary and Squires.

"That's close enough," said a voice from the car.

The car had a closed roof and the voice came from

a man in the back seat. Light from the street lamp caught his clean-shaven chin, but no more.

"Well, Miss Snow, you have given me quite the run-around," the man said. "On the other hand, you four have saved me the trouble of disposing of Mr. Ryland."

"Oh, no," gasped Honoria, looking back at the burning house.

Party-goers were running about. Neighbors came out of their houses. At the end of the street, a small group of Negroes, their instruments glinting in the street light, had gathered.

"But my drums!" one of them complained loudly. "Damn it, that's the second set this year."

"So, are you going to kill us now?" Mary asked.

"No. I am not," the man in the car said. "I only kill when it's absolutely necessary. That was Mr. Ryland's mistake. Kill too often and someone starts noticing the bodies and gets curious. Besides, even if you did try to tell the world about the president's death, no one would believe you. The rumors have been spreading for the past two years and are mostly being laughed off. I don't recommend saying anything, just in case, you understand. But I seriously doubt you will, even if only to keep your reputation and your acting career."

The sound of sirens slowly grew and the man in the car reached forward and signaled the driver.

"Time for me to go," he said. "Good night."

Squires and the other mobsters got in the car and it drove off.

Mary sank against Honoria, who waved at someone down the street. The Packard that Freddie had rented eased up the hill from the front of the street. Lowell was behind the wheel. Wearily, the four squeezed into the car and Lowell drove off just as the first fire engine pulled up.

Chapter Fifteen

Honoria, Kathy, Lowell, and Mary - or rather, Ivy, as she preferred to be known - took the train back to New York the next day. Freddie, who flew home, was waiting on the platform and allowed Kathy a chaste hug, while she smiled and held back the urge to kiss him soundly.

A week later, Freddie invited his mother to a small dinner party. Lowell was there, as were Honoria and Ivy, who was sharing Honoria's apartment for the time being. Kathy was hostess.

It was a lovely, peaceful evening, with Lowell telling outrageous stories about the movie business. Gloria informed the group that Edward Roundhouse had been collected by his father and sent to another sanitarium in New York. Ivy also had news.

"I've got a part in a play on Broadway later this season," she said. "I'm playing Hedda Gabler."

"That's amazing," said Kathy.

"That's that terribly tragic play by that Norwegian fellow, isn't it?" Gloria said. "Good for you."

"What about your contract with RiverWind?" Lowell asked.

"We've come to terms," Ivy said, in her deep throaty voice. "Having some Broadway credits will make me more desirable as an actress, so Mr. Schulman thinks. I have no idea, but I'm thrilled to have the chance. Oh, and Honoria, you've got an announcement, too."

"I don't know," said Honoria, fidgeting nervously.

"Oh, go on, darling," Ivy said, giving Honoria a friendly shove. "You said you wanted to give your mother a chance.”

“Me?” asked Gloria.

“I’m afraid you’ll disapprove dreadfully, Mother,” Honoria said. “But it’s something that sounds so very interesting and I’d really like to try and make it work.”

“What, darling?”

“I want to start my own magazine,” Honoria said. “For women. You know, advice on child-rearing, how to handle servants, how to stand up for yourself. Things that would be really useful to a woman who wants to think. Opinions on politics, even.”

“Oh,” said Gloria, who was obviously a little non-plussed. “And why would that make you happy, darling?”

Honoria shrugged. “I like publishing. I tried it once and, yes, there were problems, probably because I was trying to publish the wrong sort of thing. But I do think this magazine has a chance. There isn’t anything quite like it out there, and if I include things like fashion and cosmetics and the normal things you find in a woman’s magazine, it will sell better.”

Gloria frowned. “You don’t want to get married?”

‘No, Mother. Not at all.”

“Well, what I want is for you to be happy,” Gloria said at last. “I’m not sure I understand why this will make you happy. But if that’s what you want to do, then I say do it.”

“What about the scandal?”

Gloria sighed. “We don’t have to advertise that you’re doing it, do we?”

Honoria laughed and grabbed her mother’s hand. “No. Thank you for not being too upset.”

“You’re very welcome, darling.” Gloria shifted, then looked at Freddie and Kathy. “Any more news?”

“I’m afraid not,” said Kathy. “And I don’t expect there to be any very soon.”

“We can’t let our chief editor get herself otherwise occupied,” Lowell said, grinning.

“Lowell!” Kathy gasped, blushing furiously.

"Chief editor?" Gloria asked.

"Yes," said Freddie. "Lowell, I and three of our fellow authors are joining together in a new venture."

"Four, if we can get that ass Jennings back from California," Lowell added.

"You don't mean Pierce Jennings, do you?" Gloria asked. "Oh, his books are wonderful."

Ivy laughed. "They are, but he is not, by all accounts."

"He can be rather dreadful," sighed Freddie. "And he is occupied at the moment with writing the next big MGM film. However, the new publishing company was his idea, so I suppose we'll have to include him at some point or other."

"And I'll still be editing books," said Kathy. "Only this time, I'll be in charge. It's going to be so much fun."

Roberts slipped in and announced that dessert and coffee were being served in the living room.

"Oh, let's go put some music on," Ivy said as the group made their way there.

"I do have a radiophone in the living room," Freddie said. "Kathy convinced me to buy it so we can listen to the news in the evenings."

Ivy went straight to the radio and switched it on. A male voice emerged from the speakers. The room fell silent.

"The man in the car," whispered Kathy.

"That sounds very much like his voice," Ivy said.

"And that was Will H. Hayes, the man tasked with cleaning up Hollywood, talking about his plans to help the motion picture industry set new standards of wholesomeness in filmed entertainment," the announcer said.

"Hays," said Freddie.

Ivy switched the radio off. "It makes perfect sense. As the former postmaster, he has the connections to watch your mail."

"Will Hays?" Gloria sniffed. "Fred said that he has his fingers in quite a few pies these days. Calls him the puppet master. Always pulling the strings behind the scenes. Why is he important?"

Freddie sighed. "We just think we met him, is all. It wasn't very pleasant."

"Well, your father thinks he could get away with murder, he's so slippery."

"And that is exactly what he did," Ivy said. "But we can't prove it, so nothing will come of it."

"Oh, I firmly believe that one gets one's just desserts in the end," Gloria said, comfortably settling herself in an over-stuffed chair.

"We can but hope," said Honoria. "In the meantime, we'll move on." She smiled. "You know, it's almost as if all of us are leaving behind some wretched parts of our past and moving on to new things."

"It does, indeed," said Freddie.

"Then forget the coffee." Honoria went to the sideboard and got a bottle of whiskey and several glasses. "This calls for a toast. To our new lives."

Afterword

If you're a historian and have gotten this far without throwing my book against the wall, I profoundly thank you. Because I have to be fair - President Warren G. Harding was probably not murdered. Given some of the articles I've read about the way Harding was acting in the weeks and days before his death, he probably did have some form of heart disease and it was either that or a stroke that most likely killed him.

But here's the rub. We don't know. We will never know because Mrs. Florence Harding refused to allow the president's body to be autopsied. She also, upon arriving back at the White House from San Francisco where the president died, burnt a lot, if not most, of her husband's papers. Suspicious? You bet. Even more suspicious? Both Florence Harding and the president's personal physician Dr. Charles E. Sawyer, a homeopath, died within a couple months of each other in late 1924, within seventeen months of President Harding's death.

The rumors were out there, and even inspired disgraced Federal Agent and conman Gaston Means to write *The Strange Death of President Harding*. The book was soon debunked by Means' co-author May Dixon Thacker, but she was reportedly peeved that she hadn't gotten her royalties.

So, while it is not likely that Harding was murdered, you can see where I couldn't resist playing "What if..?"

As for Will H. Hays, he became best known as the man behind the Motion Picture Code or Hays Code, which effectively censored movies up through the early

1960s. I chose him as my bad guy because he was one of the few people in Harding's administration that came out of the Teapot Dome and other scandals relatively unscathed. Commerce Secretary (and later President) Herbert Hoover also came out of the whole debacle looking good. However, Hoover was widely touted as incorruptible and I thought that would be pushing it. As for whether or not Freddie and Kathy will come across Mr. Hays' path again, I haven't made up my mind yet. This could be fun.

About the Author

Anne Louise Bannon is an author and journalist who wrote her first novel at age 15. Her journalistic work has appeared in Ladies' Home Journal, the Los Angeles Times, Wines and Vines, and in newspapers across the country. She was a TV critic for over 10 years, founded the YourFamilyViewer blog, and created the OddBallGrape.com wine education blog with her husband, Michael Holland. She also writes the romantic fiction serial WhiteHouseRhapsody.com, with Book One now available. She is the co-author of Howdunit: Book of Poisons, with Serita Stevens, as well as the first two mysteries in this series Fascinating Rhythm, and Bring Into Bondage, and contemporary mystery Tyger, Tyger. She and her husband live in Southern California with an assortment of critters.

Other books by Anne Louise Bannon

I'm so glad you liked The Last Witnesses! Check out my other novels, available in print or ebook at your favorite retailer:

Freddie and Kathy Series:
Fascinating Rhythm
Bring Into Bondage
The Last Witnesses

Operation Quickline Series
That Old Cloak and Dagger Routine

Brenda Finnegan
Tyger, Tyger

Romantic Fiction
White House Rhapsody, Book One

And I would be honored if you left a review for this and any of my books on GoodReads or any other retail site. It really helps.

Connect with Anne Louise Bannon

Thank you for sticking it out this long! Please connect with me on the following social media platforms:

Friend me on Facebook: http://facebook.com/RobinGoodfellowEnt
Follow me on Twitter: http://twitter.com/ALBannon
Favorite my Smashwords author page: https://www.smashwords.com/profile/view/MsBriscow
Subscribe to the Robin Goodfellow Newsletter: http://eepurl.com/zH0Ab
Connect on LinkedIn: http://www.linkedin.com/in/annelouisebannon
Follow me on Pinterest: http://pinterest.com/msbriscow
Visit my website: http://annelouisebannon.com
Follow me on Google+: http://google.com/+Annelouisebannonfiction